FROM THE ASHES

NUCLEAR DAWN BOOK THREE

KYLA STONE

PAPER MOON PRESS

Printed in the United States of America

Cover design by Christian Bentulan

Book formatting by Vellum

First Printed in 2019

ISBN: 978-1-945410-35-2

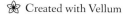 Created with Vellum

1
DAKOTA

Dakota Sloane was a survivor.

She'd survived the blast from the nuclear bomb terrorists had detonated in downtown Miami. She'd escaped the brunt of the lethal fallout, fought violent gangbangers, and braved a burning house—all to reach her sister.

She'd done it. Eden was safe; she was alive. They'd both made it. Dakota could hardly wrap her mind around it. Despite everything that had happened over the last few days, Eden seemed okay. Pale and shaken, but okay.

Maybe the radiation just hadn't set in yet.

Dakota kissed Eden on the forehead. She held her little sister tight, never wanting to let her go.

Eden pulled away first and fluttered her hands furiously, shaping them in a way Dakota recognized as sign language. She had no idea what any of it meant.

"Use this." Dakota pulled the notepad out from beneath her shirt and thrust it into Eden's dancing hands. The unicorn rainbow cover was sweat-dampened, the edges of the paper curled from the heat.

"I went into that burning house to find you," Dakota said hoarsely, "but you weren't there."

"She was with me," said a familiar voice.

Dakota stopped breathing. An icy chill skittered up her spine.

"Eden, come here," the man commanded.

Before Dakota could react, Eden pulled free of her arms, leapt to her feet, and scurried out of reach. She dashed behind Dakota, toward the house. Toward the voice of the man Dakota had hoped never to see again.

Dread pooling in her gut, Dakota rose on trembling legs and turned around.

It couldn't be. No. *No, no, no...*

The world sharpened. She saw everything, every color, every detail.

They were standing in the trimmed front lawn of someone's fancy six-thousand-square-foot house in the exclusive Palm Cove subdivision. Smoke billowed into the darkening sky. To the east, at the end of the street, the unrelenting fire raged on.

The blaze had already consumed a half-dozen houses; it would reach them soon.

Watching them quietly, Shay Harris—the nursing student— knelt a few feet away. Her brown skin was ashen above her filthy clothes, and a faint bloom of blood stained the bandage wrapped around her head.

Logan Garcia, the tough Colombian ex-con, leaned against the trunk of a shiny red Tesla parked in the brick-paved driveway thirty feet away, arms crossed over his chest. Next to him, Julio de la Peña, the stocky Cuban bartender, finished his granola bar and stuffed the wrapper in his pocket. His gold cross glinted on the chain around his neck.

Patiently waiting at the end of the driveway were the first responders they'd rescued. Yu-Jin Park rested on the stretcher parked next to the curb, his broken forearm splinted with scavenged pieces of pipe. Nancy Harlow, the female first responder and casino security guard, bent over him and held his uninjured hand. The empty M4 nestled on the stretcher next to Park's leg.

Dakota swayed on her feet as a sickening wave of dizziness lurched through her. She was still light-headed from the smoke inhalation. Her throat was raw, her lungs scorched. Her head pounded with a vicious headache, and her bandaged hands stung from a dozen cuts.

But none of that mattered.

"You should sit back down, Dakota," Shay said. "You need to rest..."

Dakota heard her voice from some distant, far place. Everything faded away—almost everything. Except him.

A man stood a dozen yards away, hidden in the shade of a magnolia tree planted in the center of the manicured lawn. He remained in the shadows, his hand slung loosely over the pistol at his hip.

She knew exactly who he was, what this meant. In her jubilant reunion with Eden, she hadn't even noticed him. Silently, she cursed her lack of situational awareness. But there was no time to berate herself now.

She could hardly force oxygen into her tortured lungs. Her heart was a fist in her throat.

No, no, no...

She'd made it so far, come so close...

"I saved her from that fire," the man said, mirth in his voice, as if there could possibly be anything to laugh about. "Good timing, wouldn't you say? Almost like a divine appointment."

"He said he's your brother." Logan glanced from Dakota's stricken face back to Eden, who nestled next to the man, happily gazing up at him with a delighted, earnest trust that twisted like a knife in Dakota's belly.

Of course, Eden trusted him. She didn't know.

Dakota had made the decision not to tell Eden the truth. She'd thought she knew better, trying to protect her sister the best she could.

But if she was completely honest with herself, she knew it was because she couldn't bear the thought of Eden discovering what she'd done. It had been so much easier to allow Eden to continue to trust her blindly, without the complications of the harsh, bitter truth between them like an unbridgeable chasm.

Deep down, Dakota was terrified that Eden would never forgive her.

Now her choices had come back to bite them both in the ass.

"Maddox," Dakota whispered in a strangled voice.

The man stepped out from beneath the shadow of the tree, Eden at his side. He slung his left arm around Eden's shoulder, his right hand still resting carelessly on the butt of his gun.

Like he was just a friendly family man. As if his every move wasn't a threat.

She knew better.

Maddox Cage was always ready, always prepared.

His movements only appeared languid and casual to the others. His narrow shoulders were slightly hunched, his neck and spine stiff. Every fiber of his being strained with tension like a rubber band about to snap.

At twenty-three, Maddox had the grim, rough handsomeness of a man several years his senior. His face was long and angular, his features even, his dirty-blonde hair shorn close to his skull.

He was lean and rangy as a stray dog—tough, powerful, and dangerous.

Over the last three years, she had only glimpsed him twice, but he remained exactly as he'd looked in her memories—and her nightmares.

Yet now his pallor was tinged a sickly, unhealthy yellow, his lips dry and cracked, his sharp blue eyes glassy with fever.

He'd been exposed to radiation. How much, she didn't know.

Not enough to kill him or slow him down. Not yet, anyway. Otherwise, he still looked as strong as a horse.

Shay clapped her hands in delight. "Oh, a family reunion! How wonderful!"

Maddox grinned at her with a flash of white teeth. "It's some kind of reunion. Isn't that right, Dakota?"

Dakota's fingers twitched, desperate to go for the Sig Sauer pistol holstered at her belt, but Eden was right there in the line of fire. And in the time it would take to draw her weapon, Maddox could do whatever he wanted to Eden. Put a gun to her head. Slit her throat.

Eden should be the last person on earth Maddox would ever hurt. But then, she'd once believed that about herself. She knew better than to discount any possibility.

Like his father, Maddox Cage was capable of just about anything.

She couldn't do a thing to stop this from happening, and Maddox knew it.

2

DAKOTA

"It's so good to see you, Dakota." His words sounded real, his smile genuine. It even lit up those feverish blue eyes, drawing her in with disarming warmth. "I can't begin to tell you how much I've missed you."

Dakota was never quite sure whether it was a ruse, or if he truly believed in his own goodness. He was a man of many faces: at turns kind, indifferent, or cruel.

He kept you off-balance, using your own weaknesses against you, twisting tenderness and affection into weapons wielded to control, to dominate.

But Dakota wasn't a scared, timid sixteen-year-old anymore. She knew better now.

She knew what he wanted, what he'd come for.

A hundred yards to the east, the raging fire consumed house after house, hissing and crackling. To the west, at the other end of the cul-de-sac, an elderly couple stood on their front porch, pointing at the fire.

A few houses closer, another couple ran out of their house

clutching several suitcases, headed for the new Ford-150 parked in their driveway. No one paid them any attention.

Some people here had sheltered in place after all. Now, with the fire, they were forced to flee.

The sun sank slowly toward the horizon, twilight hovering at the edges of the sky. The breeze cooled her feverish skin, though the heat was still oppressive. Somewhere, a bird burst into song.

It could almost be a normal, everyday evening—but for the smoky stench stinging her nostrils and the fear stuck in her throat like a hook.

She could still fix this. She had to fix it.

She dragged her gaze back to Maddox. Her bandaged hand inched toward the butt of her gun. A coughing fit gripped her. When she could breathe again, she glared at him.

"You shouldn't be here," she said hoarsely. "You don't belong here."

"I have a right to be here more than you do," he said, still smiling. He licked his cracked lips. "We both know that."

She swayed on her feet, dizzy from the lack of oxygen, from whatever damage the smoke inhalation had done to her lungs. "Eden, get away from him. Right now."

Eden gestured something that Dakota couldn't understand, her expression bewildered. She remained at Maddox's side.

"Easy now, Dakota," Maddox said smoothly. "I think the smoke inhalation did something to your head. It causes confusion and mental changes, doesn't it? You know me. We're *family*, right?"

His gaze shot to the holster at her hip, to her fingers creeping toward the butt of the Sig. His eyes sharpened, glittering like a predator's.

He gave the smallest shake of his head. *Don't even try it.*

Defeated, she lowered her hand. Helpless anger, fear, and hatred slashed through her veins. "You're nothing to me," she spat.

Logan was up off the fender of the Tesla now, on edge and alert.

7

He hadn't reached for his own weapon yet; he was smart enough to know that would instantly escalate an already tense situation. But she caught the twitch of his fingers. He was ready to draw his pistol if needed.

Shay and Julio stared at Dakota, too startled by this abrupt turn of events to say or do anything. At the curb, Harlow and Park watched silently, their faces perplexed, eyes wide.

No one understood what was really happening here.

"Dakota, what's going on?" Logan asked.

"I can explain," she said, her voice cracking, panic creeping in.

"Why don't I give it a try?" Maddox tightened his hold on Eden's shoulder. "I'm sure I can explain everything just fine."

"No," she whispered. "You can't."

Maddox smiled at her, sharp as a blade. His pale skin and sunken eyes gave him a gaunt, almost ghoulish appearance. Even sick, he still had that keen-edged hunger in his gaze.

He was the kind of man who was never satisfied, who always craved what he didn't have, who always wanted more.

All the old terrors she'd worked so hard to defeat came roaring back.

A tremor went through her body, like she was standing too close to the edge of a cliff, about to fall. Her bones vibrated beneath her skin. Her heart shuddered inside her chest.

The brands on her back throbbed—just like the moment she'd received them at Maddox's hand. The stench of scorched skin and hair. The red-hot burning jabbed into her spine, like boiling oil sizzling her flesh.

And his words, hissing in her ear: *For the Lord shall execute judgment by fire...you deserve far worse. You know that, don't you? But I am merciful, because I love you...*

She swallowed the acid stinging the back of her throat. Her knees trembled, but she forced herself to remain standing. "You need to leave. Just turn and go, right now."

Maddox turned to the others. "My name is Maddox Cage. And I am *Eden's* brother."

"Eden's—?" Logan's bewildered gaze flicked from Eden to Dakota to Maddox.

"She told you they were sisters, didn't she?"

"We are!" Dakota croaked.

"She's a liar, too," he said with relish. "And a thief."

"No," she said weakly. "No—"

"Dakota Sloane is no sister of Eden's," Maddox said in triumph. "Dakota is her kidnapper."

3

EDEN

E den stared at Dakota in confusion.
She'd been overjoyed when her brother found her,
trapped in the stifling, pitch-black bathroom, frozen in terror as the
stench of gas grew stronger, as the rank smell of burning fabric, plastic, and drywall mingled with the swirls of smoke sifting through the
cracks around the door jam.

She didn't know what she was supposed to do. The terrors
outside that closed bathroom door—lethal radiation, a bombed and
ruined city, death and destruction everywhere, her own house on
fire—loomed so large she'd been utterly overwhelmed with paralyzing fear and indecision.

At first, she thought it was a figment of her imagination—a hallucination due to dehydration and lack of food, or the choking, disori-
enting smoke.

The door abruptly jerked open, a male voice cursing. The towel
Eden had pushed into the crack was caught beneath the door.

Panic surged through her veins. She shrank back against the
cool porcelain tub. That wasn't Dakota's voice. And it wasn't her
foster parents, Jorge or Gabriella Ross, either. Jorge's voice was

higher, almost musical, while this voice was deep and rough like gravel.

Maybe it was someone coming to hurt her. A thief robbing the house or worse, looking for a girl like her to hurt...

And then she heard her name. "Eden! Are you in there? Eden!"

Her heartbeat stuttered in her chest. Was that...? Was it even possible? How could it be? If she was delirious—if she'd drifted into a fantastical dream as she lay dying—she didn't want to wake up.

She couldn't call out to him. Her mangled voice wouldn't let her. She whistled instead. Her tongue was thick and swollen, her lips cracked. It barely made a sound.

"Answer me!" the voice shouted. "Eden!"

She forced herself to sit up, fighting through the faint-headed wooziness. She banged the tiled wall over the bathtub with her fist.

With a grunt, the figure forced the door open. And then he was there, standing in the doorway, silhouetted against the dim daylight streaming down the hallway.

Maddox, her brother.

She let out a sob of desperation, relief, and joy.

"Eden!" In two strides, he was across the bathroom and scooping her up into his strong arms. He cradled her to his chest. His body was too warm, his skin burning hot and damp with sweat against her own. "I've got you. You're safe now."

She must have dropped her notepad, but she didn't notice in the exhilaration of being rescued. Maddox carried her down the long hallway, turning into the formal living room.

Smoke snaked into her nostrils and throat, and she coughed into his chest. She gazed over his shoulder, bleary-eyed. The flames danced across the glossy white cabinets in the beautiful kitchen she'd spent much of the last two years enjoying—sitting at the island, doing homework, practicing sign language with Gabriella, eating takeout together like a real family, grinning as they both danced to salsa music or laughed at Jorge's lame jokes.

All of that was gone now.

Gabriella and Jorge weren't coming back.

The fire would burn down the house she thought of as home. The bomb had destroyed the city she loved. Was anything but ashes left?

And where was Dakota?

With Eden still held firmly in his arms, Maddox dashed through the dark living room and crashed through the double front doors. She closed her eyes against the harsh blast of sunlight.

She'd been trapped in complete darkness for two and a half days. It felt like forever.

Maddox carried her across several lawns, finally stopping ten houses away. She forced her eyes open, blinking rapidly as he set her down beneath the spreading leaves of a huge magnolia tree near the front of the house.

This was the Westwood's house. They were both real estate agents, with a son who was studying engineering at Miami University. Mrs. Westwood had a green thumb and tended to her own landscaping rather than hiring gardeners like everyone else did.

Bright rain lilies and periwinkle flowers poked out of the mulch surrounding the trunk of the tree. All along the front of the house, luscious tropical plants like Florida sweethearts, white birds of paradise, and elephant palms fluttered in the breeze.

It was all so beautiful, so peaceful—except for the smoke pouring into the sky behind them.

Maddox knelt, pulled a water bottle out of his back pocket, and handed it to her. She downed half of it in one gulp. It was warm but still tasted like heaven, soothing her parched throat and wetting her cracked lips.

When she was finished, Maddox gripped her shoulders and stared at her. She looked into his vivid blue eyes.

Her brother. It wasn't a dream. She wasn't delirious. He really was here, right in front of her.

Memories of her life at the River Grass Compound came flooding back. Maddox, Jacob, her father, Sister Rosemarie, all her friends...and the Prophet.

After they'd fled, Dakota told her not to think about that place anymore, to put it all in the past—where it belonged.

She'd done her best, trying to only think of the here and now, to live her new life without mourning the old. *The past only brings heartache*, Dakota had told her. *We're going to build a new life.*

She'd thought she had. Until now.

Maddox shook her. "Are you okay?"

Slowly, she nodded.

"Where is Dakota?"

She signed, *I don't know.*

He looked at her like she'd grown two heads. "What are you doing? This isn't the time for games, Eden! Answer me!"

Fresh fear constricted her lungs. He didn't know about her voice. Would he think less of her? Would she be damaged goods to him now? Would he get angry at her? Hate her?

She loved Maddox, but he could be volatile, and fly into a rage over anything, just like their father. At the compound, she'd learned to notice the signs of a coming storm and find somewhere to hide. But she wouldn't be able to avoid this one.

She signed again, forgetting he couldn't understand her. She gestured at her throat instead, at the thick, ugly worm of the raised scar.

His eyes narrowed. They were glassy, his pupils dilated. "What did she do to you?"

Eden didn't understand the question. She opened her mouth, closed it, pointed to her damaged throat again.

"You can't talk." Her brother scowled, indignant. "You're damaged! You're handicapped!"

She shrank away from his anger. *I'm sorry*, she signed. *Please don't be angry.*

He saw her fear and his features softened—barely. "I didn't know it was that bad. I saw it, but I didn't realize..." He pulled her into his arms. "I found you, little sister. I found you and I'm never going to let you go."

For some reason, his words didn't bring her comfort.

"It won't matter," he said quietly into her hair. "I'll make it right. I'll figure it out." He pulled away and held out his palm. "Spell out the words. What happened to you? Where the hell is Dakota? You need to tell me everything."

4

EDEN

"Dakota kidnapped Eden," Maddox said.

Eden knew perfectly well that she and Dakota weren't sisters by blood, but by choice. Back at Ezra's, Dakota had sworn to love her and protect Eden like she was her own. Eden loved and depended on Dakota as much as any real sister would.

Once they'd left the compound, Dakota explained that it would be safer for them both if they called themselves sisters. In a cruel, harsh world, they only had each other.

They had already been through so much together. Dakota had already sacrificed so much for her. It was only natural to consider each other sisters. To Eden, it had become real.

But kidnapping?

"Someone tell us what's going on," the middle-aged Cuban guy said, glancing warily between Dakota and Maddox.

Dakota stood there, speechless and white-faced.

Maddox's hand pressed heavy and hot against Eden's shoulder. She could feel the heat of fever radiating off his body mingled with the sweltering temperature.

"My family has a home in the Everglades." Maddox's voice was calm, but she could sense the barely contained rage vibrating just below the surface. "A community of like-minded souls who work and live and worship together in peace.

"Dakota is an orphan who came to live with us after her own parents perished in an unfortunate car accident. Her aunt is one of our loyal parishioners. My father could have kicked her out to starve. Instead, he took her in, gave her a home, food and shelter, and welcomed her into our community."

He coughed and cleared his throat. "Instead of gratitude, instead of obligation, she chose to betray me, to steal the thing that would hurt my family the most. Eden was twelve when Dakota kidnapped her, did you know that?"

"You're the liar," Dakota said, her voice shaking. "That's not how it happened, and you damn well know it."

"She's a murderer, too," Maddox said evenly.

The blood drained from her face.

"She killed our brother," Maddox said. "Stabbed him to death in cold blood."

Eden's hands fluttered in the air like startled birds. *What? Jacob is...? No, oh no...*

Her mind struggled to decipher the words. Jacob...was dead? The older brother she adored, the one always with a ready smile and twinkling eyes, who never lost his temper or treated her like she was just a bothersome kid?

Jacob was so tall and strong, like the trunk of a mighty, ancient tree. When she was little, she would look up at him and his head would blot out the sun.

That's how she remembered him—his face fairly glowing, the sun shining all around him like a halo.

When she thought of the compound, she always thought of everyone the same as when she'd left—never aging or changing, never dying.

"Dakota murdered Jacob," Maddox said, venom dripping from his every word.

"That's a—that's not how it happened," Dakota stammered.

But Eden knew her too well. There was something guarded in her face, something she was hiding.

You knew? she signed. *All this time, you knew he was dead?*

But Dakota couldn't understand her words. No one was paying attention to her, anyway. They were all staring over her head, watching Maddox.

The others in the group—two men standing beside the Westwoods' car in the driveway, two others at the curb, one of them lying in a stretcher—watched silently, too stunned to intervene.

Eden's pulse thundered so loud inside her head she could barely hear her own thoughts. There was so much she didn't remember. The events of that night were still a blot in her memory. A black hole.

Dakota had never explained what had happened. She never told Eden her own brother was dead. Anger and confusion mingled with the grief tearing at her insides. She didn't know what to feel. It was all too much.

She wanted to clap her hands over her ears and drown it out, push it away, go back to that place in her head where Dakota had saved her, not stolen her. To go back in time until her precious Jacob was still happily alive.

"Maybe this isn't the best time to have this conversation," the Cuban guy said cautiously. "We need to move somewhere safer. It's getting dark. We have wounded people in our group. Sir, you don't look so great yourself. You need medical treatment. We have a nursing student—"

"This is the perfect time." Maddox squeezed Eden's shoulder so hard she felt his nails digging into her skin like talons. "Have you told her? Have you told Eden what happened to her throat, why she can't speak?"

"Shut up!" Dakota whispered.

"Have you told her that it was your fault?"

"Stop it!"

"What did she tell you, little sister? That she'd saved you from something awful?" He gave that laugh again—flat and dangerous. "Did she forget to mention that she *was* that something awful? Not only did she end the life of your beloved brother and stole you from us, she also cut you to ensure you were completely dependent on her, and couldn't run back to us."

Eden's eyes widened in shock. She hadn't thought it could get any worse. Her mind was a jumble of confused questions and tattered thoughts.

She longed to beg Dakota for the truth, but without her notepad, a cellphone to text, or someone who understood ASL, she was effectively voiceless.

She could only watch and listen in horror as her life collapsed in a cascade of lies.

Even if she could talk to Dakota, would she get the truth? Who was even telling the truth? Her own brother or the girl she loved like a sister? Or were they both lying?

Out of the corner of her eye, she glimpsed movement. One of the men by the red car, a tall, muscular Hispanic guy, swiftly drew his gun.

But before he could lift it and point it at anyone, Maddox had whipped out his own pistol. Instead of aiming at the other man, the cold tip of the muzzle pressed against her right temple.

"Anyone moves and I put a bullet in her brain." Maddox's voice was cold, unfeeling. Like he really would do it without a second's hesitation.

The Hispanic guy froze.

"I thought—I thought she was your sister?" the Cuban man stammered.

"She is. And if she dies now, she'll die a martyr's death and spend eternity in paradise. And so will I. Death doesn't frighten us. Not like it should frighten you."

"Julio," Dakota warned in a low voice.

Slowly, Julio raised his arms in the air. "We're not your enemies. No one needs to die today. Please, just tell us what you want, and we'll do our best to help you."

Maddox gave a mirthless laugh. "What do I want? I want my sister returned to me where she belongs." His right hand still held the gun to her head. With his free hand, he pulled a folding knife from his pocket and flicked it open.

Deftly, he slipped the knife to Eden's throat and aimed the pistol straight at Dakota's chest. "Oh, and one more thing."

"Me," Dakota said. "He wants me."

5

LOGAN

Logan stared at the incredulous scene unfolding before him in disbelief. He'd barely had time to catch his breath from the fight he'd barely survived, and now this.

"Put your guns down, nice and easy," Maddox said. "On second thought, discharge the chamber, eject the magazine, and toss them in opposite directions."

Dakota unholstered her pistol, did as instructed, and set it down on the grass. She tossed the magazine a few feet away and glanced at Logan, begging him to follow suit with desperate eyes.

Logan had no clue what was going on. Whoever this guy was to Dakota, it was something bad. Her face had lost its color, and she was trembling.

The guy had accused her of murder and kidnapping.

Maybe it was true. Maybe it wasn't.

But seeing as the scumbag was currently holding a knife to his own sister's neck, Logan made the split-second decision to leap all-in on Dakota's side.

Still, Logan despised the thought of giving up any ground. Anger burned through him as he lowered his Glock to the grass, dropped the magazine a few feet from the pistol, and straightened, both hands raised, palms out.

He clenched his jaw, barely reining in the fury boiling inside him. Dakota had a hell of a lot of explaining to do. Had she known this guy was out here looking for them? She must have. She hadn't seemed all that surprised to see him. Horrified—but not surprised.

When Dakota had taken off running toward the smoke, Logan had been forced to go after her. She was faster than he expected, and he was still hurting from the shallow gash across his ribs and multiple bruises and contusions.

By the time he reached Bellview Court, several houses were on fire. He wasn't sure which one belonged to the sister. Dakota was nowhere in sight.

He had jogged down the street, searching for an opened door, for some sign or clue.

He caught sight of movement in a yard several houses up from the fire. A man and a young girl. The man had waved to him, calm and nonchalant as could be.

Hi, friend, he'd said. *Hi, friend.*

The guy had looked just like another survivor—exhausted, sick, thankful to be alive. He'd said he was Eden's brother. Knowing Dakota and Eden were sisters, Logan assumed this guy was Dakota's brother as well.

Why wouldn't he? The girl was happy to see Maddox. She stood close to him, totally comfortable, looking at him like he was her savior.

If Logan had been well-rested, if he hadn't just nearly gotten his head bashed in, if he hadn't been so worried about Dakota...he would've been on his game. He wouldn't have taken the scene at face value.

He knew better.

He should've paid better attention. But he was operating on the last of his energy reserves, and he was so focused on finding Dakota he barely registered anything other than his goal.

"Which house is yours?" he'd yelled at the girl.

The guy had pointed down the street. "Blue shutters. It's on fire."

But Logan was already gone, tearing down the street to save the crazy waitress, who he knew without a doubt would never leave that house without her sister, even to her own demise.

She'd burn to death before she admitted defeat.

And crazier still—he knew he had to get her out. He *wanted* to get her out.

And he had. She'd been okay—hacking like a smoker from the inhalation and cut up everywhere—but alive.

He told himself it was quid pro quo, nothing more; she'd saved him by shooting Tank in the head. Now, he owed her. He was just returning the favor.

A small, insistent part of him knew it was more than that.

Now here he was—exhausted, completely spent, hurting and sick—and faced with yet another threat: one he hadn't even seen coming, in large part because Dakota Sloane hadn't bothered to warn him about her apparently psychopathic non-brother.

Fresh anger slashed through him. Whatever little game she was playing was gonna get someone killed. Possibly even himself.

He pushed aside his rage. Allowing emotions to interfere in a deadly-force situation got people killed.

"What do you want?" he asked through gritted teeth.

"Only what's mine," Maddox said. "Only what's fair."

The blonde girl—Eden—started to cry. According to Dakota, she was fifteen, but the girl was short and chubby, her angelic face sprinkled with freckles. She didn't look a day older than thirteen. She was just a kid.

"We're doing what you asked." Julio spoke with remarkable calm, like he was just soothing another bruised ego at his bar. "We put our guns down, no discussion. How about you do us a solid and lower your own weapon? Maybe you could put that knife down, too. We don't want any accidents. Your little sister looks really scared right now."

Maddox cocked his head, like he was considering it. He spat yellowish-tinged spittle out of the side of his mouth. "Nah. I'm taking them both."

"No, you're not!" another voice shouted.

Flinching, Logan whipped his head toward the sound.

Nancy Harlow stood at the curb, feet shoulder-width apart, gripping the M4 with both hands. She aimed it at Maddox's chest.

6

LOGAN

"Y ou aren't stealing a kid, sister or not," Harlow said valiantly. "Not on my watch."

Maddox gave a hollow laugh. Sweat trickled down his forehead and stubby jawline. His skin looked clammy and tinged a sickly shade of yellow. "You sure you can hit me and only me?"

The muzzle of the M4 shook in Harlow's hands. The woman was brave—Logan gave her credit for that—but she was also foolhardy. The weapon was out of bullets.

Maddox didn't know that, but he didn't seem afraid. Like he was banking on the fact that most women—most people—weren't good shots with an assault rifle.

Even fewer were willing to take a shot at a man with a child hostage.

"Don't test me, you scumbag!" Harlow spat.

"Did you not hear me the first time? I'm not the bad guy here." He dipped his chin at Dakota. "She is. I'm simply rescuing what's mine. Y'all aren't a part of this. We've all survived our own slice of hell on earth. If you're alive, it's for a reason. I've got no desire to kill you. Put your gun down and walk away."

"Whatever Dakota did or didn't do, taking revenge into your own hands isn't right," Julio said. "Neither is taking this girl by knifepoint."

Dakota didn't take her eyes off Maddox, but Logan saw her nostrils flare slightly in surprise at Julio and Harlow's support. As if she didn't expect it, or believe she deserved it.

"Remind yourselves later that I tried this the nice way the first time." Maddox shifted, adjusting his stance, and swallowed hard. His mouth contorted like he'd just tasted something nasty.

Dark circles of sweat stained his armpits. He was clearly suffering from radiation sickness. But how badly? Would it make him more aggressive or easier to take down?

Logan's own stomach lurched. He swallowed down the acid burning the back of his throat. *You're getting sick, too.*

"You don't have to do this," Julio said. "Let's stop and think things through. We're still in a radiated area. Once we're safe, we can discuss this like gentlemen, without weapons. Let's move—"

"Shut up, old man!" Maddox gestured at Dakota with the pistol. "Come on. Right now."

"Everyone, calm down—" Julio tried again.

Maddox jerked the knife. Eden inhaled sharply. Several droplets of blood puddled against the raised scar ringing her neck.

"Do I not look calm to you?" Maddox asked darkly.

Dakota took a step toward him. "I'll come with you. Don't hurt her."

Every fiber of Logan's body thrummed with tension. Adrenaline spiked through his veins. He wanted to shout at Dakota not to move, not a damn inch.

He was an experienced street fighter, but he wasn't a soldier. He didn't possess tactical or martial arts skills. There was a way out of this, but he didn't know what it was.

He was limited in what he could do. As long as Maddox kept

that blade tight on the girl's neck, Logan didn't see a way to neutralize him without risking Eden's life.

"Now," Maddox said, his gun still aimed at Dakota, "I'd prefer Dakota alive, but I don't need her that way. I don't need her all in one piece, either. Put that rifle down, lady, or I'm shooting her in the kneecap. That'll do some damage, especially without many hospitals taking patients right now."

Harlow hesitated.

Fury painted Dakota's features. If that M4 had actual bullets in it, the waitress would've told Harlow to shoot anyway, pain be damned. Logan was certain of it.

But it was just a bluff—one Maddox Cage hadn't fallen for.

"You've never seen me shoot, but trust me when I say that I put a bullet where I want it." He spoke in a flat voice, like he was reciting a grocery list. Even sick as he was, his hand was steady.

Unlike Harlow, he didn't seem like the type to bluff.

Logan could tell by Dakota's rigid expression that she was frightened of this guy. And Dakota didn't scare easy. It didn't matter that he'd known her for less than three days. They'd already survived a nuclear bomb, escaped the fallout, and battled a crazed mob.

There was nothing like fighting side-by-side with someone, both your lives on the line, to cut away the layers of B.S. and take the true measure of a man—or woman, in this case.

Dakota Sloane passed muster in his eyes. Despite the lies she'd spun, whatever games she'd played—the girl had grit, and guts.

If she was wary of this guy, then Logan was, too.

They couldn't do anything stupid. It wasn't worth the risk.

"Harlow," Logan said. "Stand down."

"Listen to him, damn it!" Park urged her. He tugged on her shirt sleeve with his good hand. "Don't be a flaming idiot like me."

The woman huffed a breath and lowered the rifle, a scowl masking her fear. "Screw you."

Maddox's smile slid into a grimace. "Unless you want me to double-tap you in the chest right now, Dakota, I suggest you get your ass in gear. Walk right up to the gun. That's it."

Julio threw a hesitant look at Logan as Dakota started to obey, but Logan had no answers for him. He despised this sickening, helpless feeling as much as Julio did.

Logan scanned their surroundings, searching for an advantage. When Maddox started to move with the girls, he'd present openings, weaknesses. A hell of a lot of mistakes could happen between now and their escape.

If Logan saw even the smallest opening, he'd take it.

His stomach roiled, and he sucked in his breath, ignoring the hot wrench of nausea.

A flash of movement drew his attention. Behind Maddox, three houses down on the right, a couple had been packing their belongings in their vehicle. They'd been loading a heavy suitcase into the rear passenger seat on the opposite side of the truck when Maddox drew his gun.

At the sight of a weapon, they'd disappeared quickly.

Now, though, the barrel of a rifle peeked over the shiny gray hood, followed by the head and shoulders of a Caucasian man with thick, black-framed glasses and slicked-back salt-and-pepper hair.

Maddox's body was partially blocked by the trunk of the magnolia tree, which had maybe a ten-inch diameter. If the guy took a shot, the rounds could easily go wide and hit Logan, Dakota, or Julio instead. Even if the round struck Maddox, he might startle and slice into the little girl's neck without even trying.

Logan gave a subtle shake of his head, trying to warn the shooter off. The man gave no indication he'd gotten the hint.

He was probably some rich CFO who went deer hunting with his buddies twice a year and believed that made him an ace shot in a dangerous, incredibly high-stress situation. Some well-fed, soft-bellied paper-pusher with Rambo delusions—which would only get somebody killed.

Before Logan could decide what to do about it, the crack of a gunshot shattered the air.

7

DAKOTA

Out of the corner of her eye, Dakota caught the glint of the rifle barrel in the setting sun.

There was no time to react. The man aimed over the hood of his F150 and took his shot.

The round went wide and pinged into the rear fender of the Tesla thirty feet behind her. A second and third shot sailed over their heads.

"Get down!" she cried.

Shay dropped to the grass, her hands over her head. Logan dove for the pistol and magazine only a few feet from him.

Simultaneously, Maddox swung toward the street. Keeping Eden locked close to his body, the blade still at her throat, he focused on Harlow and aimed his gun at her chest.

"NO!" Dakota shouted.

But it was too late.

Maddox squeezed the trigger. Once, twice, three times.

Harlow's body juddered like a puppet on a string. She staggered backward, looking down at herself, at the two red stains blooming: one on her upper right shoulder, the second one in the center of her chest. The M4 slipped from her fingers and clattered against the pavement.

Harlow collapsed.

Shay screamed.

Park yelled something indecipherable.

Maddox spun, took one step left out of the cover of the tree, and fired two shots at the man behind the truck. One bullet struck the windshield. The second skimmed the hood and narrowly missed the man's head.

The man yelped and ducked back behind the relative safety of the engine block. The woman with him let out a piercing shriek.

The gunshots blasted Dakota's eardrums. Ears ringing, she searched the grass desperately for her gun and the magazine, her fumbling, bandaged hands shaking with rage, adrenaline, and fear.

No, no, no. If Harlow was dead, Dakota would kill Maddox with her bare hands.

Logan leapt to his feet with the Glock, slapping in the magazine, racking back the slide, and chambering a round. He half-raised his weapon and froze.

Maddox had already moved back behind the cover of the tree trunk, whirled in a complete circle, and turned back toward Logan.

The muzzle of his Beretta was aimed at Logan's head. "Don't move. Drop the gun."

Logan cursed but obeyed.

So did Dakota. She was on her knees, one hand closing around the magazine of her Sig.

"Get up," Maddox said to her.

She dropped the magazine, the cuts on her palms stinging, and stood slowly.

Maddox raised his voice. "To the hero behind the gray F-150, I advise you to stay down. These people are harboring a kidnapper and murderer. You're on the wrong side of justice. I've got no problem with you, man. But if you shoot at me again, I'll kill you."

The man didn't peek over the truck's hood. He was probably cowering, completely terrified. He'd better stay there, too, or Dakota would be tempted to shoot him herself.

His recklessness had gotten Harlow shot.

Was she still alive? Dakota didn't know. She couldn't afford to take her eyes off Maddox for even a heartbeat.

"You shot Harlow!" Julio stood next to the shattered window frame, his empty hands dangling at his sides. His mouth hung open, his eyes wide in horror and shock. "You killed her!"

"It was self-defense," Maddox said flatly. "I had every right."

Shay let out a low moan. She crawled across the grass toward Harlow.

"Don't move toward that rifle, girl, or I'll put a bullet in this guy's femoral artery, and you can watch him bleed out, too."

"The gun is empty!" Dakota cried. "It was a bluff."

"I believe you." Maddox took a step back and leaned against the tree trunk. He huffed several deep, rasping breaths before speaking again. "Go ahead. Tend to your wounded. I'm nothing if not merciful. Isn't that right, Dakota?"

Dakota didn't bother to answer.

Shay reached Harlow. She checked the woman's pulse, then looked up, stricken. "She's dead."

This couldn't be happening. It was all wrong. Dakota's entire body flashed hot, then cold. Her ears rang, her breath coming in short, shallow gasps.

Nancy Harlow was dead.

She was dead because of Maddox, who was only here because of Eden and Dakota.

This was Dakota's fault.

Something inside her shriveled. Black hatred colored her vision. The scars on her back burned with white-hot fire. "Go to hell."

Maddox smiled. "Let's go together."

She forced herself to breathe, to focus. Dakota still had her knife sheathed at her waist, but she wasn't willing to risk Eden's life. As long as Maddox held the knife to Eden, she was helpless. They all were. She had to turn the tables somehow, and quickly.

Against every instinct screaming at her to run in the opposite direction, she took a step toward Maddox.

"Dakota, what are you doing?" Logan asked, his voice strained.

"It's no use," she said softly, playing to Maddox's ego. "He's better than you are, Logan. He's bested us. If we try to fight him, he'll kill more innocent people."

"Still just as smart, I see," Maddox said.

"I don't understand what's going on," Julio said.

Dakota coughed and cleared her throat. She met Eden's frightened gaze. "It's okay. Everything will be okay. If we go with him, he won't hurt you. It's for the best, okay?"

Eden couldn't nod with the blade against her throat. She just stared at Dakota blankly, like she was a complete stranger, like Eden didn't know her at all.

Slow tears leaked down her chubby cheeks. Her eyes were filled with confusion—and betrayal.

It felt like a blade slipping between her ribs. Dakota couldn't blame her. Maddox twisted the truth to his own ends, but he wasn't lying, either. She *had* murdered Jacob. She *had* caused Eden's wound.

Maybe Eden would never forgive her. Maybe she'd even hate her. Dakota had to live with that. But first, she needed to get them out of this alive.

Every muscle ached with exhaustion. But she couldn't rest. Not yet. She took another step and moved between the gun and Logan. "Take me as the hostage."

Maddox tightened his grip on Eden's shoulders and chest. "Why would I do that?"

"You've got to keep your attention on both Eden and me. If your attention—and that knife—slips for even a second, I'll be on you. But if I'm your hostage, you only have to worry about me. Eden won't try anything, you know that. But I will."

His vivid blue eyes brightened. "You've gotten more feisty since we last spoke. I always did like that about you."

She suppressed a flinch. She wouldn't let him see her fear.

His eyes were glassy with fever. She detected a slight tremor in his gun hand. He was weakening. She could use that against him.

"I'm the expendable one." She took another step. The metal barrel touched her forehead. "Take me."

In one swift move, Maddox released Eden and seized Dakota, drawing her to him so her spine pressed against his chest. The whole time, he kept the gun on her.

Something large crashed behind them. Seven houses down, a portion of a burning house's roof collapsed in on itself. Flames surged into the sky, spitting and sparking.

Maddox cursed and jerked Dakota backward. "Eden, follow me. Anyone tries anything, Dakota gets the first bullet."

8

DAKOTA

I nstead of turning toward the road and Harlow's crumpled body,
Maddox hurried Dakota and Eden between the houses, through
several backyards to the next street over, and the next, following the
same path Dakota had taken to reach Eden less than an hour ago.

Eden stumbled beside them, crying silently.

Maddox's sweat-dampened shirt rubbed against Dakota's skin.
She inhaled the sour, pungent stench wafting off him and
suppressed the urge to vomit.

The haze of smoke dissipated as they traveled further from the
burning cul-de-sac. They rounded the corner of a beige stucco mini-
mansion, skirted the huge screened lanai and pool, and stumbled
between two large yards lined with six-foot fences.

"There." Maddox pushed her roughly toward a house with three
vehicles parked in the brick circular driveway. "The keys to at least
one of them should be inside. Let's go."

Maddox would likely put Eden in the back seat, take the
passenger seat himself, and force Dakota to drive with the gun
pointed to her head.

Once they were in the vehicle, it'd be that much harder to make a move. She couldn't risk forcing an accident with Eden in the car with them.

She wasn't worried about her own life. But Eden couldn't return to the Prophet. Dakota would do anything and everything within her power to save Eden from that fate.

No matter what.

"Hurry it up," Maddox panted. He was breathing heavily. Sour sweat poured off his feverish body.

Whatever move she was going to make, it needed to be soon.

They passed between two houses, their lawns divided by a small pond about twenty feet wide and just as long. The grassy walkway between the side of the closest house and the pond was only four feet wide.

Every Florida resident knew to steer clear of any body of water, no matter the size. Anything deeper than a puddle was liable to contain an alligator or two.

Maddox, Dakota, and Eden crowded together.

This was her chance. Maybe the only one she was going to get.

Panic clawed at her throat. For a moment, she couldn't breathe. What if she made a mistake? What if it was the wrong move?

She had to be calm. She had to focus. *One, two, three. Breathe.*

What if Maddox decided she was more trouble than she was worth and simply put a bullet through her brain? Then he'd be free to take Eden right back into that viper's nest he called home.

And Dakota would have failed at the only thing that mattered.

Breathe, damn it! Breathe.

Her muscles tensed. Dakota lowered her right hand to the knife sheathed at her side, the knife Maddox either hadn't noticed or hadn't deemed a legitimate threat.

She stretched out her leg and tripped Eden.

Eden lost her balance and tumbled against Maddox, striking the arm holding the gun to Dakota's head. She felt the cold metal scrape across the back of her scalp, then disappear.

Maddox expected something from Dakota, but not from Eden. It took him by surprise. "What the—"

But Dakota was already spinning and slashing at the closest piece of Maddox she could reach—his face. Her hands stung as the knife handle gouged into the cuts marring her palms.

He threw up his arm in time and the knife glanced off his forearm.

Maddox grabbed for her knife hand. He seized her wrist and slammed her hand against the stucco wall of the closest house.

Her fingers went numb. The knife dropped to the grass.

She jerked her leg up and kicked him in the kneecap as hard as she could.

His leg buckled. He released her arm.

"Eden, run!" she screamed.

Eden didn't move. She stood next to the pond, her arms hanging limply at her sides, a silent tear trickling down one blood-smeared cheek. Frozen in shock.

Dakota flew at Maddox again, going for the gun even as he raised it. She ducked in under his gun arm and head-butted him in the gut as the weapon discharged.

The blast exploded in her ears. Pain vibrated through her skull. Sounds faded.

They wrestled for the gun. She sucked in ragged mouthfuls of air, her scorched lungs begging for oxygen. Even sick with radiation poisoning, Maddox was physically stronger than she was. He jerked it out of her hands.

"Get behind me, Eden!" she cried. "Now!"

Startled out of her fugue, Eden shuffled like a sleepwalker toward Dakota.

Dakota shoved the girl behind her, against the wall.

Maddox stood, but he didn't come after her. The gun was in his hand, but it was aimed low, at her knees. He swayed on his feet. His face was so pale she could make out the blue veins beneath his skin.

He spat a string of yellowish spittle.

"You're sick," she said. "You have acute radiation syndrome."

"I should be dead a thousand times over."

That part, she couldn't disagree with. Maddox Cage was a cunning creature. Maybe he never came out on top, but he always made it out alive somehow, even when lesser men would've fallen.

"The Lord spared me," he said.

"The radiation will still kill you."

Even sick as he was, he managed to sneer. His steely blue eyes bored into hers. "It won't. I have a holy mission. This is only a test. One I will pass."

"You should've killed me when you had the chance. Isn't that what you promised?"

He laughed, spittle flying from his lips. "I wanted to. I've imagined a hundred ways to make you suffer."

"Then why didn't you?"

"I've missed you," he said, ignoring her question. "You know that?"

Her stomach clenched. Her head swam with memories—the two of them in their early teens, sneaking around the docks, stealing one of the airboats to explore the Glades for a lazy afternoon, for a few moments of escape from their stifling, restrictive lives.

Maddox's face was younger then, boyish and unlined, his dirty blonde hair spilling into those sly blue eyes. His features were more mischievous than cunning, but there was still a sharpness to him even as a boy.

They had been something like friends, once upon a time.

He was the one who offered her a reprieve from the exhausting toil of endless tasks the Prophet bestowed upon the females of the compound. He was the one who shared her doubts, who appreciated a barbed jab at the compound leadership—and even God Himself—on occasion.

The black sheep of his family, Maddox was the only one who

understood the shame, the loneliness, what it felt like to be ostracized, singled out, scapegoated and punished for the sins of someone else. Though he was several years older than Dakota, that shared experience had connected them somehow.

At least until his father ordered Maddox to conduct her punishments in the mercy room.

Then Maddox began to hate her almost as much as he hated himself.

"It didn't have to be this way," she said.

"Wrong again." He shook his head slowly, resigned. "It always had to be this way."

Three feet above Maddox's head, a bullet struck the side of the house.

9

DAKOTA

Maddox cursed and crouched. Another bullet sang through the air and cracked a Spanish tile from the roof above them. Broken pieces rained down on Maddox's head.

Dakota spun and went for Eden. She pulled the girl down beside her and pointed past the pond, the way they'd come but to the right, out of the line of fire.

Across the backyard, she glimpsed movement. Logan was crouched at the side of a huge two-story house behind a large AC unit.

More bullets sailed over their heads as Maddox returned fire.

Logan couldn't have many bullets left. If they were going to make the most of this, they had to go now. "Come on!"

Eden crouched, gasping, her eyes glassy. She was panicking, hyperventilating, rigid with terror. Dakota looped her arm beneath Eden's underarms and dragged her back. "Hurry!"

Half-bent, they dashed around the pond and across the manicured lawns. Dakota's muscles ached with exhaustion, her heart pumping sluggishly. She couldn't go much further before her body gave out on her.

They ran between two houses and came out one street over from Bellview Court. She looked back as she ran, searching for Maddox. Logan had him pinned. No one was chasing them. But she was terrified to stop. He was still too close. He could—

Abruptly, Julio was there, grabbing her shoulders. "Hey! I've got you! It's okay!"

She longed to sag into the comfort of his embrace. Instead, she used her remaining strength to hoist Eden up beside her. "We've got to get out of here. We need a car."

"Come with me."

She twisted to look back again. "But Logan—"

"Can take care of himself. Come on."

For once, she gave in. She let Julio take her by the arm and pull her back toward the others.

Shay crouched beside Harlow's body. Park had raised himself into a sitting position on the stretcher, his shoulders hunched, legs hanging over the sides. He stared down at Harlow's limp form.

"She's dead," he said in disbelief. Tears leaked from the corners of his eyes. "She was just here, and then she wasn't. She's just...gone."

Julio crossed himself. "I'm so sorry for your loss, Park. May I say a prayer for her soul?"

"She wasn't religious. She always said she wanted to be Buddhist 'cause she loved the idea of reincarnation, of coming back in the form you deserved, you know? But I guess it doesn't matter now, does it?"

"What would she come back as?" Shay asked as she gently closed Harlow's vacant eyes.

"Knowing her?" Park choked out a half-sob, half-laugh. "Probably a rhinoceros."

Dakota's gut twisted. She didn't feel grief. She didn't know the woman well enough to grieve for her. But anger, she knew well.

Maddox had no right to take Harlow's life. Or anyone's life. He talked all virtuous and self-righteous, like he believed the utter crap he spewed—just like his father, the Prophet, Jacob, and all the rest.

She should've found a way to kill him. She shouldn't have run. She should have ended it with him, right there, right then. *But Eden...*

The girl had been standing in the line of fire. It was the innocent bystanders who always paid with their lives. She had chosen to protect Eden over taking vengeance. No matter how it ate at her now, it was a choice she'd make again.

Eden pulled away. Dakota let her go.

Eden trudged to the spot where she'd dropped her notepad, the pen tucked inside, and picked it up. She clutched the notepad to her chest and stood there, staring glassy-eyed at nothing.

Dakota retrieved her Sig, inserted the magazine carefully with her bandaged palm, and chambered a round. She didn't holster the gun but kept it in her hands, ready.

Her vision went blurry with fatigue. She blinked hard, scanning the houses and yards behind them, searching for Logan and Maddox. She hadn't heard a gunshot in a few minutes.

Something moved near the rear of a yellow house opposite them, about forty yards away. She stiffened, adrenaline spiking. She raised her pistol, finger on the trigger, and sighted the corner wall. "Come out slow and steady."

Logan stepped into the yard, both arms up, the Glock in one hand. "It's me."

She lowered her gun, relieved.

Logan stomped up to her, his face livid. Anger radiated off him in waves. "Who the hell was that asshole I just risked my life to run off? What the hell are you doing?"

Guilt skewered her, but she lifted her chin. "Not now. There's no time."

Logan leaned in close, his eyes spitting fury. "We're not finished here."

She ignored his outrage. There were more pressing concerns. "What happened with Maddox?" Her throat tightened. "Did you— did you kill him?"

"He got away."

"What do you mean, 'got away'?" Dakota asked, her breath catching at the thought of Maddox still out there. Circling them, hunting, closing in.

Logan holstered his Glock. "I'm out of bullets. He wasn't. Luck- ily, he turned tail and ran instead of attacking again. Otherwise, I'd be telling a far different story."

Dakota shook her head. Dread and confusion coiled in her gut. "No. That doesn't make sense. That's not Maddox. He doesn't run away."

Logan shrugged, his eyes hard. "I don't know what to tell you. I followed him for several blocks. He was staggering, clutching his stomach. Maybe I hit him, but I doubt it. He looked sick as a dog. Hopefully, he crawls into a hole somewhere and dies."

"He might be gone now, but he'll come back," she said. "He won't give up. Maddox never gives up. I have bullets. I should go after him. I should kill him."

"We don't have the time." Julio gestured at the sun hovering just above the tree line. "We're still in the hot zone. We have multiple wounded people who need to get to the EOC and receive medical care, including you."

"I'm fine," Dakota rasped.

"And your so-called sister?" Logan asked.

Dakota spun around.

Eden had sunk to her knees. Her face was gray. She turned her head, gagged, and spewed a sickly string of yellow vomit into the grass.

10

LOGAN

L ogan watched Dakota run to her sister.

"She has radiation sickness," he said. "And I think I do, too."

His guts felt like some unseen hand was tying his intestines into knots. His skull was pounding. Even though the evening air had cooled, it felt like he was trapped inside a sauna.

"I feel okay," Julio said. "What does that mean?"

"Nothing," Shay said dully from beside Harlow's body. She rose heavily to her feet and leaned against the stretcher for balance. "With radiation exposure between one and two gray, some people will get sick; others won't. Some will live long, healthy lives, but five percent will die within months."

She tilted her chin at Eden. "She was exposed to higher radiation, but I can't tell you how much, not until we get her to a doctor."

Shay tried to stand on her own and walk to Eden. She swayed and sank back down onto the curb.

Julio rushed over to her. "Are you okay?"

She touched her bandaged head. "Yeah..."

"This isn't the time for optimism," Julio said. "If you're hurting, we need to know."

Helping Park set his broken bones and then tending to Dakota after the fire had taken a lot out of her. Her face was ashen. She was sucking in rapid, shallow breaths.

"I'm...dizzy from the blood loss," Shay admitted. "I'm sorry."

Dakota looked back one more time in the direction Maddox had fled. She obviously wanted to go after him and empty a mag into his chest, or worse. The desire was written all over her face.

Logan hadn't wanted to let him go, either. He hated the threat of a hostile out there somewhere. Even if Maddox was sick enough that Logan could hunt, ambush, and overpower him without a weapon, it would take precious time they didn't have.

Dakota let out a frustrated breath and set her jaw. "You're right. We've got to get to medical care. That's our first priority."

"What about Harlow?" Park stared down at her body with glassy, unfocused eyes. "She is—was—a good person. We can't just leave her like this."

Julio exchanged a glance with Logan. "What if we carry her into a house across the street, wrap her in a blanket, and leave her on a bed? We'll write down the address, and as soon as we get to the EOC, we can report it to the authorities. They'll come take care of it."

Park nodded in weary resignation.

Something thumped behind them.

Logan and Dakota whirled toward the sound.

Someone moved behind the gray F-150.

"Is it safe?" a man asked in a quivering voice.

"Yes," Shay said at the same time Dakota snapped, "No!"

"Come out, but leave your weapons behind," Logan called, his adrenaline spiking. "Keep your hands where we can see them."

"I'm putting down my Remington. Just...don't shoot." A

Caucasian couple stood up slowly, moved around the truck, and walked toward them.

"This is my wife, Vanessa," the man said, tense but not hostile. Dressed in pressed khakis and a golf shirt, he was average height and weight, with black-rimmed glasses and graying hair. "We've lived in this neighborhood for twelve years. Just who are you people, and what do you want?"

"I came here to get Eden," Dakota said. "We were attacked by...a looter. Now, we're getting the hell out of the hot zone."

The woman, Vanessa, looked from Dakota to Eden. She was in her forties and trim with short, carefully styled auburn hair and tasteful makeup. She wore diamond earrings and a pearl necklace draped around her neck. The fear only partially faded from her expression as she realized they weren't a threat. "And how do you know these people, dear?"

"Eden is my—" Dakota cleared her throat uncomfortably, then scowled. "She's my sister."

Vanessa smoothed her hair with shaking fingers, regaining her composure. "Oh, the sister! We've heard so much about you. Eden is such a lovely girl. She walked our little Yorkshire Terrier, Munchkin, every day after school until he passed last month."

"It was cool of you to try and defend us, but you nearly shot me." Dakota looked like she was restraining herself from punching the guy in the teeth.

"I *was* trying to shoot you. I thought you were thieves and looters."

"Have you been here since it happened?" Julio asked Carson, trying to change the subject.

"We've been sheltering in place," Vanessa said, "just like the emergency broadcasts instructed. We were at Carson's office for the first day and a half, but we just wanted to be home. We drove back yesterday afternoon..." Her voice faltered. "I...I work on Brickell Key as a litigator for Juniper, Hollandale, and Associates. I just finished a huge case and took the morning off to surprise Carson at his office for lunch...I was supposed to be right there, when it happened. On any other day, I would've been there."

She looked crushed, stricken. "All my co-workers are dead. All of them...I heard what they said on the radio. My building...it's not even there anymore."

She hugged herself, her movements slow and jerky, like a sleep-walker moving through a nightmare she couldn't escape from.

None of them could.

Carson slipped his arm around her shoulder to comfort her. "Where are Gabriella and Jorge Ross?" he asked, as if he'd just realized his neighborhood was completely abandoned. "Eden is their foster child."

Eden scribbled something on her notepad and held it up. *They never came back.*

Vanessa blinked rapidly, a distant, vacant look in her eyes. "I'm sure they're fine...in a hotel somewhere, perhaps..."

"We're heading to the airport to catch a plane to stay with Vanessa's brother in Chippewa Falls, Wisconsin," Carson said. "We can't stay here with this fire, and there's no way to call 911 with the power out. It should be safe there."

"Planes are grounded all across the country." Julio quickly explained everything they knew so far, with Park adding a few things they'd missed. "The airport is the acting Emergency Operations Center. They have food, shelter, and medical care."

Julio didn't say anything about Dakota, Eden, Shay, and Logan moving on to Dakota's friend in the Everglades, which was wise. It wasn't their business.

Vanessa raised a trembling hand to her mouth. "The government is there, at this emergency place? It'll be safe?"

"Yes," Dakota said. "That's where we're going now."

The husband and wife exchanged weighted looks. The wife tilted her chin, still trembling, but the husband shook his head in some long-practiced non-verbal communication only they understood.

Carson straightened his thick glasses and cleared his throat. "Look, I'm an orthodontist. I run a successful family-owned business in Buena Vista. We aren't prepared for what's out there. I'm smart enough to know that. I have my Remington rifle, but I admit I'm not a great shot. My wife can't shoot, and if I'm driving...we have no way to protect ourselves if bandits try to carjack our vehicle or steal our things."

"You all seem like decent folk who know what you're doing. And you're well-armed. If you'll escort us to the Emergency Operations Center, we can offer transport. We've got a Ford F-150 Super-Crew that seats six in the cab, with room in the bed if needed."

He looked at Logan, his apprehensive gaze straying to the tattoos snaking up his arms. He cleared his throat again. "It seems to me there's safety in numbers."

Julio and Shay looked to Dakota and Logan. Logan figured Dakota was adding up their lack of bullets and able-bodied manpower in her head, just like he was.

They were running out of options. They could waste time searching for a van or SUV in the neighborhood, along with the matching key fob, but the sun was setting fast.

If they wanted to get out of here quickly, they didn't have much choice.

"Fine," Dakota said. "But you defer to Logan on matters of security."

Logan raised his brows, pleasantly surprised, but didn't say anything. No way she was winning him over that easily.

"Deal," Carson said.

"I need more ammo," Logan said.

"What about my .308 Remington 700?" Carson offered. "My father passed it down to me when he died. You're welcome to use it. I have four boxes of ammunition."

A bolt-action rifle was accurate, dependable, and trouble-free. Logan wouldn't get off as many rapid-fire shots as with a semi-auto, but the rifle would hit its mark.

"Done," he said with palpable relief.

Dakota cast a sharp glance at the darkening sky. "And we leave in five minutes."

11

DAKOTA

Dakota and the others hurried as they prepared to leave. Vanessa provided several blankets from her guest bedroom, and Julio and Logan helped Park and Eden into the bed of the truck so they could lie down.

"What about the radiation contamination?" Julio asked, gesturing at the blankets.

"We'll get rid of everything we can as soon as we get out of the hot zone," Shay said. "But they need comfort right now. The hard truck bed could jostle Park's arm and cause further injury."

While Julio and Logan quickly attended to Harlow's body, Dakota checked on Eden. The girl stared blankly up at the sky, listless, maybe in shock. Or maybe she was too angry at Dakota to even look at her.

Dakota opened the rear passenger door. Several expensive-looking suitcases and overnight bags stuffed the seats and every spare inch of space. There wasn't room for one person to squeeze back there, let alone three.

"This isn't gonna work." She grabbed the first massive suitcase, lugged it across the seat, and dumped it on the driveway, touching as little of it as possible. It must have weighed fifty pounds.

The effort made her lungs and throat burn even worse. Her palms stung, but she ignored the pain. She'd already added a second and third suitcase to the pile when Vanessa dashed around the truck, waving her arms in agitated distress.

"What are you doing?" she asked, horrified.

"You can't take this stuff with you."

"It's *mine*. I most certainly can!"

Dakota didn't stop unloading the back. She turned to drop some fancy Vera Wang bag that probably cost a small fortune.

Vanessa tried to jerk it out of her hands. "You are *our* guests! We're the ones helping you—"

Dakota released the bag. The woman wasn't expecting it and stumbled backward.

"Lady," Dakota said with barely restrained impatience, "everything in your house is contaminated with radiation. *Everything*. Do you understand? Including that bag in your arms."

Vanessa's face drained of color. She dropped the bag like it'd just sprouted fangs and claws. "What?"

"You won't be taking anything with you into the EOC, probably including the clothes on your back. You'll need to be decontaminated."

"Everything I own is in that house," Vanessa said, her voice shaking. "Everything that *matters*."

"You're welcome to stay," Dakota said. "But we're leaving."

Vanessa began to cry. "I can't just leave everything! I've lived here twelve years! All my memories are here. My grandmother's fine china collection. My wedding dress. The letters from my mother before she died—"

"I'm sorry, dear, I'm so sorry," Carson repeated, like he was personally responsible for this hell.

Maybe Dakota should've had more sympathy for a woman

who'd just lost friends and co-workers, who was now leaving every earthly belonging behind, but she didn't. It was 'survive or die'.

She had no time or patience for this. She dumped the last bag on the driveway and gestured at the truck's open doors. "Get in or get out. Make up your mind."

Carson took Vanessa's arm and gently guided her into the front middle seat. "It's alright. Everything will be alright."

Logan took the front passenger seat with the Remington rifle and the ammo boxes at his feet. Dakota slid in the opposite side with her pistol and six remaining bullets. Shay and Julio followed.

The sun slipped behind the palm trees as they drove away from Bellview Court.

Dakota twisted in her seat and stared through the rear window at the splotch of red staining the road.

Harlow was dead. Maddox killed her.

Don't ever forget that. Not for a second. Don't forget what he did.

Dakota's buried past wasn't so buried. Maddox had plunged from her nightmares into the real world, devasting everything in his path.

He was still out there. Still dangerous. Still deadly.

If she ever saw him again, she would hunt him down and kill him.

No hesitation. No remorse.

They had a long way still to travel before they reached safety. They had to get everyone to medical care at the airport. Then make it to Ezra and his cabin in the Everglades—home.

So many ways for things to go wrong. So many opportunities for Maddox to find them again and attack.

Dakota shook the dark thoughts from her head. She'd made a grave mistake, and someone else had paid for it. She couldn't be this stupid again.

How easily that might have been Eden's lifeblood spreading in a crimson halo around her lifeless body. Dakota saw Eden's face again in her mind's eye, her stunned, disbelieving expression as she realized Dakota had lied to her, that the woman she loved and trusted wasn't who she thought she was...

The look of betrayal in her eyes seared Dakota to her core.

She forced herself to remain stiff and alert—ignoring the fatigue, the aching muscles, the pain in her body, in her soul. It didn't matter whether Eden hated her; she still depended on Dakota to keep her alive. So did Shay and Julio and the others.

Dakota would keep fighting with everything she had. And when she was completely spent, she would dig down deep and fight some more.

1 2

LOGAN

As Logan expected, SR 1 1 2 was a parking lot.

"We could take US 27 or even SR 944 west to the airport," Carson suggested.

"We need to stay off all the main roads." Logan shot a glance at Carson. "Residential only until things clear up."

He looked nervous as hell, even though he'd insisted on driving. Sweat slicked his forehead and stained the ironed collar of his golf shirt. "Okay, yeah. That's probably a good idea."

"If we can get on 28ᵗʰ Street, we can take it to South River Drive," Julio said as he studied the paper map he'd kept in his shoulder bag. "21ˢᵗ Street will take us the rest of the way, avoiding the highways."

"Do it," Dakota said.

They carefully maneuvered west along the side roads until they reached 28ᵗʰ Street. They had barely enough clearance to squeeze the truck through the congested roads. At one point, 28ᵗʰ Street was so crammed with abandoned vehicles they had to backtrack and do several loops through neighborhood side streets.

The going was tough and slow, especially in the gathering darkness. Often, they were forced to veer onto the curb, the truck bumping and bouncing, jostling the passengers against each other. More than once, they had to stop so Eden could vomit.

Logan felt ill himself, the nausea churning each time the truck swerved and jolted. The cab stank of sickness. The humid air was sticky and cloying. Logan's nerves were on edge. He wasn't claustrophobic, but he'd give his left nut to get the hell out of that truck.

Carson flicked on the headlights.

"We're sitting ducks with those lights," Logan growled. "Anyone can see us a half-mile away."

"And without them, we can't see at all," Carson argued. "It's too dark without the street lights or ambient light from houses and buildings. We need to see."

"Still not a good idea," Logan said.

But Carson insisted. It was his truck.

Logan wasn't ready to overpower the man in his own vehicle. Not yet. But he didn't like it. In all this darkness, the headlights were targets.

They made it one mile. Then another.

Occasional lights run by generators pricked the night, but the rest of the city was completely black as far as he could see. On all sides, buildings hunched dark and shadowed, like huge creatures— beasts and monsters—taking on new, sinister shapes in his imagination.

The sky was empty of stars. Thick clouds covered the moon.

It felt like they were the only people in the entire world—though of course, they weren't. There were people still here, hidden behind their curtains and closed doors. Scared, numb, grieving, and angry. A few seethed with hate and vengeance.

Not all of them were friendlies.

Carson let out a muttered curse. The whites of his eyes were huge. The man looked like he was balancing on the brink of panic.

Beneath his shaking hands, the Ford lurched and jolted. He

could barely keep the wheel straight. He kept jerking his feet on the gas, then the brakes.

"Careful, please!" Shay said. "We've got injured people here."

"I know, I know." With a squeal of burning rubber, Carson wrenched the wheel and veered between two rows of cars on both sides of the road.

Fenders scraped either side of the truck. A moss-green Hyundai leaned against the passenger side door. On the other side, a Civic was pinned against the rear tire.

Carson swore under his breath.

"I'm happy to drive if you'd like a break," Julio offered from the back.

Carson's hands tightened on the steering wheel. "It's my truck. I'm driving it. I'm fine. Everything is fine."

Logan twisted in his seat, checking and rechecking the dark yards and buildings, the empty cars huddled along the sides of the road.

His pulse hammered in his throat. This was a perfect spot for an ambush. If hostiles leapt out of any of these dark buildings, they would be trapped, as easy pickings as fish caught in a barrel.

He despised feeling this helpless. "We've got to get out of here."

Carson reversed, flinching at the rasping grind of metal against metal as the truck wrenched free of the vehicles on either side. They scraped past several more cars and turned left at the next light. Without electricity, it was nothing more than a dark blob in more darkness.

"Could we turn the radio on?" Julio asked, his voice tense. "Maybe there's an emergency broadcast."

"Good idea." Carson switched the radio on and turned the dial.

After a belch of static, a female voice broke through. "...Keep listening for the emergency processing center nearest you. You will receive food and water, medical care, and shelter. No personal belongings will be allowed. Please wear protective clothing, eyewear, and gloves to protect yourself from the radiation. Use only sealed food and water."

"This is an emergency alert broadcast. If you reside in the following counties, please make your way to the nearest processing center only if you are injured or need assistance. You are located within a safe zone and do not need to evacuate. Please do not panic. Keep listening for a list of emergency centers..."

She rattled off a list of locations several miles away in Hialeah Gardens, Kendall, and Miramar. "If you are located within three miles of the coast north of Hobie Island Beach Park and east of 22nd Avenue north through Fort Lauderdale, please evacuate and find your nearest emergency center. Survivors in downtown Miami, Brickell, East Little Havana, Overtown, and Wynwood, when you can safely do so, please evacuate to the Miami International Airport for assistance..."

"See?" Carson said to his wife. "That's where we're heading, dear. Everything will be fine."

"Nothing is fine," Vanessa whimpered. "Don't you see that?"

"I'm just trying to make the best of things."

Vanessa shivered and stared straight ahead through the windshield. "It's not working."

Logan raked his hand through his unruly hair, gritting his teeth to hold back a curse.

These two were barely holding it together. It was a whole different world they lived in—where life didn't kick you every chance it got, where high-dollar promotions, luxurious vacations, and homes that belonged on the covers of magazines were the norm.

They'd probably never met a problem they couldn't throw money at to fix. Until now.

Maybe joining up with these people was a mistake. But with Park, Shay, and Eden injured, they needed the vehicle. Dakota had inhaled so much smoke, it was a wonder she was on her feet at all.

And Logan didn't want to admit how sick he was, not even to himself.

They needed the truck until they reached the airport and the EOC.

Then all bets were off.

13

LOGAN

C arson turned the radio dial. More staticky stations. Then a deep male voice with a prim British accent came on the air: "...in this, the single greatest catastrophe and humanitarian disaster the United States has ever seen.

"In the L.A. attack alone, experts estimate that the radioactive fallout has contaminated a three-hundred-square-mile region. Two to three million residents will require relocation facilities, unable to return to live and work in the affected hot zones for anywhere between three to twenty years."

"What can you tell us about the astounding numbers of refugees being reported?" asked a female radio announcer in a grave, raspy smoker's voice.

"In the Los Angeles Basin, more than half of the six million people who fled their homes are now stranded, strung out along the major interstates to the north of the San Gabriel Mountains and along the north and south coasts of L.A."

"Holy hell," Logan breathed.

"Where are they going to put all those people?" Julio asked in disbelief. "This is just for one city...There are twelve more..."

"Hundreds of schools, hotels, warehouses, and stadiums have been opened for displaced persons," the announcer continued as if he'd heard Julio's question, "but these facilities are already overwhelmed. Most refugees are critically low on water and food. Some have set up tents or are simply camping in their vehicles on the side of the road, in parks, and on public property. Many have run out of gas and have nowhere else to go."

"Similar stories are coming out of every attacked city, from Charleston and New York City to New Orleans, Norfolk, and Seattle," the female announcer said. "Surrounding states are reporting mass food shortages, rolling brownouts and blackouts, and increased crime and looting as officials try to deal with hundreds of thousands of displaced refugees.

"FEMA is working around the clock in conjunction with the Red Cross and other humanitarian aid organizations to provide emergency temporary shelters, but the demand for housing for tens of millions across the country has far outstripped their capacity."

"What about medical care for the injured, Rebecca?" the male announcer asked.

"State officials report that functioning hospitals within a two-hundred-mile radius of the thirteen affected cities are overwhelmed, with severe shortages of personnel and medical supplies. Dozens of mobile military medical units have been deployed to help relieve the overload, utilizing stadiums and gyms as emergency clinics."

"My parents are in Charleston," Vanessa said. There was no whine in her voice now, only grief. "We couldn't get through at all before our phones died. I have no idea if they're even okay."

"I'm so sorry," Julio said.

"They'll be fine," Carson said. "I'm sure they're fine."

"You don't know that," Vanessa said. "No one can know that."

They fell silent again, listening to every horrible snippet of news, each seemingly worse than the last.

"...Criticism intensified with calls to President Harrington to recall a significant portion of our four hundred and fifty thousand forward deployed troops. Texas Governor Omar Harris's quote to the Washington Post yesterday has gone viral: 'We don't need them in Syria protecting the Syrians, we need them on American soil protecting Americans.'"

The announcers continued talking, but Logan only caught bits and pieces. "...Over a hundred thousand people are presumed dead in Miami alone, not counting the injured or those expected to die of radiation poisoning...social media blowing up with images of mass graves of thousands...Nightly rioting in Miami-Dade has reached a fever pitch...statewide curfews have been enacted as Governor Blake urges President Harrington to declare martial law..."

"May God help us all," Julio said.

To Logan, the mind-numbing numbers and horrifying statistics were white noise. He couldn't wrap his head around it, and he didn't want to.

What was happening in L.A. and New York and D.C. meant nothing to him. Even the disaster of greater Miami meant little.

He cared only for what was happening in this neighborhood, on this street, in this cab.

Everything else was a distraction.

And distractions could get you killed.

"The country is falling to pieces!" Vanessa said, shocked. "What are we going to do?"

"We have to take care of ourselves, now," Dakota said.

"What if it's all over?" Vanessa's voice rose with a tinge of hysteria. "What if we never recover? What if the U.S. becomes another collapsing, war-torn country like Syria and Venezuela—"

"Maybe we should turn it off," Julio said gently. "Just for a while."

Silence filled the cab. Vanessa stared straight ahead, trembling, lost in whatever future horrors gripped her imagination.

Logan didn't have time to envision the horrors of the future. There were plenty right in the here and now.

He kept his gaze on the houses creeping by outside.

Two shadows stood on a dark front porch. They were large and bulky—men. One held a flashlight.

As the truck passed, the man aimed the light at them. The beam slowly swept the truck, pausing on Logan and the Remington in his hands.

He squinted against the glare. The men didn't have guns themselves, but they had weapons. The one with the flashlight gripped a crowbar in his other hand. The second guy held a long kitchen knife.

"We may have trouble," he murmured. "Stay alert."

Beside him, Vanessa sucked in her breath.

Logan tensed, watching them carefully as the truck rolled past.

The men didn't move, just watched.

Most likely, they were guarding their own families from hostiles rather than plotting mayhem themselves. But you never knew.

"We should be out of the hot zone now," Julio said a few minutes later. "Harlow said it was only a mile west of us, didn't she?"

"Yeah," Shay said, "she did."

Logan knew he should feel relief that they were out of danger from the radiation, but he didn't feel anything of the sort. The radioactive particles were already on them, inside them—invisible, deadly, doing their dirty work with silent, lethal precision.

It made his skin crawl, made him want to vomit until his stomach turned inside out in a vain effort to rid his body of the hideous toxins.

Damn, he wanted a drink. Wanted to forget for just a few minutes the poison roiling in his gut, the thousands of corpses hidden in the dark, the death and destruction hanging over the city like a black shroud, that clung to him like a shadow he couldn't escape.

But he couldn't have a drink. In a misguided moment of gallant good intentions, he'd stupidly dumped it out on the road. Idiot. He'd take back every vow and promise he'd ever made for a shot of vodka right now.

They'd driven well over an hour when he heard it. The sound was unmistakable—the *rat-a-tat* of automatic gunfire.

14

MADDOX

R age burned through Maddox Cage's veins.
He fled the Palm Cove subdivision, staggering between houses, around huge screened lanais and pools, across trim lawns and manicured gardens, clutching his gun with one hand, his nauseous stomach with the other.

One bullet had grazed his arm, but it was a surface wound. The sickness wrenching his guts was another matter. Sour sweat matted his hair to his scalp. Every inch of his intestines felt like they were on fire. Waves of dizziness wracked his body.

He'd been forced to run. If he hadn't, that man with Dakota— Logan, he'd called himself—would've hunted him down and killed him.

Normally, Maddox could hold his own. He'd been trained by combat soldiers. His father had made him learn to shoot and fight and kill when he was ten years old.

He feared no one.

But things were different now.

He'd thought he could overcome it on his own, through sheer force of will—and Maddox Cage had considerable will—but once again, he was wrong. The debilitating radiation had made him weak. In his weakness, he'd allowed that slut to slip through his fingers yet again.

How dare she? How could she? He'd trusted her once. Even— but now? She'd betrayed him. Now she deserved nothing but suffering.

His vision went black with fury and righteous indignation. He paused, leaning heavily against the stucco side of some beige monstrosity, and cursed until spittle ran down his chin.

It was several minutes before he'd calmed himself enough to think clearly. This was a test. He'd thought he passed it. But weren't the most arduous tests reserved for the most devoted followers?

As long as he still held breath in his lungs, he would let nothing stop him.

At least he'd gleaned one nugget of information he didn't have before. It would be enough to placate his father. He was sure of it.

He pushed himself from the wall and kept walking, forcing one weak, trembling leg in front of the other.

It grew darker. Long purple shadows stretched across the pavement.

Occasionally, he saw people. A family stared out a broken front window, several lit candles on the window sill. A skinny, ragged woman hugged herself and chain-smoked on her front porch while two little kids in saggy diapers rode tricycles on the cracked side-walk. An old couple slumped in lawn chairs, sweating and dull-eyed from heat stroke.

Maybe they knew they were out of the hot zone. Maybe they were too numb and resigned to care.

Several cars weaved between the stalled vehicles crowding the road, their trunks crammed with suitcases, pillows, clothes, toys, photo albums—the remnants of a life. With no electricity, no A/C, and no water, some of the families that had remained behind to shelter in place had given up, choosing to flee like everyone else.

An overweight shirtless guy in striped boardshorts stood on the street corner next to the road sign. He was in his late thirties, with tan lines circling his neck and arms, his soft, flabby beer-belly fish-white. He held a cell phone high in the air with both hands.

Maddox staggered toward him.

The man noticed him and stepped back, his face blanching. "Hey, man, you don't look so good."

Maddox stopped ten feet away so as not to alarm him. He forced a disarming smile to his lips. "You have service?"

The guy relaxed. "Barely. It really sucks. I've only managed to get one call through. Several texts, though. It goes in and out. The first few days, there was nothin'. I kept my phone off and let everyone else drain their batteries trying to connect every other second."

"Smart."

"Yeah, man." The guy grinned at his own genius. "Now if we could just get the damn power back on. My old lady's about to crap a brick, you know? Seriously, though. My mom's not doing so well in the heat without the A/C. No one can live in South Florida without air conditioning. Not for long."

Maddox hid a wince with a wider smile. He kept walking, stepping off the sidewalk to avoid the loser with the phone.

"Hey, man, take care of yourself, okay?" The guy called after him. "Miami needs to watch out for Miami, amiright?"

At the end of the street, Maddox caught sight of an elementary school. Next to the school stretched a huge set of soccer, football, and softball fields.

He stopped and took in the sight. He blinked to clear his blurry vision and let his gaze travel across the empty, darkened fields.

It gave him an idea.

15

LOGAN

L ogan stiffened. He peered out the window, looking ahead and behind them. They were leaving a mostly residential area.

On every street, maybe three or four houses on each side had some sort of glow from candles or the occasional swipe of a flashlight beam across a window.

The rest were dark. It didn't mean they were empty.

The smart ones wouldn't give their presence away, not on a night like this.

Shouts and screams echoed in the night, followed by another string of gunfire, this time from a different direction. A dim glow flickered over the rooftop of a squat condo complex maybe a hundred yards away.

Another fire.

"Oh, hell," he muttered.

"That was gunfire!" Vanessa cried.

"Rioting," Julio said from the back seat. "Or looting. Maybe both."

"Or a gang turf battle," Logan said.

"It was only a matter of time," Dakota said.

"You think it's the Blood Outlaws?" Shay's voice was soft. She sounded frail—and terrified.

"Hopefully, we don't have to find out," Julio said.

"Switch off the headlights," Logan said. "Turn off the car."

Carson obeyed. He slowed, easing to a stop before a stop sign at a quiet intersection. "Can we go around it?"

Logan kept his eyes on the street. "Julio, keep the flashlight low. You see anything on the map, any way to avoid this?"

"We're in Allapattah," Julio said. "Looks like mostly residential to the north. To the south, we've got businesses, grocery stores, pharmacies, and warehouses. We'll hit 22nd Street in a quarter mile. There'll be heavier traffic, more people. We're more likely to run into trouble."

"What are the options?" Shay asked.

"We should keep going," Carson said. "We've got a vehicle. We can gun it and power through any dangerous areas."

"The truck's going to draw attention," Dakota said. "Even in the dark."

"We could find somewhere to hole up for the night," Julio offered.

"What about our sick and injured?" Dakota asked. "We need to get Eden, Park, and Shay to a doctor as soon as possible."

"And if we get shot on the way?" Logan demanded. "That won't help anyone."

"We can't stay out here," Vanessa said. "These gangs are crazy. We hear it all the time on the news. They're animals! It isn't safe."

As they talked, Logan scanned the street ahead and behind them, then the yards, the houses, then back to the street.

Thirty yards ahead on the right, two dark shapes materialized around the corner of a small house. They were barely distinguishable in the darkness. Logan squinted, trying to make out details. They were hunched, moving stealthily. Up to no good.

"I've got three—no, four—possible problems in a backyard just behind us," Dakota said tensely. "They just scaled the fence."

Something thudded against the rear of the truck.

Logan's adrenaline skyrocketed. He whipped around, gun up, searching for the culprit.

"What was that?" Vanessa cried.

"Shhh!" Julio hissed. "Please."

A loud crack echoed in the night air. Something shattered.

"Oh no. No, no, no..." Vanessa ducked and covered her head with her hands. "They're shooting at us!"

"I think that was our taillight breaking," Dakota said. "They're throwing rocks."

Another fist-sized rock struck the rear windshield. A tiny, spidering crack appeared.

Logan didn't intend to waste precious bullets on rocks. That didn't mean things wouldn't escalate fast. He couldn't tell whether they were all unarmed, or whether this was just a test run—the same way a shark circled and bumped its potential prey before taking a bite.

"Go!" he said. "Go now!"

16

LOGAN

With shaking fingers, Carson turned the keys and restarted the Ford. The engine rumbled to life. A few more rocks bounced harmlessly off the roof and sides of the truck as they pulled away.

"Look out!" Julio cried.

Carson wrenched the wheel to the left, tires squealing as he overcorrected. The truck bounced sharply left, narrowly avoiding crashing into the back of a Toyota Forerunner.

The driver's side scraped past a row of parked cars. The mirror struck something and bent with a screech, the glass cracked, the frame dented.

Carson slammed the brakes, hurling everyone against their seatbelts. Logan wasn't wearing his in case he needed to leap out of the vehicle quickly to defend the group. He knocked into the side door, smacking his shoulder and head on the glass. Pain spiked up his spine.

"Damn it!" Dakota cried. "Do you or do you not know how to drive?"

"Be careful!" Shay said. "You could do permanent damage to Park's arm!"

"Everyone shut up!" Logan roared.

To the south, he had a clear view of the wide thoroughfare of 22nd Street. Four or five buildings were on fire. Dozens of shadows darted here and there. The sounds of screaming and shouting grew louder.

Dozens of people climbed atop abandoned cars, jeering and yelling, hoisting beer bottles and crowbars above their heads. A few held semi-automatic rifles and pistols.

A bunch of thugs took baseball bats to various vehicles, slamming windshields and taillights, denting hoods and fenders.

The destruction wasn't limited to cars. More figures hustled in and out of the stores lining the streets, carrying boxes of electronics and other goods. At least ten bodies lay prone on the sidewalks or in the street—either dead or beaten to within an inch of their lives.

They couldn't drive through this. It was suicide.

"Keep driving," Logan said. "Take a right here, away from that madness."

"It's north of us, too," Dakota said. "And west. I can hear it. Just a bit further away. And not as crazy. Yet."

"We have to stop somewhere," Logan said, not a question.

He half-expected Dakota to argue with him—it seemed to be something she enjoyed—but she didn't. "A house?" was all she said.

Logan shook his head. "Some of these houses that're dark still have people inside them. The way things are headed out here, they'd probably shoot us before we even finished knocking on the door. I would."

"Then where?"

"Is that something ahead on the left?" Julio said, leaning forward and pointing through the windshield. "Are those lights?"

Two blocks ahead, a small, rundown two-story Best Value Motel appeared, the sign written in Spanish. Lights glowed in the lobby and a few of the windows.

A fire station stood across the street. It was also running off generator power. A few lights flickered in the windows, and one of the firetrucks was parked sideways in front of the entrance for protection and cover if the gangs ventured further out.

"I think that motel might be open," Dakota said.

"Maybe," Logan allowed.

Every muscle in his body ached with tension. His eyes burned with exhaustion. He needed to rest—his body demanded it. If they didn't stop now, he wouldn't be in any shape to defend them.

It was his job, his duty, to protect them. He'd been an enforcer in his old life, a killer dog on a leash. Dakota was tough and street smart, and she could hold her own. But Logan had the skillset to keep them all alive.

Something had happened in the last day. He felt connected to them, somehow, to Julio and Shay and Dakota, even Park and the girl, Eden. Obligated to see this through in a way he hadn't felt in years.

He studied the building, straining to remain alert. "Drive around the block first, slowly. And keep the lights off. I want to avoid walking into a trap."

Carson followed his instructions. A gas station squatted beside the motel, along with a sagging dollar store and an orange-painted laundromat, both signs in Spanish.

Behind the motel stood a long, low row of single-story office buildings—all dark. The hotel parking lot boasted several dozen cars. The motel itself was one of those low-budget affairs with external doors and rickety metal stairwells.

He didn't notice anything suspicious—other than the pop of gunfire and shouting in the distance.

On their second pass, Logan directed Carson to pull into the entrance.

Two cars blocked the sides of the road, leaving enough room for only a single vehicle to pass through at a time.

A dark figure leaned against the side of a white Kia Rio. He stiffened and stood at attention when the truck pulled off the road. A holster at his waist carried a handgun, and he cradled a Ruger American rifle in his arms.

He didn't point the weapon at them, but the threat was all too clear.

17

LOGAN

V anessa gasped. "Turn around!"

"Not yet." Logan flicked on the interior lights to show the figure with the rifle that they didn't intend harm. "Stay calm."

"Carson, roll down your window," Dakota instructed. "Nice and slow."

It was difficult to twist and aim the rifle inside the cab, so Logan left it loosely leaning against the passenger door frame. He knew Dakota would have a bead on the guy from the rear passenger window.

With a shaking hand, Carson buzzed down the driver's side window as an Indian guy strode up to them. He was young, maybe in his mid-twenties, dressed in jeans and an old Metallica T-shirt, with a friendly but guarded expression. "How can I help you?"

"We—we need a place to stay the night," Carson stammered, staring at the Ruger only a foot away from his face. "We're headed out of the city. But things are getting dangerous."

The guy peered into the interior of the cab, checking them out. He nodded to himself, satisfied with what he found. "You've got that right. I'd advise not traveling at night right now."

"How bad is it?" Carson asked.

"You can hear for yourself," the guy said. "I haven't seen a cop car since it happened."

"Has the rioting and looting affected you yet?" Julio asked.

"Nah. There ain't much over here they want."

"Not yet, anyway," Dakota said.

It wouldn't take long to go through all the food and goodies in the upscale businesses and stores. Then the mobs would be looking anywhere and everywhere. Especially places with electricity.

But they only needed one night. It was a risk, but so was continuing on.

"How come you aren't closed down like everyone else?" Logan leaned slightly over Vanessa to get a better look at the guy.

He had short, buzzcut hair and black fuzz on his upper lip and chin. He gave a little shrug. "My father is the owner. We have a good generator. Most people don't have electricity, water, or A/C. He wanted to help the refugees trying to get out of the city."

"How benevolent of him," Dakota muttered from the back seat.

The guy tilted his chin at the fire station across the street. "They went out the first night to try and protect the local businesses. Not all of them came back. There's four of them left at the station. Too dangerous to go home, and they've got no families to search for. We've been watching out for each other."

"We'll stay the night," Carson said.

"It's cash only," the guy said. "Credit card machines aren't working."

"Fine," Dakota said. "We need two rooms. How much?"

"Two hundred cash a night. Per room."

"So not that benevolent," Dakota said.

"Are you serious?" Carson sputtered. "This place is normally, what, seventy bucks a night, if that?"

The guy only looked at him without smiling. He'd gone through this song and dance plenty of times already. "Gas for the generator is very expensive and hard to find. My brother and I will be up all night to offer security. You can pay, or you can go. Up to you."

"We'll pay," Logan said.

"I need to see the cash. Just to be safe, you know."

Carson muttered to himself as he pulled out his wallet. "I have two hundred."

"I've got fifty," Julio offered.

"I have it." Frantically, Vanessa tugged out several crisp twenties and thrust it at him. "There. Take it."

The guy shook his head and stepped back. "Go on ahead to the lobby and my father will get you situated. Have a great night."

Carson put the truck into drive and rolled carefully between the two parked cars. He pulled up beneath the roof overhang in front of the lobby doors. The glass in the door and window frames were broken, but everything had been swept up.

Another young Indian guy, likely the brother, lounged against the check-in counter with a Mossberg shotgun in his hands. His pockets were bulging—probably with spare shells.

"Stay in the cab," Logan said. "I'll go in."

Once inside, he paid the balding, older man behind the counter. "Give us two end rooms with two beds in each, next to each other on the second story, as far from the lobby as possible. Do the rooms have a connecting door? Can we have it opened?"

"Yes, of course." The owner set four keycards down on the counter. "Rooms 239 and 240. We have limited power, but the city water's off. My wife put gallons of water in every room. Not for drinking. For the toilet."

"Got it." Logan stuffed the keycards in his pocket with his free hand. With the other, he still held the Remington pointed at the floor. "How's the smell?"

"The smell?" The man wrinkled his nose. "It's fine."

It wouldn't be for long. Not with nonworking sewers backing up soon. Not with mountains of uncollected trash piling up. But that wasn't Logan's concern right now.

"Check out is at ten a.m.," the man said as Logan headed for the door.

Logan nodded at the brother, who stared back at him impassively, attempting to appear tough and intimidating to protect his father's business.

Logan didn't need their protection. He provided his own.

18

LOGAN

Once they reached their hotel rooms, Logan and Julio offered to carry Park.

"I can walk," Park muttered weakly. "My arm is broken, not my legs."

"Clearly, your pride is wounded as well," Dakota said.

"It'll recover just fine," Park said. "After a week of sleep. Maybe a month."

"You get ten hours. Sorry to disappoint you."

Park still needed Julio's arm to steady him as he stumbled up the steps. "Why are we on the second floor again?" His face was bone-white from the effort of climbing. "This is literally torture."

"If there's any trouble, it'll likely begin at the lobby," Logan explained. "Most people intent on robbing and looting always start with the easiest targets, i.e. the first floor. We'll hear it before it reaches us, and can take the stairs on the east end, the west end, or through the central stairwell. If we really had to, we could jump the railing. Plus, if we're forced to defend ourselves, we have the higher ground up here and can better pick off any hostiles."

"Color me impressed." Park settled onto the mattress, shook his head, and winced. "Well, this has been a ballbuster of a day."

Julio helped Shay, while Logan offered Eden his arm. The girl threw up on the sidewalk—barely missing Logan's shoes—but made it into room 240 without further incident.

Kids made him uncomfortable. Too many bad memories. Too many nightmares. As soon as he could, he disentangled himself and stepped away swiftly.

Dakota glanced at him, her eyes narrowing.

He stared back at her. She had no right to judge him. No right at all.

She turned back to the girl. "Eden, let's get you into bed."

Vanessa settled gingerly on the closest bed, gazing at it in consternation like she expected fleas to start dancing on her pillow. Her face contorted, and fresh tears tracked down her cheeks, smearing her mascara. With a whimper, she jumped up, rushed into the first bathroom, and slammed the door shut.

"Use the jugs of water to flush," Logan called after her.

She didn't respond. The sounds of muffled sobs filtered through the thin door.

"Please bear with my wife," Carson said quietly to Logan. "She's a successful, high-powered lawyer in her firm. In the world she knows, she's confident, efficient, and in control. But this—she's never dealt with anything like this. Neither of us have."

Logan didn't have the time or patience to coddle anyone. "No one has."

"We still have to keep it together," Dakota said. "All of us."

"We will." Carson nodded stiffly. "We get it."

"Let's get everyone situated, "Julio said. "Women take the beds, men take the floor. Except for Park, since he's injured."

"I'll take it," Park said. "I have no shame. Not anymore." He looked around for a moment, as if he expected Harlow to pipe up with a sarcastic comment. He stiffened and inhaled sharply like he was realizing all over again that she wasn't coming back.

"I'm truly sorry for your loss, Park," Julio said, watching him.

Park didn't say anything after that. He just lay flat on his back, cradled his broken arm, and stared up at the ceiling, his eyes wet.

"There's room for everyone to have a spot if we don't mind sharing," Shay said.

"I'm fine with the floor," Logan said.

"Shay, you need to lay down," Julio said. "You're swaying on your feet."

Shay shook her head wearily. "I need to monitor Park's vitals and see to his wounds. Logan needs a new dressing on his laceration. I need to check on Eden and Dakota."

"And we need to change your dressings, too," Julio said. "Let me help. Just tell me what to do."

"Are you sure?" Shay asked. "There might be blood."

"I'm just gonna have to get used to it, aren't I?" Julio said with a small, rueful smile.

"Thank you," Shay said, managing a shaky grin back at him.

While the two of them focused on the group's injuries, Logan focused on security. He scanned the cheap motel room: ocean prints hanging on the beige walls, threadbare brown carpet, a small round table and two chairs by the window, two queen beds covered with thin, flower-print bedspreads, and a faux wood entertainment center against the far wall with a tiny fridge and ancient TV.

At the end of the room was the yellowed counter with the sink. The toilet and shower were in their own small room to the right. The second room had the same layout but flipped.

As requested, the connecting door was unlocked.

Dakota angled her chin at the door. "More exits?"

"Exactly. Keeps our options open and everyone together."

In each room, he grabbed one of the chairs and wedged it beneath the door handle.

"Locked doors won't matter much with the windows broken," Dakota said.

"That's why we'll take turns on watch," Logan said. "Two five-hour rotations. We need to sleep in. We're all exhausted, which lowers alertness and reaction time. Tomorrow is gonna be a long day."

A scream echoed in the distance, followed by a rattle of gunfire. It sounded almost celebratory, like fireworks.

Dakota stared at the window, her expression stony. "Tonight is going to be a long night."

"I'll take first watch." Logan lowered his voice. "You take second. I don't know or trust the Wilburns. It needs to be us."

His gut twinged at the use of *us*.

Dakota didn't seem to notice his discomfort. She nodded tightly. "Good."

19

DAKOTA

Dakota sat next to the broken window in one of the chairs in room 240, her pistol aimed at the door. The lights were switched off inside the motel rooms to better see outside. The air was hot and stifling. Someone was snoring.

The night outside the window was black. A fire glinted from somewhere several blocks away. Then another. She'd been on watch for over an hour and hadn't seen any movement. She couldn't see the motel entrance from here, but she hadn't heard any cars drive in, either.

Muffled voices echoed outside. Laughter and shouting. Occasionally, shots rang out. Some in the distance, some much closer. And other noises: things crashing, things being smashed, car alarms screeching.

And then there were the screams—deep, guttural, terrifying.

Eden slept in the bed closest to her, which she'd shared with Dakota until it was Dakota's turn for watch. Shay and Park shared the second bed.

In the other room, Vanessa and Carson had one bed, while Julio slept alone in the other. Instead of sleeping in the bed with Julio,

Logan lay on the floor next to Dakota's chair with only a pillow beneath his head, the hunting rifle locked and loaded at his side.

No one had spoken much before falling into exhausted sleep—each person fighting off their own demons of despair and desperation. They'd escaped the hot zone, but it was little comfort.

The world was still crumbling around them.

Other than Julio, Vanessa, and Carson, most of them were sick. Dakota's lungs felt scorched, her throat raw from the smoke inhalation. The knot on her head ached furiously. Shay was weak and glassy-eyed. Logan admitted to nausea, but only after Shay had lectured him into submission.

The radiation exposure had caught up to them. The theater shelter had saved their lives, but it hadn't completely protected them. For the last day, the radiation levels had been low, but not non-existent. It all added up.

Except for Julio and Dakota, they'd barely eaten anything for dinner. Dakota scarfed down two candy bars and a bag of Baked Lays simply to keep her energy up.

Before going to bed, everyone had scrubbed down with soap and water and the alcohol wipes as best they could. There was nothing else they could do.

Logan told them to sleep with their shoes on in case they needed to flee fast in the middle of the night. Vanessa complained of blisters and removed hers anyway—a pair of impractically high-heeled, strappy red sandals—but everyone else slept completely clothed.

After she'd repacked the medical supplies, water, and food, Dakota had put the bags next to the door. She wiped Eden down and helped her into the bed closest to the window. She placed the notepad on the nightstand next to her.

Dakota studied her with growing concern. Eden's face was slack. Her arms and legs were limp, her eyes unfocused as she stared vacantly at the ceiling.

She'd thrown up a few times in the motel wastebasket. Shay had given her some Pepto-Bismol from their first aid stash, but she'd warned Dakota it probably wouldn't do any good. Radiation poisoning went far deeper, was far more insidious than a mere stomach bug.

But this was worse even than radiation poisoning.

Eden was in shock. It was too much for her to handle. After two days trapped in a bathroom, she'd barely survived a fire. She'd found one brother after years—only to have him put a knife to her throat and reveal that her other brother was dead. Then she'd watched someone get shot and killed right in front of her.

"Eden," she whispered. "Please talk to me." She'd even take the sign language she couldn't understand if it meant Eden was communicating *something*. "You know I'll never leave you, right?" she whispered. "Never, ever."

Eden's eyes were shiny and unfocused. She didn't blink. She didn't show any sign that she'd heard Dakota at all—or that she wanted to.

It didn't matter that Eden wasn't her real sister; Eden was Dakota's only family, all she had. For the last three years, her every thought had been to protect this girl.

What if Eden hated her now? What if she'd lost her? The thought was unbearable. Dakota felt it like an incredible pressure, like an immense rock crushing her lungs. A little more weight and she might crack wide open.

It was too hot. She hated listening to everyone's breathing. Dread twisted in her chest, winding tighter and tighter, until her whole body thrummed with it.

She needed air.

She left the chair in place and the door locked. Silently and carefully, she moved the curtain aside and stepped over the low, jagged window frame, and slipped out onto the balcony.

With the Sig in her hand, she walked thirty feet down the balcony to the set of rickety metal-grate stairs and sat down stiffly.

She'd been able to get several hours of much-needed sleep, but it was a restless, uneasy sleep, filled with nightmares of Maddox and her years at the compound, years she wished she could erase from her mind.

She scanned the darkness—the dim shapes of cars in the parking lot, the road, and the squat buildings beyond it—and listened to the sounds of the city slowly descending into chaos.

What was Ezra doing right now? Was he safe at his cabin, rocking on the porch, his rifle in his lap while he listened to the nighttime sounds of the Glades? Was he on his ham radio, checking in on the state of things around the country?

Or was he thinking about her, wondering if she was safe, too? Did he even want her to come back? She hoped so with every fiber of her being. She closed her eyes for a moment, imagining the warmth and the peace of the only place she'd ever considered home.

A *thump* came from behind her.

Adrenaline surging, she whipped around, gun up but her finger still off the trigger guard.

She recognized the shape prowling toward her. Her heart gave a little jolt. She licked her dry lips and lowered the gun to her lap.

He wouldn't be happy with her. He had every right to be furious.

She was furious with herself.

Logan said, "We need to talk."

20

DAKOTA

Dakota didn't say anything, just scooted over to make room for him. She swallowed hard, her throat burning. Her muscles tensed like she was preparing to go into battle.

Logan held two bottles of water by the neck in one hand, the rifle down next to his thigh. He offered one to her. She took it.

A slight breeze rustled her hair and cooled her hot cheeks. It was still above eighty degrees, just another typical muggy night in July.

Logan sank down next to her, his body tense and rigid. He stretched out his legs on the stairs so they were only inches from her own. He was close enough that she could feel the heat radiating off him—and the anger.

He took a long swig of water, capped the bottle, and set it beside him next to the rifle.

"That guy is the reason you were so bent on having a gun." His voice bristled with anger. "He's the reason you wanted me with you, for protection. Matt or whatever his name is. Your brother."

She stiffened. "Maddox. And he's not my brother."

"You knew he was out here. You knew he was looking for your— for the girl, and you didn't tell me."

She glared back defiantly. "I don't have to defend myself to you."

"There's a dead body back on that street that says you do."

It was like she'd been sucker-punched. The pain left her breathless. A dull ringing echoed in her ears. She wasn't a monster; she felt guilty as hell over Harlow's death.

He was right. She knew he was right. What the hell was wrong with her? She longed to pull away, to run, to do anything to avoid this conversation, but she resisted. She deserved this.

Besides, she knew how to endure rage, contempt, hatred, even violence. She had the scars to prove it. She could take whatever he threw at her.

"I love that girl like my own sister," she forced out. "What does it matter whether she's blood or not? My own aunt—my *real* blood —did nothing when they...she did nothing. We only had each other, and we did what we had to survive. I don't care what anyone says. That girl is my sister in my heart and soul, and I'm hers."

"I don't care about that," he said slowly, every word enunciated, like he was fighting to keep his voice even. "You knew someone was out there looking for you, someone dangerous, and you didn't bother to tell me?"

"I—I didn't trust you."

"You brought me on for protection but kept me in the dark."

"I—it sounds ridiculous."

"It is ridiculous!"

"I thought I had it under control."

"Under control?" he hissed. "Are you kidding me? There are so many things wrong with that statement I don't know where to start."

She felt him staring at her in the dark. The hairs on the back of her neck prickled. Again, it took everything in her not to run, to escape him, to flee the anger and judgment in his eyes—and the hot, wriggling shame within herself.

She stared straight ahead, her eyes stinging. "Maybe I should've done things differently."

He snorted. "You have this hero complex, Dakota."

"What does that even mean?"

"You want to save everyone. The people in the Beer Shack and the theater. That woman with the dead baby. The first responders. Eden."

"What's the problem with that?"

"The problem is that you're so pigheaded you try to do it all on your own."

"Don't act like you know me. You don't know anything about me."

"No?" His voice rose. "You think you're in control, but you're so desperate to be the hero that your heart scrambles your brain and makes you impulsive and reckless. You end up putting people at risk instead of saving them. How am I doing so far?"

She flinched. His words left her reeling, like she'd been kicked in the teeth. "At least I'm not a drunk," she shot back.

"Don't you dare turn this around on me," he snapped, livid. "This is about you and what you did. You play the hero, but you don't trust anyone else to help you. You try to control everything, but you can't. You didn't want to trust me, so you purposefully kept me in the dark, even though you wanted to use me for protection."

It was true. Every word of it. She hadn't trusted him.

She couldn't trust anyone else with her fate. She'd learned that the hard way. The people who were supposed to care for you the most were the ones with the most power to hurt you. The ones who died and left you behind, alone and defenseless. The ones who trapped you, who lied and betrayed you. The ones who hurt you, just because they could.

"You can't have it both ways!" Logan said.

She bit her lip, suddenly unable to speak.

"I didn't know some psycho was after you. I didn't know he was dangerous because *you* didn't tell me. I was unprepared. I was unprepared and someone got killed. Do you understand that? Nancy Harlow is dead. And it could've been Eden. It could've been all of us."

That finally got through to her.

Her mask disintegrated. Her face crumpled. Everything she'd been holding back behind a tough, stoic wall collapsed.

She was left as raw and vulnerable as an open wound.

"I know." Her voice cracked. "I know."

21

DAKOTA

Dakota wasn't any good at apologies, but she *was* sorry. She was sorry with every fiber of her being. She'd take it back if she could. All of it.

Logan was right. He'd read her like a book. She was stubborn, shortsighted, and cagey. She was distrustful of everyone, and her skittish, suspicious nature had put them all in danger. She'd tried to control a situation that was far beyond anything she could handle.

It had cost a life. Next time, it could cost even more.

But the thought of trusting him, of being vulnerable, filled her with complete and utter terror.

"I'm not asking you to tell me your life story," he said, as if reading her mind. His voice softened. "But I can't do what I need to do if I don't know what's going on."

Her heart throbbed, bruised and tender. Hot tears stung her eyes. She blinked them back furiously. "That's...fair."

"Will he keep coming after you?"

"As long as he's alive."

"Anyone else? Or is he alone?"

She ran her finger along the cool, hard metal of the Sig in her lap. "I don't know."

That old fear clawed at her, strangling her throat, filling her with cold terror. She yearned to run until her legs collapsed, to scream and scream until her voice box gave out, to hit and punch and batter something with her bare hands until her flesh was mangled, bruised, and bloody.

Until her outsides hurt as much as her insides did.

Her fear still gave them power over her. She hated that. She hated how they'd changed her, made her afraid to depend on anyone but herself, made her suspicious and distrustful of everyone and everything—like a beaten dog, wretched and cowering, always expecting the next blow.

It was pathetic and mortifying, and only left her miserable, bitter, and alone.

She risked a sideways glance at Logan. He was still watching her. Quiet, waiting.

She looked quickly away. Her throat was dry and painful. She opened the bottle of water he'd offered her and took a swig.

Off to the east, another fire had started up. Now there were five fires burning on the horizon. From this distance, they looked like campfires, the glow warm and inviting.

Maybe she could take it back—everything the compound had stolen from her. Take herself back; one slow, halting step at a time. Maybe it started with a stop to the lies—layers and layers of lies piled so high she couldn't begin to dismantle them.

Except she could. She could start by telling the truth. If not all of it, then at least in part.

Her resolve grew with each ragged breath.

Just breathe. That's how you got through things. One breath, then another. She could get through this, too. *One, two, three. Breathe.*

"You wouldn't have believed me." She couldn't stop her voice from trembling. She hated that weakness in herself, but she couldn't stop it. All she could do was keep going. "You wouldn't have come. If I said, 'Hey, I was trapped in an abusive cult, but I ran away with the cult leader's daughter. I didn't have their permission, so yeah, call it kidnapping if you want. Oh, by the way, the leader's son is also after me, and he just happened to find me right before the whole damn city exploded. He's a tenacious psychopath, so he's probably still after me and the girl I stole. You want in on this hot mess?'

"What would you have done? You would have run in the opposite direction. You would have thought I was crazy. You probably do now."

He didn't speak for a long time.

She listened to his slow, steady breathing and the beat of her own heart.

"Tell me," he said finally.

She shivered despite the heat. It felt like she was hanging over the edge of a cliff with no rope and no spotter. One false move and she'd plummet hundreds of feet, splitting her skull open on the harsh, unforgiving rocks.

She couldn't break through her own tough, impenetrable exterior she'd been forced to cultivate to survive the compound, the streets, and the group homes, couldn't unravel the beliefs that kept her going: *Everyone's out to use and abuse you. Trust no one but yourself. Survive at any cost.*

Rosemarie's words came back from all those years ago. "I'm scared," Dakota had said in the moments before Rosemarie had thrust the gate keys into her trembling hands and told her to take Eden and run. "The fear won't go away."

"Child, the fear never goes away," Rosemarie had said gently. "You just have to do it anyway. Do it afraid."

Do it afraid.

Something released inside her chest. She opened her mouth,

and before she could think better of it, the words spilled out. "I moved to that place with my aunt when I was ten, after my parents and my—after my family died in a car accident. I didn't have a choice.

"They live like the Amish—living off the land, homesteading. I'm not saying that's bad, that wasn't it...it was everything else. They're crazy religious people. Strict and...terrible."

"Where does Eden come into all this?"

"Eden's father is Solomon Cage. He's the leader of the River Grass Compound. He's—he's a horrible man. But he's not the leader of the whole thing. That's the Prophet, his brother. He's worse. He says God sent him to save America. Everyone worships him like he's an angel...or maybe even God himself.

"The Prophet travels around. He has other compounds. It's a big group. I don't know how big. They're Shepherds, what the 'chosen ones' call themselves. They have weapons. They act like soldiers. God's army. I don't know the details. The women didn't get to know that stuff.

"All I know for sure is that Solomon isn't going to forget about his daughter. And the Prophet...he's not going to forget about her either."

It was quiet for a moment.

A car alarm went off. She watched the fires glowing on the horizon.

"What do you mean?"

Her words were bitter as ashes on her tongue. "It's what every cult in the history of the world does, doesn't it? Use and abuse its women and girls. It's the same old twisted story. The leader manipulates his adoring, brainwashed followers for money and sex.

"The Prophet picks certain girls to be one of his wives, says God chose them. He preaches that the Bible is literal. If the so-called heroes of the Bible did it, then as the chosen prophet of the Lord, it's okay for him, too. Jacob had two wives. David had a bunch. Solomon had like seven hundred."

"Are they Mormon?" Logan asked quietly.

"No, they're something else. Do you remember the David Koresh cult in Waco, Texas? All those kids that died? We've got a couple of men who survived that cult in the compound. They splintered off another religion around twenty years ago. I don't remember which ones. Mennonites or something like that. I doubt it matters, anyway.

"The Prophet started preaching God had revealed a new present truth to him, that certain people were special, the pure, the chosen ones, called out of the church to begin something new, ordained by God to save them from the time of trouble—the reign of fire and brimstone that's coming."

She stared down at her hands wrapped around the grip of the Sig. She wasn't helpless. She wasn't back there anymore. Still, even talking about it filled her with anxiety and flooded her mind with the awful memories—the constant fear, shame, and guilt.

Her chest tightened. It was hard to breathe.

"It sounds crazy when you say it out loud," she whispered. "But to live it...these people actually believe in him. They believe he speaks for God. They believe he's going to save them from the end of the world. So whatever he says...it's like God Himself is saying it."

She took a deep breath. "Right before we fled...The Prophet said God told him to take Eden as his bride."

Beside her, Logan stiffened. "She's this Prophet's niece."

"Maddox told me once his father was adopted, that they weren't birth brothers, so he's not her blood uncle. But that doesn't make a difference to me. Not when Eden's just a kid. She's fifteen but she's been so sheltered and traumatized that mentally, she's more like twelve."

"Fifteen is still a kid no matter who they are or what they've been through."

"Mary was only fourteen when she married Joseph. That's how they justified it." Dakota felt sick even speaking the words aloud. "They were going to wait until she started her period, the sacred mark of womanhood or whatever. But she was promised to the Prophet immediately. She was going to live with his other wives in one of his compounds.

"As soon as I found out, I knew I had to do something. I...I couldn't just let that happen."

"No," he said slowly. "I guess you couldn't."

She couldn't tell him the rest. It was too much, too dark and ugly.

"And the brother? The one Maddox said you murdered?"

She closed her eyes against the vision of the body, the wide staring eyes, the blood so red it was almost black. "Collateral damage."

22

DAKOTA

Neither of them spoke for several minutes.

"I know it sounds unbelievable," Dakota said.

"I believe it," he said without hesitation.

She barely heard him. "I know it feels like the world is ending right now, but atrocities on a smaller scale happen every day. You just don't hear about them on the news or Facebook or Twitter." She took a breath. *Just say it.* "The Prophet was going to take her to Missouri to marry her."

"How is that even legal?"

"With a judge's consent and a parent's signature, it's allowed in about half of the states. There's no minimum age that's against the law. With parental consent, even twelve-year-olds can do it—thousands of children get married here every year. No one thinks it happens *here*, but it does. Out in the boonies, in rural areas like the Everglades, no one cares what happens anyway. Not the governor, not the sheriff, no one.

"They make you think it's normal. That that's how it's supposed to be. Girls and women are good for cooking and cleaning and raising babies. Men are the ones made in God's image. The Prophet only allowed women to read certain parts of the Bible. He said some parts were written 'beyond our comprehension'."

She smiled bitterly. "He left out all the parts about love, forgiveness, and equality. And mercy."

Memories of the mercy room stained her mind like blood. She pushed them away.

"What about Maddox?" Logan asked.

"Maddox, he...wasn't always like this. He was angry and possessive, but not a killer, not like he is now. He was the black sheep of his family, always breaking the rules and getting in trouble, like me. We were the only ones who didn't fully drink the Kool-Aid—who doubted the hogwash the Prophet shoved down everyone's throats.

"He used to take me out in the airboat when no one was looking. We spent hours and hours in the wilderness of the Glades. Out there, it didn't matter what his father said about either of us. He was...different.

"But his father twisted him with his hatred and his guilt, made him believe love was a weakness to be snuffed out with a good whipping. And when that didn't work, his father forced him to..." Her voice trailed off.

Logan went completely still. "What do you mean?"

But she only shook her head, unable to speak the ugliness into being.

The Prophet's idea of discipline was biblical. If your eye sinned, carve it out. If your hand sinned, cut it off. He didn't actually go that far, but he went far enough.

Beatings, whippings, brandings. Given to save the souls of the wicked, so it could be called merciful.

The skin of her back prickled, the scars suddenly itchy and painful. The images rushed in, whether she wanted them or not. The dark, rank room, the concrete floor stained with spatters of red like paint. The thick wooden plank table in the center. The handcuffs.

For the rest of her life, she would never forget the distinctive, singed stench of burnt flesh. That, and the pain—pain throbbing through her body, each burn pulsing like a tiny heart, with a furious, white-hot heat.

Sweat would pour down her face and back, her heart pounding so hard she felt it in her toes, her fingertips, her skull; her legs trembling and kicking in vain, her body writhing uncontrollably, the metal of the handcuffs abrading her wrists; her breath jerking from her chest in short, ragged gasps, her lungs collapsing as the pain clamped over her whole body.

She could never get enough oxygen. It felt like drowning on dry land.

She would fight to focus on something other than the pain, to anchor herself to something, anything. *One, two, three. Breathe.*

Each breath another moment, another second she'd endured, that she would never have to endure again. Get through this breath, this moment, and then the next and the next.

I'm sorry, Maddox would whisper, out of earshot of his father. Or, *It's over now. It's over.* Only toward the end would he say, *You made me do this. You deserve this. It's all your fault.*

It was a twisted curiosity of psychology that a tortured soul could ever bond with her torturer, and yet it happened. A moment of softness, a bit of compassion in the midst of agony, like manna in the desert.

Logan cleared his throat, bringing her swiftly back to the present.

"It was bad," she said softly. "For both of us."

"You...did you love him?" he asked.

She sucked in a sharp breath. "Not like that. But he did. I didn't understand it at the time. But looking back...I know he did, in his own broken way."

"And now he wants to kill you?"

She didn't say anything about the look on Maddox's face when he'd strode into the room and caught sight of his brother bleeding out on the floor. The betrayal in his eyes. The fury. "Sometimes love twists into an even stronger hate."

"I guess that's true."

"There are people who endure horrific things. Things other people can't even imagine. Some can break free and forge a different life. Some are broken, lifelong victims who never believe anything different than what they've been taught. Others see the truth, but are too hurt to do the hard work to fix themselves."

"Which one is he?"

"Maddox Cage is the last one. They twisted him all up until they snapped something crucial inside him, something that can't be repaired."

"That's... a lot to take in," Logan said.

"I didn't understand it back then. I was just a teenager."

"Aren't you still?"

"What?"

He cocked his brows. "How old are you?"

She grimaced. "Still nineteen, though sometimes I feel like I'm forty."

"You act like it."

"A person can endure a lifetime of suffering before they're old enough to drive."

He stared out in the darkness. "True enough."

Gunfire chattered several blocks away. It sounded closer.

Dakota's heartbeat quickened. Her eyes strained to make out any potential threats. They were both quiet for a full minute as they studied the dark shadows all around them, searching for movement.

There was nothing.

"Those people in that place." Logan's voice was soft, the anger from earlier gone. "They're wolves masquerading as sheep. They're pure evil."

"That's the crazy thing. They weren't all bad. They weren't all evil." She turned the gun in her hands, over and over. Her fingers were trembling. She couldn't make them stop.

She kept seeing the mercy room, kept feeling the scorching burns.

One, two, three. Breathe. She breathed in, breathed out. That place was gone. She'd escaped them. They couldn't hurt her anymore—not unless she let them.

"It made the evil things that happened that much worse," she said. "Because the rest of the time, people were kind and almost normal."

"Sounds like you've forgotten the definition of normal."

She let out a snort. And then, before she could stop herself, she laughed. It was a high, hysterical sound, bubbling up from the center of her chest. She covered her mouth with her hand to keep from waking anyone inside the motel.

"It wasn't that funny," he said.

She could see the gleam of his teeth in the dim moonlight. He was grinning.

On the streets and in the group foster homes, she'd learned to keep to herself real fast. Self-preservation at all costs was the name of the game.

Be tough, show no weakness, never reveal an ounce of vulnerability to anyone. Keep your spine to the wall or you were liable to get stabbed in the back.

It was an incredibly lonely way to live.

But now, for the first time in a long time, she didn't feel so alone.

"I'm sorry," she said, meaning everything. "I'm sorry."

"I know," Logan said.

23

MADDOX

Maddox staggered back to the street corner, to the man on the phone.

With shaking hands, he pulled out his Beretta and aimed it at the man's chest. "Give me the phone."

The man's mouth dropped open.

"Now!" Maddox shouted.

Terrified, the man held out the phone. Maddox snatched it. "What's the passcode?"

"14502." The guy raised his hands, his eyes bulging with fear. His jiggly white belly sagged over his shorts. His armpits were as pale as his prodigious stomach. "Hey man, I thought we were cool. I gave you what you wanted."

Maddox smiled, keeping the gun trained on the man's chest. The guy's fear energized him. He was the one in charge. He had complete control over this man's future. Life or death, at the flip of a coin.

"Don't shoot me," the man begged as pathetic tears leaked down his fat cheeks.

Maddox watched him, but he wasn't seeing the loser in front of him. He imagined Dakota on her knees, begging for her life, imagined finally enacting his revenge for all the pain and the suffering and the humiliation she'd caused him.

A blazing fury swept through him, a red mist of rage exploding behind his eyes.

"You don't need to—"

Maddox squeezed the trigger. The gunshot rang in his ears. He watched with great satisfaction as the man's eyes widened in surprise. Men were always surprised when they died, like it hadn't happened to every human being throughout all of history.

The man sank to his knees, his mouth opening and closing like a fish. He collapsed to the sidewalk and didn't move.

A curtain fluttered in the front window of the house on the corner, but no one came out.

"Thank you for the phone," Maddox said to the body. "Blessings upon your soul."

He straightened his shoulders, already feeling better. The anger and adrenaline burning through him provided the strength to stumble across the street to the school property. He checked the address embossed in a brass placard by the front of the school's front doors.

He swiped the phone on and punched in the passcode. His hands were so sweaty he had to redo it three times. Two signal bars in the upper corner of the screen. Good.

He called the number he'd memorized by heart. *Service is not available at this time, please try your call again...* He dialed a second number. Same response. *Service is not available...*

He sank down against the stucco side of the school building, his butt on the grass. The grass was thick, stiff, and prickly. A red anthill grew against the wall a few feet away. He eyed it warily. He wasn't sure if he had the strength to move, even if the ants started biting him.

Maddox decided to text. The phone's former owner had said

texts went through even when calls didn't. It was all he had left. He texted both numbers. *This is Maddox. Need an immediate evac. Address 1333 5ᵗʰ Court in Wynwood. A school. Plenty of space to land.*

He didn't know how long he waited. Maybe a minute, maybe thirty.

The phone vibrated in his hand. *Do you have the packages?*

He grimaced as he texted the response. A minute after he tapped "send," the bars in the upper corner disappeared. *No service.*

Now, he waited again.

Dusk faded to night. Clouds covered the stars. The trill of cicadas filled the hot air.

He drifted in and out of consciousness. In his fever dreams, Dakota was still kneeling in front of him, her hands clasped in desperate pleading, almost in worshipful adoration.

And then she was laughing at him, mocking him, scornful of his cowardice, his failure, his weakness. His impotence.

He awoke to gunshots and screaming in the distance. He was too sick to even crawl around the corner. He remained where he was.

Sometime in the early morning, he opened his exhausted eyes to discover dawn pinking the sky over the palm trees.

The *thump, thump, thump* of a helicopter descended above him. The chopper dropped to the ground in the middle of the football field, the rotors surging, the palm fronds whipping, the wind slapping him in the face and stinging his eyes.

The chopper was white with blue lettering: *Miami Sand and Sea Air Tours.* His father's men had come for him.

His father would be furious. But it didn't matter.

All was not lost. He would still find Eden. He would still bring Dakota to justice. There'd be no mercy for her this time—of that, he was dead certain.

Maddox knew exactly where they were going.

2 4

EDEN

E den's stomach was hot and queasy, her guts twisting like she'd swallowed rancid meat. She was shaky, her skin cold and clammy even as fever burned through her insides.

Her notepad lay beside her on the seat, but she didn't feel like drawing. She didn't feel like doing anything except curling into a ball and forgetting about the broken world, her sickness, Maddox—forgetting about everything.

She sat in the back seat of the truck cab behind Logan. Shay took the middle, and Dakota hunched in the far seat with her gun, keeping watch. Mr. Wilburn was still driving.

The Asian guy with the broken arm, Park, was in the back with the older Cuban man named Julio. Julio had offered to ride in the truck bed so Eden could have the air-conditioning inside the cab. He seemed nice.

Everyone seemed nice, but she was scared of Logan. He was intimidating—big and muscular, with a whole bunch of tattoos all over his arms. He never smiled or even looked at her.

Dakota seemed to like him, though. They talked a lot in low, rushed whispers.

But she didn't want to think about Dakota.

With bleary eyes, she stared out the window at the scenery passing by. It was nothing like she'd ever seen before.

Most of the stores had been looted. Crushed cardboard boxes, bits of Styrofoam, and shreds of plastic wrapping were scattered along the streets and sidewalks, mingling with the glass shards glinting in the sun.

Plywood was nailed across building windows, as if everyone was bracing for a hurricane. Graffiti sprawled across the storefront walls. A few people were picking up the trash in front of their businesses. Others came out of grocery and convenience stores carrying the remnants of whatever they could find—Gatorade, candy bars, diapers, toilet paper.

In the neighborhoods they passed through, more people were outside. Some huddled in clumps, others pulled out their lawn chairs and just sat in their yards or carports, fanning themselves and drinking the last of their water or beer.

Everyone stared back at them, sweating, dull-eyed, shell-shocked.

There were no manicured lawns or fancy in-ground pools here. Weeds choked the cracked sidewalk. The dull, squat houses sagged, rusting chain-link fences surrounding tiny, scabby yards. A Rottweiler on a chain barked viciously, running back and forth in the groove his paws had worn into the dirt.

Logan and Dakota held their guns in clearly visible positions, so no one tried to approach the truck. A few other cars were driving around, but not many.

Heat shimmered off the asphalt. The sultry air was pungent with sweat, smoke, and the stink of rotting garbage inside empty, overheated houses and in overflowing bins at the curb. There was no one to pick up the trash.

The radio was on for a while, but it just repeated the same old information, providing evacuation routes and locations of emergency camps to receive food, water, and medical care.

The only new thing was a mandatory citywide curfew for all citizens, excluding emergency and law enforcement personnel, at seven p.m. sharp. Anyone out after dark was subject to arrest, prosecution, and imprisonment.

Finally, Logan turned it off.

"You doing okay?" the nursing lady, Shay, asked her quietly.

Her whole body felt like it was burning up from the inside out. Prickly sweat gathered at her hairline. Her damp shirt clung to her skin. But she'd managed not to throw up into the small plastic trash bin Dakota had swiped from the motel room. Yet.

Eden forced herself to nod.

She didn't remember much of yesterday. When she thought about it, her stomach cramped with dread, terror, and confusion. Nothing made sense.

She'd been overjoyed to see her brother, but that joy had turned to brittle terror when he'd held a knife to her throat—and then horror when he'd killed that lady.

Just as quickly, horror transformed to grief. Her other brother, Jacob, was dead. Dakota had killed him.

That was crazy. Why would Dakota do something like that? But Dakota hadn't denied it. Had Dakota really kidnapped Eden? Dakota hadn't denied that either. If it was true, then Dakota had betrayed her, had betrayed her entire family.

A sudden anger surged up from somewhere deep inside her. She sucked in her breath, desperate to tamp it down. With the anger came the shame and that immediate, reflexive fear of those forbidden emotions—resentment, bitterness, hatred, rage.

You couldn't get mad in the compound. You weren't allowed to. Anger was a grave sin, a sign of the devil himself gaining a foothold in your soul. Her whole life, she was taught to be meek and mild and accepting, for everything came from the Lord or the Prophet—both good and bad was the Lord's will.

It didn't matter that it had been three years since the compound. Sometimes all the old thoughts and feelings came flooding back in a heartbeat.

Her mind swam, everything disoriented and muddled. She didn't know what she was supposed to do or how she was supposed to feel. She couldn't even begin to process it all—her whole world flipped upside down at the same time the real world was falling apart.

She just wanted everything to go back the way it was before. She missed her foster parents, Gabriella and Jorge Ross. They always knew how to make her feel better. They made her feel safe.

They're never coming back. They're as dead as Jacob.

She bit her bottom lip to keep from crying. When she was trapped in the bathroom in the dark for those two days, she thought everything would be okay once she was rescued.

But that wasn't true.

She was scared and sick and surrounded by strangers. Dakota was the biggest stranger of all. Eden had so many questions, but she was too terrified of the answers to ask a single one.

A thought niggled at the back of her brain, dark and ugly. Something she couldn't bear to think about. So she didn't.

She leaned her head against the seat, fighting back a wave of sickness. Her stomach cramped. Her brain felt like it was boiling from the inside out.

"There's something ahead," Logan said tightly.

Everyone tensed.

The truck jolted onto the curb as Mr. Wilburn jerked the wheel to the right to miss a garbage truck stalled in the middle of the road.

"What the hell..." Dakota said.

"It looks like a checkpoint," Mr. Wilburn said.

"It *was* a checkpoint," Dakota said.

Mr. Wilburn stopped the truck in front of a long line of cars. Four police cars were parked across the road, six concrete barriers angled in front of them. Several large white Red Cross tents were clumped together in a parking lot just off the road. They appeared empty.

There were no people anywhere.

No people still alive, anyway.

"Bodies," Dakota said quietly.

Little bits of metal glinted all over the road. From her time at the compound, plus the movies her foster parents let her watch, Eden knew what they were—shell casings.

The police cars were riddled with bullet holes. Some of the regular cars had bullet holes in them, too. Some of the cars had people inside them. Dead people. Blood stained the road like paint splotches.

Logan stuck his head out the window and studied the scene. "Looks like they tried to set up a checkpoint to control traffic and got overrun."

"By who?" Mr. Wilburn asked. "Who would shoot at police officers?"

Mrs. Wilburn shot her husband an incredulous look. "Who else? Gangs."

"The Blood Outlaws are trying to take over the city," Dakota said.

"Why am I not surprised?" Mrs. Wilburn said. "They've been attempting that particular feat for a decade."

"I only see four uniformed bodies," Logan said. "They were understaffed. A bunch of gangbangers firing automatic weapons jumped them. It's not hard to see how they got overwhelmed."

"How far are we from the airport?" Dakota asked.

Shay looked down at the map in her hands. She traced her finger along one of the tiny lines. "Looks like about three miles still. We can backtrack and go around."

"Let's go," Logan said.

Mrs. Wilburn gave a pained sigh.

Mr. Wilburn reversed the truck and eased backward, banging into the fenders of a few cars on the way. With each jolt and jerk, sickness clawed at Eden's insides. Beads of sweat trickled down the sides of her face despite the air conditioning.

She closed her eyes. Lights danced behind her eyelids, everything lurching and sliding with vertigo. She tried not to see all those dead bodies in her mind's eye, tried not to feel the razor edge of the knife against her neck.

And she tried not to imagine the radiation invading her internal organs, slowly poisoning her from the inside out.

It didn't work.

25

LOGAN

Logan scanned the area warily, alternating between the road ahead and the side streets. They'd been forced off 28th Street when it turned into a parking lot. Now, they wove west along 36th Street.

This road wasn't as congested. Dozens of vehicles still clogged the shoulder, but there was enough room to squeeze past. More people wandered around outside, too, which made Logan nervous.

Occasionally, they drove past bodies on the side of the road, their skin blistered and burnt, chunks of their hair missing, their eyes hollowed, glassy—dead. These people had fought as hard as they could to escape the hot zone, giving up everything they had, only to discover it wasn't enough.

It didn't matter how far or how fast they ran or where they went. The poison was already inside them—an invisible, insidious enemy silently eradicating cells and tissue, destroying the body from within.

Logan couldn't help himself; he shuddered. Was this the fate that awaited them, too?

It was all anxiety and dread, conjecture and speculation—the fear of the unknown. What he wouldn't give for a few shots of vodka to drown it all out. To get that fine buzz going, that soothing warmth that hushed all the dark voices, the vile whispers, the hideous images always slithering into his brain...

He shoved those thoughts out of his mind. He had to stay alert, had to focus on what was right in front of him.

To his right, a strip of palm trees separated the street from a small park and a block of apartment buildings. A bunch of people congregated beneath one of the picnic shelters, fanning themselves or smoking cigarettes.

Without A/C, life in South Florida was quickly becoming unbearable. It was probably close to a hundred and as humid as ever. How many people were suffering from heatstroke? The elderly would struggle. Some would probably die, if they hadn't already.

A headache throbbed at his temple, joining the nausea roiling his gut. He was supposed to rest last night during Dakota's watch; instead, he couldn't sleep.

He'd tossed and turned on the hard floor, the lumpy pillow beneath his head as comfortable as a rock, until finally he'd given in with a muttered curse and stalked out to the balcony to confront her.

It hadn't gone anything like he'd planned.

A part of him wished he could despise her, dismiss her, expel her from his mind and be done with it. She was nothing if not an infuriating headache.

But she'd sat there, refusing to justify herself, and she'd told him the truth. Not all of it, but enough.

Enough for his anger and frustration to dissipate and something else to take root.

He knew what it was like to be betrayed by the people who were supposed to love and protect you. Just like he knew what it was like to be the betrayer.

And he knew what it was like to trust no one but himself. Wasn't that how he'd lived the last four years? Completely alone. Isolated. And if he were honest with himself, incredibly lonely.

As much as he wanted to hate her, he couldn't. He understood her.

He had his own past to answer for. His own darkness. His own demons. He couldn't blame Dakota for hers.

Movement snagged Logan's attention. Along the right side of the road, two teenagers pedaled by on bicycles, eyeballing the truck as they passed. The butt of a gun bulged from the back of the largest boy's waistband.

Logan watched them until they turned into an empty parking lot and disappeared.

A few minutes later, a long line of cars appeared ahead of them. The line stretched on and on. Though drivers were at the wheel, none of the vehicles were moving.

"There must be fifty cars at least," Shay said. "Maybe a hundred."

"What are they doing?" Vanessa asked.

Carson pointed ahead. "Gas."

He slowed as they approached a gas station on the corner. A young Cuban guy stood beside the road, sweating and holding a large handwritten sign scrawled in black marker: "Five-gallon limit. Thirty dollars a gallon. Cash only. No exceptions."

"Thirty dollars a gallon?" Vanessa asked incredulously. "Are they out of their minds?"

"They're charging what the market will bear," Carson said. "From a business perspective, it's smart."

"It's taking advantage of people in a crisis," Shay said from the backseat. "It's not right."

"Why the five-gallon limit?" Vanessa asked.

"Because people will hog it all," Dakota said. "If things stay bad,

111

the government will probably close most of the gas stations to civilians and restrict the gas to emergency and government vehicles."

"Can they do that?" Shay asked.

"Of course, they can," Vanessa said. She seemed slightly more composed today, though her eyes still held that stunned, deer-in-the-headlights look. "They're the government. They have to do what they must to keep the peace. As far as I'm concerned, they can shut down every gas station in Florida if it puts a stop to this madness."

At the gas station, vehicles clogged every available square foot of pavement. The area around the pumps was a mess. Cars parked sideways, blocking the exits. People were leaning out of their windows, shouting at each other.

A big Suburban nosed into a smaller Chevrolet Spark, forcibly shoving it out of line to squeeze in front of the nearest pump. Metal scraped against metal as the Spark driver screamed insults at the Suburban and shook his fist.

No one had brandished a gun—yet. Everyone looked tense, angry, and afraid. The whole place looked like it was ready to explode into violence.

"We've still got more than two-thirds of a tank," Carson said.

"Don't stop," Logan said.

A battered Toyota was parked along the grassy shoulder between the road and the gas station's lot. Two young white guys dressed like rednecks leaned against the hood. They smoked cigarettes and watched the chaos at the pumps.

As the F-150 drove past, they both turned to stare at the truck with hungry, hooded eyes. They were probably out of gas already or lacked the cash to pay the outrageous prices.

The first one—shirtless and so skinny Logan could've counted his ribs—reached for the handgun tucked into the saggy waistband of his shorts.

Logan lifted the Remington and rested the barrel on the passenger window frame.

The second punk's eyes widened. He elbowed his friend and shook his head. *Not worth it.*

"It's sure as hell not," Logan muttered.

He kept his eye on them until the truck was out of range. Those two were going to carjack someone—if not today, then tomorrow.

The more desperate people got, the more they were willing to risk violence. And the longer the city went without a law enforcement presence, the more emboldened the punks and thugs and douchebags of this city would become.

"They're acting like...animals," Carson said, clearly shaken.

"They *are* animals," Vanessa snapped. "Did you expect them to behave any differently?"

"They're scared like the rest of us," Shay said quietly. "They're trying to take care of their families. They're just trying to survive."

"I would never behave like that," Vanessa insisted. "Never."

"You never know," Dakota said. "When you get desperate enough, you do things that surprise even yourself."

No one said anything after that.

They drove past a family trudging along the sidewalk pulling an empty wagon behind them. A middle-aged Haitian woman swept up glass and debris in front of a hair salon. A teenage girl with a giant orange knit bag slung over her shoulder shuffled down the street, staring mindlessly at the pavement, her dark, stringy curls limp in the heat.

A Volkswagen Beetle appeared in the rearview mirror about two hundred yards behind them. The car didn't speed up or appear to be a threat.

Still, Logan didn't let his guard down.

About fifty feet down a side street, a dozen cars were crammed together in the middle of the pavement. On the next street, it was the same.

At first, it seemed like an accident—some kind of major pileup. But the cars looked as if they'd been pushed there by something big, like a kid organizing his Hot Wheels into a reenactment of an accident rather than the real thing.

The fine hairs on the back of his neck stood on end.

"Logan," Dakota said. He heard it in her voice—the same uneasiness he felt.

"I see it." Logan's muscles tensed. "Something's wrong."

26

LOGAN

Logan scanned the buildings alongside the road—everything was quiet and still.

Too still.

"We should go around," Dakota said. "Backtrack."

"Not again," Vanessa whined. "We've wasted the entire morning! At this pace, we'll be trapped out here with the hoodlums till nightfall!"

Carson gestured toward the windshield. "It's clear ahead and much faster."

"I've got a bad feeling about this." Logan's pulse thudded in his ears as he studied the buildings and streets, searching for movement, for anything amiss. "It's worth it to go around."

"Every second we stay out here just adds to the danger!" Vanessa argued, her voice rising in panic. "You saw those people at the gas station. And what happened last night. It's not safe!"

"Doing something stupid without thinking things through won't change that," Dakota said.

"It's our truck," Vanessa said. "We decide. Carson, just go."

Carson pursed his lips and put the truck in gear. "We're going through."

They drove forward.

"It could be a trap," Dakota said, anger and disgust in her voice. "What's the point of bringing us along if you're not going to do what we say? This is bull—"

"We said no!" Vanessa cried, her eyes bulging. She looked desperate and panicky, ready to do anything to escape the city, including clawing someone's eyes out.

"Dakota's right," Logan said. "It's your truck, but I'm not getting killed for your stupidity. Turn the car around."

"Did you not hear what we just said—"

"Turn it around!" Logan clenched his jaw as he twisted in his seat and raised the Remington.

Carson glanced at him, appalled.

Vanessa didn't. She looked at him like a cockroach crawling out of a garbage can—something grotesque, but not surprising. Like she'd known all along he was nothing more than a violent criminal.

"You're hijacking us," she said flatly.

"I don't want to, lady. But you're not leaving me any choice. Now back up and turn around."

Carson gripped the steering wheel. "I can't turn around with that huge dump truck ahead of us. Just let me pass it and I'll do what you want."

"Back up," Logan growled. "Right now—"

"I can't. Just—I'm doing it, okay! Point that gun somewhere else!" Carson slowed the truck as he maneuvered around a large yellow dump truck taking up half the road.

Dakota swore loudly.

"Oh, no," Carson breathed. "No, no, no."

On the other side, two dozen men armed with semi-automatic weapons waited for them. The men stood in front of an SUV and an old dusty red pickup parked sideways in the road. One of them stepped forward and waved for them to drive forward.

"Go back!" Vanessa cried.

"Too late," Logan said.

There wasn't space to do a U-turn, not with the dump truck blocking most of the road and another car already stalled in the left lane. Whoever these guys were, they'd planned it this way.

On their right, the Airport Expressway, or SR 112, ran parallel to the side street, which hit 32nd Avenue in a T-junction. 32nd Avenue ran beneath the expressway. Just beyond the Airport Expressway wound the elevated rails of the Metrorail train.

To the left on 32nd Avenue squatted a bank, a Taco Bell, a McDonald's, and a Publix, all screened by a row of tall, skinny palm trees.

Logan adjusted his grip on the rifle. He lowered it so it was hidden by the passenger door to anyone glancing at the truck from outside. "Whatever you do, be polite," he said under his breath. "If they ask for something, if it's in your power, give it."

Vanessa's face went slack. "Those aren't police officers. They can't walk around with those kinds of guns. They can't stop us like this!"

"It'll be okay, dear," Carson murmured. "Just—just do what Logan says, okay?"

Vanessa didn't answer.

Carson eased the Ford toward the guy waving them down. He buzzed down the window.

"Where ya headed?" the man barked, aiming the muzzle of his AR-15 at Carson's head. He was Hispanic, maybe mid-twenties, tall and skinny with a do-rag and a giant tattoo of a tiger inked across his shoulder and chest.

The twenty or so guys guarding the road were Latino. They wore baggy shorts and tanks, bling draped over their chests, and tattoos sleeving their arms, necks, and faces.

Logan's gut—already nauseous—tightened.

Two more gangbangers sauntered up along Logan's side. The taller one's AR-15 was slung loosely over his shoulder. He was just a kid, fifteen, maybe sixteen, with huge ears sticking out on either side of his head like a jug.

The second one was shorter but bulkier, his Miami Dolphin's T-shirt straining against his bulging belly. No more than fourteen, he gripped an AR-15 in his fleshy hands.

Both kids wore ammo pouches belted around their low-slung waists and carried shortwave radios; a pistol grip stuck out of the chubby kid's pocket.

"What you doin' with these gringos, *ese?*" Dolphin said with a grin.

"You guys Blood Outlaws?" Logan asked casually, not even meeting the kid's gaze.

"Yeah," he said proudly. "We're the new Kings of Miami."

Blood Outlaws. Exactly the gang they didn't want to run into.

He'd shot a Blood Outlaw in the Old Navy after they left the theater. The thug had threatened them; Logan did what he had to. It was self-defense, but no gangbanger would see it that way.

Worse, there'd been a witness, a second thug who escaped out the back door. Logan had wanted to chase him down then and there, but the first Blood Outlaw shot Shay in the head. To save her life, he'd remained behind.

He hadn't seen the second thug's face. He didn't know who he was looking for. But if the thug had gotten a good look at him...

Cold iced his veins. He felt exposed, completely vulnerable.

Logan didn't want to draw any extra attention to Dakota, Eden, and Shay in the back. He didn't turn around in his seat, but he could feel their eyes on him, could feel the tension ratcheting up inside the cab.

No way he could take on twenty guys with a hunting rifle and the few bullets remaining in Dakota's Sig. The Blood Outlaws would riddle them with high-powered gunfire and kill them all within seconds.

One wrong move. One mistake. One thug glancing at him the wrong way.

That's all it would take.

Logan kept his expression carefully neutral. Hopefully, none of these scumbags would recognize them. But just in case this all went sideways fast, he was already forming a crazy-ass plan.

27

LOGAN

"There's a tax," said the guy with the tiger tattoo. "Pay the tax, you're free to go."

"What's the tax?" Logan asked evenly.

"It depends. What do you have?"

Two more guys circled the truck like sharks, eyeing it for anything of value. "What you got in the back?"

"Just two injured people we're trying to get to a hospital," Carson said.

"You and everyone else." Tiger Tattoo snorted. "Good luck, *ese.*"

"We're looking for food, mostly," the kid with big ears like a jug said. "And water."

"We'll take cash, jewelry, watches." Tiger Tattoo let his gaze roam over the Ford F-150. "And sweet rides. Which you've got."

Carson stiffened. Logan flashed him a look, warning him to shut the hell up. Luckily, he did.

"We're taking care of our own," Jughead said, even though no one asked what the tax was for. There was a slight waver in his voice —and his movements. His bronze skin had a yellowish tinge to it, and his eyes were wide and glassy. He took a step back from the window and pointed across the street. "No one else doin' it. So we will."

Radiation sickness. Logan pretended not to notice and looked where the kid pointed.

A bunch of Hispanic kids—a few black kids, too, all in their early teens—were standing around a bunch of pallets and two forklifts in the Publix parking lot. The kids were busy handing out packages of bottled water, along with crates and cardboard boxes stuffed with boxed and canned food.

A straggly line of people—the elderly and families with little kids climbing all over their legs—waited to receive their boxes. They were mostly Hispanic, but not all of them. Some had battered cars or bicycles, others were walking. Everyone left with several grocery bags or a box or two of supplies.

"We worked most of the night gettin' it all done," Dolphin boasted.

He wiped sweat off his forehead with the back of his bare arm. A constellation of raw, red cuts and welts marred his arm from his wrist to his shoulder. A few peppered his throat and chin as well. He must've been standing near a window during the blast, and hadn't escaped the shattering glass.

"We've got outposts all over the city now," Dolphin said. "I mean, not downtown. But everywhere else. Some of the churches are helpin', too. They don't wanna know where it's from, but they still take it."

"Father Michael says a prayer over it." Jughead snorted like that was the funniest thing in the world. He was clearly sick but doing his best to act like he wasn't. "Says it 'sanctifies' the food, whatever the hell that means."

"What about everyone else?" Vanessa asked sharply, unable to contain herself. "What're they supposed to do now that you've stolen all the food from the stores?"

Dolphin's eyes hardened. "No one else ever cared nothin' about us. Why should we care 'bout anyone else?"

"Let the rich gringos starve," Tiger Tattoo said. "What'd we care?" He narrowed his eyes at Carson and Vanessa, at the pearls circling Vanessa's throat. "You got places to go, fancy-ass hotels and second homes and yachts. What'd we got? No one can afford to leave here, man. This it. This our home."

Logan looked past Tiger Tattoo at the group of restless thugs. Most of them were leaning against the two cars parked on either side of the road about thirty yards away. A few men sat on the hoods, drinking beers. Several coolers were pushed up to the front wheels of the SUV.

These guys didn't seem intent on mayhem. On closer inspection, at least half of the gangbangers looked physically ill. They were hunched or slumped, their thousand-yard stares listless rather than malicious.

They were hot and miserable and just wanted to keep the line moving.

All Logan's group had to do was pay the stupid tax and the gang would let them go. If they were lucky.

"It's a really good thing you're doing here," Carson stammered. "Don't misunderstand us."

Tiger Tattoo scowled. "Man, I ain't askin' your permission or your approval."

On Logan's side, Jughead tapped his rifle nervously. "We got another car behind this one. We gonna let 'em go? What about their guns?"

Logan stiffened, his finger moving toward the trigger.

"Relax. We don't need your guns, *ese*. We collected us plenty of donations from Charlie's Pawn and Gun Shop and Pantera Brother Firearms." Tiger Tattoo patted the bandolier slung across his chest, which bristled with shiny ammunition. He lifted his rifle and mimed shooting at several invisible people over the roof of the truck. "Bam, bam, bam!"

Vanessa flinched.

Tiger Tattoo saw it and gave a hard chuckle. "Those pearls real, lady? I'll take 'em. My *abuelita* will like those just fine."

Vanessa went rigid. "This was *my* grandmother's. This is all I have left."

"So what? Give it up, lady. Now."

Carson coughed.

She still didn't move.

Tiger Tattoo took a hand from his rifle and rubbed the back of his neck, grimacing. "We don't got all day—"

"Hey!" One of the thugs leaning against the SUV thirty yards away stood and took a few halting steps toward the truck. Tiger Tattoo looked back at the guy, who waved a hand and gestured him over.

"You two take care of this. I gotta see what Spider wants." Tiger Tattoo jogged over toward the other gangster, a spindly punk who couldn't have been taller than 5'6. His skinny arms were almost black with ink. His long, narrow face was inked with a skull on his right cheek, charcoal tears on his left.

Sometimes the small ones were the most dangerous.

"Gotta get that necklace," Jughead said. "Then you're all good."

"We're fine," Carson murmured. "It's fine, honey. We're gonna be fine."

Logan could hear someone breathing heavily in the back—short, shallow breaths of panic—but he couldn't afford to pay it any attention.

"Give it to them," Logan said.

Reluctantly, Vanessa unclasped her necklace and handed over the pearls. Jughead grabbed them, thrust them in his pocket, and smiled. He looked a lot younger when he smiled. Like he belonged in school, an ice cream shop, or even a damn church choir, not on the streets.

He stepped back, Dolphin beside him, and gestured with the muzzle of his rifle. "Move on through."

Logan expelled a breath through his teeth.

"Finally," Dakota muttered. "Drive. Let's get the hell out of here."

Carson shifted the truck into drive. They rolled slowly forward.

Tiger Tattoo stood next to the skinny, inked thug, who turned to stare straight at Logan.

Electricity exploded through Logan's body as he caught the flash of recognition in the other man's eyes.

28

DAKOTA

Dakota sat in the rear left passenger seat, tense and alert, scoping out three half-drunk gangbangers who kept eyeballing the truck in between swigs of warm beer.

Logan let out a string of curses.

Her stomach sank to her toes. She knew what it meant. One of these low-life gangbangers had recognized them. The crap was about to hit the fan, now.

Logan slapped the dashboard. "Go, go, go!"

"What?" Carson asked, blinking. "They're letting us through! They're—"

"Hey!" The small, scary one with the teardrops inked on his cheeks pointed at them. "They the ones that killed Potillo!"

"Stop!" Tiger Tattoo shouted. He spun and raised his M4. "Get them!"

The rest of the gangbangers snapped to attention. They leapt from the cars' hoods and jerked to their feet, immediately spreading out to block the lane between the two vehicles.

Within two seconds, a dozen assault rifles were aimed at the truck's windshield.

"What happened?" Vanessa cried. "What are they doing?"

"Reverse!" Dakota shouted. She punched the back of the driver's seat. Going forward was suicidal. They were seconds from a rain of high-octane gunfire.

The stalled cars along the left side of the road next to the expressway kept them from going left, while the row of palms blocked their exit on the right. They were trapped.

"Go back! Back!"

Dolphin and Jughead took several swift strides backward, almost tripping over their own feet. Jughead's face turned ashen and his eyes widened. The kid could've shot them all dead right there, but he didn't raise his weapon—just gripped it tighter and held it in front of his chest like a shield.

Logan leaned across Vanessa's frozen body and shifted into reverse. "Punch the gas!" he shouted.

Carson blinked and obeyed. The truck jerked backward, tires slewing to the left.

Gunfire exploded. Vanessa screamed. Beside Dakota, Shay went rigid in fear.

"Get down!" Dakota cried.

Shay grabbed Eden's arm and pulled her down. Eden bent at the waist, covering her head with her hands. Shay leaned over and covered Eden's small body with her own.

A burst of gratitude toward Shay thrummed through Dakota. With Eden as safe as she was going to get, she focused on keeping them all alive.

She twisted in her seat and looked behind the truck, the seatbelt rubbing against her neck.

The Jetta was idling about fifteen yards behind them. Thirty yards behind the Jetta, the dump truck was parked at a forty-five-degree angle, blocking the entirety of the right lane. They had to get past the dump truck for cover, then they could do a U-turn and get the hell out of here.

Gunfire and shouting erupted. While Dakota gave directions, Logan racked the bolt action and returned fire with the Remington. *Boom.* The crack of the rifle reverberated in the enclosed cab.

The truck squealed backward, swerving into the left lane, then the right. Park and Julio were both lying flat in the truck bed, Park on his back, eyes squeezed shut, Julio on his stomach, his hands pressed over his head.

Three rounds punched through the side of the truck and out the other side. She didn't have time to see if Park and Julio were okay.

The Jetta saw them coming and hastened into reverse. Dakota glimpsed two stricken faces—one male, one female—in the front seats.

Pop, pop. Two holes appeared in the Jetta's windshield. The woman driver's head jerked backward. She slumped against the seat.

The Jetta swerved left, tires squealing as it canted off the shoulder. Its backend slammed into the trunk of a palm tree. The fronds shook. The rear bumper crumpled.

Several more rounds smashed into the Jetta's windshield and side passenger windows. Safety glass spidered and broke into pieces. The male passenger's mouth hung open in a red O.

Two people dead—their only fault being in the wrong place at the wrong time.

The truck careened toward the Jetta.

"Go right!" Dakota yelled. She could barely hear her own voice over the bullets, the screaming, and her ringing ears.

Carson jerked the wheel too far. He overcorrected and the truck lifted onto two tires. It spun as Carson slammed the brakes, tires squealing.

A bullet pinged into the grille of the F-150. Another drilled through the rear window, six inches to the right of Dakota's head. She ducked instinctively and popped her head up—only to watch in horror as the truck smashed into the back of the Jetta.

29

DAKOTA

Dakota's body was flung against the back seat. Her head smacked against the rear window, and pain flashed through her shoulder and skull.

Everything went dark and blurry. For a second, sound seemed to fade away. She tasted blood in her mouth. She'd bitten her tongue.

Someone was calling her name.

"Dakota!" Logan shouted. "Dakota!"

The rear window had shattered. Gummy shards of safety glass clung to her clothes and spilled on her lap. How had that happened? Was it from the crash? Or the bullets?

She blinked and shook the fuzz from her brain. Fresh pain radiated from her head all the way down her neck and spine. But she could move. Nothing was broken.

Carson had slammed on the brakes, so luckily they'd slowed significantly before striking the Jetta. She fumbled for her seatbelt and freed herself. Her gun had slipped out of her hands in the crash. She twisted and frantically searched the floor at her feet.

More gunfire chattered from outside the truck.

She snatched the Sig and wrestled the door open. "Eden, get out!"

Eden sat rigid in her seat. She didn't move. Blood dripped from a small cut on her forehead.

"Eden!" Dakota screamed.

Shay reached over, unbuckled Eden's seatbelt, pushed her out, and stumbled after her.

"Wait for cover!" Logan growled.

Shay, Eden, and the Wilburns cowered behind the truck, their arms over their heads. On the opposite side, Logan slammed open the door and crouched behind the engine block for protection.

Rounds screamed over their heads. Twenty yards away, five gangbangers rushed the truck. With the stock pressed firmly against his shoulder, Logan aimed and fired.

The gangbanger on the right dropped his carbine and clutched his shoulder.

Logan cycled the bolt action, chambering another round, and fired again.

His second shot struck another thug in the stomach and he went down with a scream.

Dakota forced herself to focus, exhale, and aim her Sig. Six bullets. She had none to waste. She fired a double tap. The middle thug's head jerked. Red mist sprayed from his skull as he dropped.

The next shot went wide, but it accomplished its task. Abruptly realizing they'd bitten off more than they could chew, the Blood Outlaws scrambled for cover.

It gave the others the precious seconds they needed to escape the line of fire. Julio helped Park scramble out of the truck bed and drop to the pavement.

"Get behind me!" Dakota cried.

She fired off two more shots as a handful of thugs scurried from the cover of the pickup and SUV to one of the cars parked along the shoulder—and only forty feet away.

She nailed one in the leg as he dove for cover. He screamed, fell, and dragged himself behind the car. She aimed and fired at him again but missed.

She pulled the trigger. Nothing.

Out of bullets, with no way to reload.

Panic swirled in her gut as she ducked down low and shoved the useless pistol in its holster. *Damn, damn, damn!* What now?

The other thugs stayed down as Logan ejected another shell, racked the load, and blasted the car. The metal frame juddered, safety glass cascading from the windows.

Out of the corner of her eye, she glimpsed her group rise and dash for the protection of the dump truck ten yards behind them.

Thirty feet. It felt like forever.

When she knew they were safe, she signaled to Logan.

Logan was still crouched behind the F-150's engine block to protect himself from oncoming fire, but he'd angled his body to the left, leveling the hunting rifle at the two gangbanger kids.

They were standing ten feet away, slack-jawed, their hands on their weapons but not in the ready position, not aimed at anything. They must've run after the truck, but once they'd reached it, they froze, unsure what to do, hesitant to kill.

Logan didn't hesitate. He cycled the bolt action and blasted the heavy kid in the chest. He shifted, cycled again, and shot the one with the big ears.

The round punched through the boy's throat. Blood sprayed everywhere. The AR-15 clattered to the pavement as the kid sank to the ground in slow motion, clutching at his mangled neck.

Within a few seconds, both teenagers were dead.

"Cover me!" Logan shouted.

Dakota darted forward, grabbed the Remington from Logan's hands, and popped up just long enough to rack the bolt, aim, and fire at two thugs rounding the fender of the rusty red pickup. Her shot missed—she didn't have time to aim properly, and the kickback was stunningly powerful—but the thugs jerked back and dove for cover.

Logan kept low and dashed out into the open. He ran for the assault rifles, seized one, then crouched, grabbed one of the bodies by the leg, and dragged it back with him behind the truck, the AR-15 attached to the sling around the boy's shoulder clattering after it.

A couple of shots blasted his way, but Logan moved fast and low. They missed.

He squeezed in beside Dakota, pressing against her side as he swiftly stripped the ammo pouches on the dead boy's belt and stuffed two large, curved magazines in his pocket. He handed one semi-automatic AR-15 to Dakota and kept the second one for himself.

"Thirty rounds each magazine," he panted.

It was a good thing. The Sig was completely out, and the Remington was nearly empty.

"Go!" he said. "I'll follow."

Bullets zipped past their heads, pinging the asphalt in front of them and the sides of the truck. Another boom cracked the air. Three feet away, the pavement erupted in an explosion of concrete shards.

"Go!"

She leapt to her feet, turned, and ran.

Legs pumping, hair flying behind her, ragged breath torn from her scorched lungs—she ran with everything she had. The large, heavy rifle banged against her ribs.

Her back was an exposed target. She expected a bullet to the spine at any second.

She made it ten feet, then twenty, then thirty. Behind her, Logan kept the gangbangers locked down under steady fire. *Boom, boom, boom.*

She sprinted around the dump truck and pressed herself against a giant wheel, her pulse a roar in her ears. She longed to stay there, to stay safe, but Logan needed help.

She pivoted around the edge of the fender, kneeling and resting her elbows on her leg to better steady her aim. The rifle was much heavier than her pistol. She needed to keep it braced or she'd tire quickly, and her shots would fly wildly off-target.

She flicked the safety off, quickly adjusted the stock, and wedged it tight against her shoulder. She peered through the scope.

Thirty yards away, a head popped up behind the red pickup, preparing to shoot at Logan as he hustled toward the dump truck, facing backward, aiming and firing with every step.

She squeezed the trigger, tensing as the recoil slammed against her shoulder. The thunderous *crack* boomed in her ears.

The shot missed the thug's head but struck the hood a foot away. She squeezed off three more shots—all missing, but close enough to scare the living crap out of her target.

The thug ducked low, giving Logan time to reach cover.

Logan angled himself just left of the enormous truck's cab. He aimed in the space between the cab and the large yellow hopper.

With Logan protected, Dakota risked a glance around her. Two feet away, Carson and Vanessa knelt, clutching each other, Carson's arms wrapped around his wife. Julio, Park, and Shay huddled together behind the second wheel below the cab.

Dakota's throat constricted. "Where's Eden?"

30

DAKOTA

S hay's eyes widened, and her hand flew to her mouth. "Oh, no. I thought she was right behind me—"

Dakota whirled, wanting nothing more than to run back into the line of fire to rescue Eden.

"Wait!" Julio reached out and grabbed her arm. "It's too dangerous!"

Logan moved forward, took a quick peek, let off a volley of shots, then pressed himself back against the truck. "She's under the Ford. I can see her foot."

Dakota couldn't breathe. "I'm not leaving her."

"Of course not," Julio said. "How do we help?"

"Don't get yourself killed," Logan said.

Julio touched his gold cross. "That's not good enough! Let me help!"

A bullet whizzed by and clipped the edge of the front grille. Another shot grazed the outside of the huge tire Shay and Park hid behind. Shay flinched and let out a whimper.

"This isn't safe enough. We've got to get them out of here first." Logan craned his neck to look behind him. "When I say go, run and get behind those big concrete columns beneath the overpass. No bullets are getting through those. Dakota and I will cover you. Then we'll go get Eden."

He was right, and she knew it. She had to fight off the panic, the gut-wrenching fear, and regain control. *One, two, three. Breathe.*

She pulled away from Julio, forced herself not to run for Eden.

"Dakota?" Logan asked. "You good?"

Dakota gave him a tight nod. "Let's do this."

Dakota and Logan covered them while Park got his arm around Shay's waist. They hobbled toward the nearest concrete column. Carson seized his wife by the wrist and pulled her along. They ran past Shay and Park, who were helping each other. Park was pale but on his feet.

"Julio, go!" Dakota said.

"You two cover me. I'll get Eden."

"Julio—"

Julio's soft, friendly face hardened into something Dakota didn't recognize. His hands clenched into fists at his sides. "This is the best way! There's no time to discuss it!"

"Listen to him." Logan's rifle clicked. He swung back behind cover, ejected the magazine, and pulled a fresh one out of his pocket. He slapped it in. "Dakota, you take that side. You've got everything right of center. I'll take the left."

Fresh gunfire zipped over their heads. Dakota swore as she scurried to the right edge of the truck, knelt, adjusted the AR-15 and prepared to provide a fresh volley of covering fire. She would have to trust Julio with her sister's life. She had no other choice.

She settled her nerves, just like Ezra had taught her. *You're no good to anyone if you panic.* Her hands stung, her palms damp with sweat and blood beneath the bandages. It made it harder to grip the rifle and keep it steady.

Her chest and lungs still ached from the smoke inhalation. She couldn't suck in enough oxygen. But it didn't matter. None of it mattered.

She shut out the pain, the fear, the gunfire—everything but the task at hand.

Five gangbangers had left the cover of the SUV. Two crept forward, rifles aimed at the F-150. They let fly a few shots. Bullets pinged the rear fender and punched through the driver's side door.

Julio was down low, scrambling on his hands and knees, only a few feet from the truck now. She focused between the sights. Took a breath. Exhaled. Squeezed the trigger. *Boom!*

The recoil smacked her shoulder. She shifted an inch and adjusted her aim to the left. Exhaled again. Squeezed the trigger.

The first thug's head jerked back like an invisible hand had slapped him. The second man spasmed, jittering like a puppet on a string, then slumped to the ground.

She panned for another target.

The remaining thugs sprinted for the cover of the Taco Bell fifty feet west. They were shooting sideways as they ran, guns bobbling in their hands, rounds whizzing harmlessly over the Ford's roof.

Out of the corner of her eye, she saw Julio reach the crumpled fender. He crawled past the front wheel, stretched between the undercarriage, and grasped Eden by the ankles. He gave an unceremonious yank and dragged her out.

Eden was shaking and crying. Julio covered her body with his own and started the arduous crawl back to shelter. Dakota could see his lips moving but couldn't hear a thing over the cacophony of bullets and the tinny ringing in her ears.

She centered her sights on a tall guy in a lime-green shirt running across the grassy patch between the buildings. Sweat dripped into her eyes. She blinked and exhaled. Squeezed the trigger. Missed. Shot again, missed again.

Her hands were shaking. The rifle was heavy, and shooting moving targets was incredibly difficult. The last few years, she'd only practiced at the range. She'd gotten rusty, and now it was going to cost her.

Lime Shirt was almost to the cover of the building. She panned ahead of him and fired two shots. He stumbled and fell face-first to the ground. He dropped his M4 as he squealed, body contorting, and clutched his leg. She'd hit him in the thigh.

She blinked. Took one more shot—the stock slamming against her bruised shoulder, the *boom* rattling her ears—and ended him.

Julio and Eden scrambled safely around the side of the dump truck. Dakota glanced at them only long enough to check them for bullet holes.

One side of Eden's face was scraped from the pavement. Vomit stained her shirt and dribbled down her chin. The sour stench mingled with the stink of gunpowder. She was trembling like a leaf. But they were both unhurt.

"Get behind the columns with the others!" Dakota scanned the area for more threats. "Go, go, go!"

Julio wrapped his arm around Eden's waist, and they half-ran, half-stumbled beneath the underpass to the shelter of the concrete columns.

The chatter of gunfire ceased.

Shell casings littered the asphalt. The F-150, the SUV, and the red pickup, and every car along the east shoulder of the road were riddled with bullet holes. The scene looked like a war-zone from a movie.

She took a second to wipe the sweat out of her eyes. The heat drained every ounce of her energy. Her arms felt like heavy weights; she could barely hold up the rifle.

"I think we got most of them," she panted.

"Maybe," Logan allowed.

He didn't lower his gun. Neither did she.

Boom. Boom. Boom. More gunfire—but it wasn't the Blood

Outlaws. Or at least, not these Blood Outlaws. The shots came from farther away, echoing in the still, heavy air. *Boom, boom, boom.*

A bullet whistled past her head, so close she felt it like a wind in her hair.

Three more rounds struck the pavement a few yards behind her.

Behind her? The angle was all wrong. How could that be?

At least ten dead bodies littered the road. Several more were alive, but barely. The rest were hidden behind the three bullet-riddled vehicles. By her count, there couldn't be more than five gangbangers left.

Unless there were reinforcements...

She twisted, craning her neck, searching for movement behind her or to the left, near the Taco Bell and McDonald's.

More shots blasted. Closer, now. Too close.

"Logan! What's going on?" she cried between pops of gunfire.

"Somehow, they're flanking us...oh, hell."

"What? What is it?"

Logan swore. "We've got company."

31

LOGAN

L ogan turned to see a horde of bodies swarm out of the Publix entrance about seventy yards away—at least thirty gang-bangers with assault rifles.

The makeshift emergency aid center was long gone. The pallets and forklifts sat abandoned in the middle of the parking lot. The crowd had fled.

A second group was coming from the west behind the restaurants. More gangbangers. But—no. That wasn't right.

He peered through the scope. The figures wore uniforms. Soldiers, maybe the National Guard, and a few police officers.

They were moving fast, engaging the first group from the Publix. The gangbangers took cover behind the dozen or so abandoned vehicles spread across the parking lot.

Somehow, their own scuffle had collided with a larger battle between law enforcement and the Blood Outlaws.

Dakota risked a peek over the hood and ducked back down. "No one's pointing any guns at us."

"They're distracted," Logan whispered. "We can get the hell out of here."

Dakota hesitated. He recognized the look on her face—stubborn determination, that wild ferocity in her eyes.

She wanted to do something insanely stupid.

"No way," he said. "Don't even think about it."

"There are two officers taking cover between the McDonald's and the Taco Bell, on the Taco Bell side, near the drive-thru window," she said. "Forty yards, maybe. At your nine o'clock."

He shook his head. "Hell, no."

She ignored him and motioned to the west. "Their backs are to us. They don't know we're here—or the Blood Outlaws. The gang-bangers aren't all dead, Logan. I glimpsed a few of their heads through the shattered pickup window. Five of them left. Tiger Tattoo is still out there."

"We need to leave while we still—"

"Those scumbags aren't paying attention to us anymore because they're going after the officers. The good guys."

"I know," Logan said. "That's the point. We need to run while we still can."

"We will. After we end those maggots."

"Dakota—"

"Logan." Sweat dripped down her forehead, strands of her long auburn hair stuck to her cheeks. Her face was pale, her pupils too wide, her voice still raspy from the smoke.

But her expression was as fierce as it'd ever been. "I'm doing this."

He saw the stubborn tilt of her jaw, the steely determination in her eyes. He resisted the urge to argue with her. He knew her well enough by now. She wouldn't bend.

He wasn't sure if he'd forgiven her for her lies and deception, but he harbored no anger, either. They understood each other. Something had happened in the last few days. Something he didn't understand.

All he knew was that now they were in this together.

He wasn't going after her again.

This time, he'd go first.

"Fine," he said.

Surprise flashed across her face—then relief. "Really?"

He shrugged. "You with the hero complex again."

She gave him a grim smile. "You with the bitching. You're worse than a whiny teenage girl."

"Yeah, yeah." He jerked another loaded magazine from his pocket—he had two more—and handed it to her. "You need to get beneath the overpass and protect the others."

She ejected her spent magazine and slapped in the new one. "I'm coming with you."

"There's no time. We've got hostiles and gunfire coming from all directions. Our people are sitting ducks. Save them."

She scowled. "What're you gonna do?"

"Exactly what you want me to do. I'll save your guys."

She didn't argue. She didn't say anything, just gave a single sharp nod, then moved into a crouch and scurried away.

A sickening rush of dizziness lurched through Logan. He blinked and pushed it away. He couldn't afford to be sick. Not until he'd finished this.

He peeked around the edge of the dump truck's front fender, then immediately jerked back. Dakota's intel was good. Five Blood Outlaws were left standing, including Tiger Tattoo and the runt who'd ID'd Logan—Teardrop.

They were inching toward the dump truck along the center of the road about twenty yards away. But they weren't coming for him. Their heads were turned to the west. They edged off the road, toward the fast food buildings.

Five against one. And they all had M4s and AR-15s just like he did. Not great odds. He didn't have a good angle from his position, either.

There wasn't time to think, to strategize a better plan. In a few seconds, they'd be off the road and headed between the palms. He'd have to get creative—and quick.

Before he could think better of it, Logan dropped and rolled beneath the dump truck. It was tight. He couldn't move very well, but he could do what he needed to do. Hopefully. The stench of gasoline and gunpowder singed his nostrils. He could barely hear a thing over the tinny ringing in his ears.

He braced his arms against the asphalt and aimed low. All he could see were feet and shins. He scanned left to right. Five pairs of feet in his line of sight.

Here we go.

He pulled the trigger. Hit a right ankle. The thug dropped his gun and buckled with a shriek.

Logan shifted, re-aimed. Fired. Hit a shin. A spray of red mist. Fragments of bone exploded. The man fell back onto his ass. The second bullet struck his inner thigh, blood spurting. The rifle clattered to the pavement.

Logan didn't pause to see what the hostile did next. He was already shifting his focus, aiming the sights at a pair of neon-yellow Nike high-tops and multicolored track pants. The third gangbanger jumped back after the first volley and took off running to the north.

Logan fired a shot, missed, and quickly searched for another target.

The fourth thug was close, only ten feet away. He crouched low, searching underneath the vehicle.

Boom! Logan missed.

The thug darted around the rear of the truck.

"Shooter beneath the car!" he screamed, already dropping to the pavement himself, a suppressed pistol in his hand.

Logan's finger was damp on the trigger, the grip slipping in his palms. He fired again, missed again.

He couldn't twist easily to aim down the length of his body and find his target. He was too big, too bulky.

Logan was trapped.

32

LOGAN

Logan contorted his body. His right shoulder, arm, and side ground into the asphalt. Tiny chunks of rock and gravel jutted into his hips and ribs as he awkwardly dragged the AR-15, smacking his wrist against the undercarriage.

He aimed down past his feet though he couldn't see anything, hoping he didn't shoot his own toes off. Anything to make it harder on the gangbanger at the rear of the truck.

He fired. *Boom!*

Someone screamed. Then a thud, like a body collapsing.

He waited a moment, every muscle tensed, straining his ears for any sounds, frantically scanning the narrow sliver of space he could see.

The rat-a-tat of gunfire came from the west. No bullets found their mark anywhere near him.

He shoved the AR-15 in front of him, his finger still on the trigger, and inched out from beneath the truck, worming himself up between the rear wheels so he came out head—and gun—first. Staying to the rear of the truck also gave him protection from any stray gunfire from the Publix battle.

As he clambered carefully to his feet, then scooted into a crouched position, his knees popped in protest. The oily stench of gasoline burned his nostrils. He spat sour spittle and wiped his sweating face.

He eased around the rear left fender, gun up and ready to fire, and took in the scene.

One of the Blood Outlaws he'd shot in the thigh was already bleeding out. The one at the rear of the truck was crawling away with low, anguished moans, his bloody leg dragging uselessly behind him.

Logan shot him twice in the back of the head.

The third thug with the shattered ankle was on the ground, fumbling for the pistol at his side. Without hesitating, Logan fired off a burst of five shots. They ripped through the guy's chest. He went down and didn't move.

Logan moved across the road, rifle up and ready, finger on the trigger. He stepped over the bodies of the two teenagers. The two kids he'd shot and killed in cold blood.

They hadn't been hardened criminals. Maybe they'd joined the Blood Outlaws out of necessity, out of desperation to survive—just like him all those years ago.

He didn't care. He couldn't afford to care. They chose the wrong side.

To save his own skin and the people with him, he'd needed their weapons. He couldn't afford to wonder if he'd made the right choice.

He hadn't felt a thing when he'd killed them, when he fired lead into soft flesh and bone, ending their pathetic, pitiful lives.

The darkness was inside him. The monster. He felt no anger, no blinding rage. The doubt was gone. The shame erased.

His mind was clear. He was a machine. Cold, efficient. Lethal.

He would kill anyone and anything in his way.

Two scumbags were left. Where were they? Logan quickly swept his surroundings. Teardrop was nowhere in sight. He was the one in the neon-yellow Nikes who'd turned tail and fled, just he like had in the Old Navy store.

Logan glimpsed movement between two palm trees on his left. He recognized the do-rag, the snarling big cat tattoo. Tiger Tattoo had his back to Logan and was headed toward the McDonald's and the Taco Bell, intent on taking out those soldiers.

There was a pop of gunfire. It sounded suppressed.

Logan ducked behind a stalled car. He slunk stealthily around the side and inched around the front fender.

A man lay on the ground. Blood stained the right shoulder of his army combat uniform. A soldier.

Tiger Tattoo stepped over the downed soldier, grasping what looked like a Beretta M9A3 with a suppressor in both hands. He rounded the corner of Taco Bell, edging close to the wall.

For half a second, Logan wished he'd asked Dakota to remain behind and cover him.

Too late now. He had Tiger Tattoo in his sights. It was time to take him out.

Logan followed in a crouch, slipping between the palm trees. He didn't have a good shot yet. He couldn't afford to waste the element of surprise.

The soldier on the ground was injured—unconscious, but still breathing. Logan crept past him. A side door inset in a shallow alcove along the western wall of the building provided a bit of cover. He hid as much as he could, then anchored himself against the stucco wall, the stock firm against the tender muscles of his shoulder, and peeked around the corner.

The soldiers were kneeling, focused on the battle in front of them. One wore an Army combat uniform; the other was dressed in khaki pants and a bulletproof vest emblazed with "ATF Police" over a navy T-shirt.

Twenty feet ahead of him, Tiger Tattoo planted his feet on the asphalt and aimed his weapon at the soldier's head.

Logan had only a second to act. He found the center of Tiger Tattoo's skull in his sights, exhaled, and squeezed the trigger twice, the rifle kicking back hard.

The Blood Outlaw's head exploded in a cloud of red vapor. He toppled onto his back. He didn't get up.

Both the agent and the soldier whirled at the sound of the gunshots directly behind them.

They pointed their weapons at Logan.

"Don't shoot!" he shouted.

33

LOGAN

Logan knew he looked like a gangbanger himself, with his bronze skin, hard face, and sleeves of tattoos. His only chance at remaining alive was to obey immediately—and hope they weren't so hyped on adrenaline that they shot first, asked questions later.

He flung the AR-15 to the ground, knelt on the pavement, and laced his hands behind his head. "I'm unarmed! I'm not one of them!"

The soldier and the ATF agent rushed forward, guns aimed at his chest.

"Down!" shouted the ATF agent, a tall, bald black man. "Down! Get down!"

Logan complied. He dropped and lay prone against the road, the right side of his face scraping gravel. His pulse thundered inside his head. His ears were ringing.

"I have a pistol in my holster," he said. "It's unloaded."

The soldier—a short, fierce woman—bent down and pulled it from his holster. "Got a Glock 43."

"It's empty," Logan said.

"No one said you could talk!" the soldier snapped.

Logan bit down on his cheeks in frustration. They were as stressed and hyped on adrenaline as he was. One false move and he'd be dead. No one had the time to analyze a situation—or a potential killer—in the line of fire.

They were shaky with nerves. They'd messed up, letting a hostile get behind them. The third soldier was likely watching their six before he'd gotten shot.

Logan remained limp and docile and let them do what they needed to do while he gritted his teeth and tried not to vomit on the soldier's boots. She probably wouldn't care for that.

They were frisking him roughly when footsteps approached.

"I'm friendly!" Dakota called. "I'm coming around the corner, now. No weapons."

"On your knees! Hands above your head!" the ATF agent ordered.

"We were attacked by that gang you were fighting," Dakota said evenly from somewhere behind Logan. "This dead gangbanger was sneaking up to kill you, along with a few others. That guy you've got there is my friend, Logan Garcia. He risked his life and managed to kill them first."

"Kinsey?" the agent said, keeping his weapon trained on Logan.

Logan heard the soldier walking away, back toward the road. "Holy mother of..." she muttered. A radio clicked. "Mueller, I've got at least a dozen dead hostiles over here. Maybe two dozen. You'd better bring the team and come up."

Her footsteps returned. She nudged Tiger Tattoo's dead body with her boot and rolled him over. He'd been lying on top of his M4.

"Damn it all to hell." She glanced at Logan, her tense expression softening. "We got surprised by an ambush. Turned into an ugly shootout. Cheung had our six—until he didn't."

Her gaze flitted to the guy leaning against the wall, groaning and clutching his shoulder—hurt but alive. Another soldier was bending over him, administering first aid.

"Tunnel vision," she said. "It's a real bitch."

"We got caught with our pants down," the agent said.

The soldier frowned up at him. "Speak for yourself."

The ATF agent held out his hand. Logan took it and rose heavily to his feet.

Now that the battle was over, his adrenaline was fading fast, replaced by the familiar shaky, gut-wrenching nausea.

"I guess I should thank you for saving our bacon." The man grinned. "Name's Trey Hawthorne. My friends just call me Hawthorne. I'm with ATF, Miami Field Division."

His skin was a warm chestnut brown, his face lean and chiseled beneath a full beard. In his late twenties, Hawthorne was lanky and extremely tall, about six and a half feet. Even Logan had to crane his neck to gaze up at him.

The female soldier looked faintly Middle Eastern. Her inky black hair cut in a tousled pixie and the dimples in her round, ruddy cheeks gave her an impish look, though the fine lines around her eyes betrayed her age as closer to forty.

She stuck out her hand. "Captain Rachel Kinsey, National Guard."

Logan and Dakota introduced themselves as several other Guardsmen strode up from the Publix parking lot. They were all dressed in ACUs and gripped rifles. Two soldiers held paddle-shaped electronic devices: Geiger counter meters to detect radiation.

"We lost three of ours," one of them said. "Four injured. We've got about thirty gangbangers DOA and another fifteen escaped."

"Clear the area here, too," Kinsey instructed. "And arrest any punks still alive."

Hawthorne ran a hand over his smooth, bald head and turned back to Logan and Dakota. "I'm serving as the Preliminary Damage Assessment Coordinator for the Joint Field Office and Recovery Emergency Operations Center. Our team was tasked with providing initial assessments of the infrastructure damage, residual fallout zones, civil unrest activity, and analyze community needs.

"We received reports that several checkpoints were overrun last night and came to verify what we were up against before we put more boots on the ground."

Kinsey shook her head. "We expected some gang activity, but mostly at night. These guys are brazen as all hell. They attacked us without hesitation or provocation, in broad daylight."

"Same here," Dakota said.

"It took everything we had to fight them off," Logan said. "And then some."

"You did this?" Kinsey said, her eyebrows raised as she surveyed the scene, all the dead and broken bodies.

"Me and her together," Logan said grimly.

"I'm impressed."

Dakota dipped her chin at him in acknowledgment. Then she turned to Kinsey. "There are six others in our group. All civilians and unarmed. Three are wounded, and several of us have acute radiation syndrome. We were heading for the emergency center at the airport when we were attacked. We crashed our truck trying to escape." She cleared her throat, shifting uncomfortably. "We...we could use some help."

34
LOGAN

K insey rubbed her chin and frowned. "We're not a rescue operation. That's not our mission."

"They saved my ass," Hawthorne said. "And yours."

"Yeah, I know. I was there."

"It's the least we could do." Hawthorne elbowed her playfully in the side. "Come on, now."

Kinsey sighed. "Okay. Let's get the rest of your group. We've got a military transport a few blocks back. We'll provide you and your group an escort to the EOC."

Logan felt relieved—but also wary. Less than five minutes ago, these people had guns trained at his head. He was still strung taut with nerves—his body hadn't received the message that the threat was over yet.

"Thank you," Dakota said. She whistled and shouted for the rest of the group. They shuffled cautiously out from beneath the overpass and made their way to Dakota and Logan.

Carson slung his arm around his wife, holding her up. Vanessa's eyes were wide and stunned. She kept clutching at her bare neck, unconsciously seeking the pearls that were no longer there.

Park and Eden weren't doing so well. Julio had to hold Shay steady to keep her on her feet.

Maybe help was a good thing. They needed it.

"What's it like?" Julio asked. "Is it safe?"

"It's a chaotic mess, but it's better than anywhere else right now," Hawthorne said. He was looking at Shay with a big, dumb grin on his face. "We do have power and warm food, at least."

"That sounds wonderful," Shay said weakly.

Hawthorne's smile brightened, then faltered as his gaze strayed to the blood seeping through Shay's bandaged head. "Looks like we need to hurry."

Dakota swayed on her feet. She looked as weary as Logan felt. "Sounds good to me."

"Is there room for us?" Julio asked.

"We'll make room." Hawthorne winked at Shay. "I know a guy."

Kinsey rolled her eyes. "Kill me already, why don't you?"

"What about our truck?" Carson asked.

"We hit the Jetta at less than ten miles per hour," Julio said. "It hurt us more than the F-150, I think. The grille and fender are beat-up, but it should still run."

"Great," Hawthorne said. "We can provide medical transport for your injured and escort the rest of you in the truck."

They kept talking, but Logan didn't hear them.

He bent over, resting his hands on his thighs, breathing deeply to fight the dizziness rushing through him. His legs felt watery, like his muscles couldn't hold him up anymore.

The aftereffects of the battle were on him now—the utter exhaustion and the nausea, both made worse by the radiation sickness. Plus, a blistering headache and tremors in his hands.

He had no idea which symptoms were from the radiation and which were from alcohol withdrawal. The thirst was in him. The need. To feel that familiar, welcoming warmth buzzing through his veins. To give in and forget the pain and suffering and the constant, torturous whispers of the demons lurking in his own mind.

It was all he could not to bolt for the nearest liquor store he could loot. He raised his arm to wipe the sweat from his brow and froze, staring at the Latin words strung around his forearm, bristling with inked barbed wire: *et facti sunt ne unum.*

Lest you become one.

The faces of the teenage boys he'd just killed flashed through his mind. Their frightened faces, their weapons pointed at the ground. Then the images of the other bodies crashed in—the blood and guts and shattered bones, the agonized expressions frozen forever in death.

The regret and remorse came then. The shame, hot and wrenching, washing over him in excruciating waves, the bitter self-loathing clawing at his throat.

He was nothing but a killer. Twisted and ugly at his very core. Barbaric and savage. He'd never escape the brutal violence. It was the only thing he was any good at. The only thing that fed the ravenous darkness inside him.

There was no shutting it out now. No drowning it in the bottom of a bottle.

This was the monster, who slaughtered without guilt, hesitation, or remorse. Who mowed down anything and everything in its path, including children.

Including the little boy of his nightmares.

Tomás Canales-Hidalgo was his name. Tomás: the neighbor kid with the musical laugh and the too-big head and those tousled black curls always falling into his eyes.

You did this. He saw the kid clear as day, heard him like he was standing right there in the sunlight and the heat and the carnage. A hallucination from his detox. It must be. The boy watched him with those dark, accusing eyes. Judged him and found him wanting. *You murdered me.*

Tomás, who loved Nascar and Hot Wheel cars. Tomás, who always snuck Logan the orange from his lunch box when he got home from school, so the boy's mother wouldn't find out he never ate his fruit.

Tomás was seven years old when Logan shot him in the back of the head. That boy's face had haunted Logan every day and night since.

"Logan?" Shay asked. "Are you okay?"

Logan turned his head and vomited.

35

MADDOX

Maddox Cage drifted in and out of consciousness. His body burned with fever. His skin was seared a blistering red, radiating heat and pain. Blisters burst on his arms, legs, and face.

He dreamed of fire, of charred corpses, of destruction and ruin and death.

Someone was murmuring to him. An angel? Was he in heaven? Had he finally received the reward he deserved?

But no, the fire returned, a raging inferno ravaging the world, burning everything as the people screamed and shrieked for mercy. There was no mercy to be had, only a scorched and blackened wasteland devoid of all life.

Hours passed. Days passed. There was light, then darkness, then light again.

He floated in a sea of blazing fire, flames devouring him, consuming him piece by piece, cell by cell, bone by bone.

But he'd been promised eternity. This was a cruel trick, a betrayal. *And why shouldn't you burn?* A voice whispered in his fevered mind. *Just like the Prophet warned you would? After all, you failed, didn't you?*

"No!" he rasped.

His eyes snapped open. Everything was too bright, blindingly white. He blinked rapidly. The world was a fuzzy, indistinct haze.

Pain wracked his body. He licked his cracked, blistered lips as his bleary gaze slowly focused. It felt like coming to the surface from a deep, deep lake.

With great effort, he turned his head and took in his surroundings. He was lying in a bed with a mattress and a pillow. A thin sheet covered his body to his bare chest. An IV hooked to a pole fed into a vein in the crook of his elbow.

The room was simple, with a wooden floor, four plank walls, and a low ceiling. Daylight streamed through high windows on three walls. A row of cabinets was set against the fourth wall beside a small fridge.

A cart with a stainless-steel countertop stood in the middle of the room. There were baskets, tubs, and containers filled with scalpels, trauma shears, rolls of gauze, and other medical supplies.

Maddox recognized the medical clinic. He had spent many days of his youth here, recovering from his beatings.

He was home.

He let out a low, painful breath.

A figure in white bent over him. "You're awake."

The answer was obvious, so he said nothing. He focused on the blurry figure: a plump woman in her sixties, with a kind, wrinkled face and blue eyes still sharp with intelligence. She had the deep, raspy voice of a former smoker.

Though all were prohibited from speaking of the past before the compound, Maddox had overheard his father talking—he knew she'd both lived in sin as a heathen and in idolatry as a Catholic nun before finding The Way.

She'd lived at the compound as long as Maddox could remember, caring for the children and nursing them back to health when they were sick. With her sharp wit, easy smile, and the forbidden candies she'd smuggle them, she was every kid's favorite sister. Well, almost every kid.

"Sister Rosemarie," he croaked.

"So, you remember me."

He attempted a grin. "How...could I forget...my favorite Sister?"

She frowned. Less gullible than the others, she had never been taken in by his charm. "And where are you right now?"

"River Grass...Compound..."

She sniffed. "I see you have your mental faculties, at least."

"How...long?"

She dropped a clean washcloth into a bowl of ice water on the counter, squeezed it out, and placed it gently on his forehead. "You've been out for four days."

"Four...?" His heart jolted. He tried to push himself into a sitting position but collapsed onto the bed. Fresh pain exploded through him. It felt like his back was being scraped raw. "That's too long...I need to speak to the Prophet—"

"I know, and I will call him. You have much to do, but not until you rest. You have radiation sickness. You're lucky you're still alive."

"I feel better. I can get up."

"You're not well, yet. Your skin is red as a lobster, with blisters and sores. It will hurt to move."

He snorted. He wouldn't let her see his pain. She'd seen enough of it as it was. She'd seen him weak, crying and blubbering like a child. He loathed that weakness. "I'm strong enough to handle a sunburn."

"This is like no sunburn you've ever seen," Sister Rosemarie muttered. "You had a high fever along with vomiting and diarrhea. You were bleeding from your gums. I'm no expert, Maddox, but you should go see a real doctor, in a hospital. Radiation damages your stomach and intestines, blood vessels, your bone marrow and red blood cells..."

He pushed himself into a sitting position, willing his shaky muscles to hold him up, gritting his teeth against the pain. "That is blasphemy, Sister Rosemarie," he hissed. She knew as well as anyone that outside hospitals—hospitals run by heathens—were forbidden. "Surely you didn't say what I thought you did."

Sister Rosemarie's face contorted—not in fear, but in concern. Wrinkles appeared between her graying eyebrows. "Maddox Cage, I've cared for you since you were a toddler. You and I both know you were a troublesome boy, to say the least. But I've always treated you like the child of God that you are. I've no desire to see you die, or to see your father lose both of his sons."

Maddox flinched at the mention of his brother's death. "That is not for you or any man to decide. God chooses who lives and dies. Everything else is a test. To suggest otherwise is a grave sin, isn't it?"

Sister Rosemarie frowned like she was going to say something else. Then she bit her lip and simply nodded. She knew the punishment for blasphemy as well as he did. A visit to the mercy room—*if* his father was feeling gracious.

"I'm not of my right mind right now," he said. "I must still be hallucinating. I was mistaken."

"I'm sure you're right," she murmured, her raspy voice appropriately docile and meek. But she watched him with those clear blue eyes, with that gaze that always unnerved him, like she could see straight through to his traitorous black heart.

He jerked back the sheet and forced his legs to the side of the bed. He wore only boxers. His skin was raw and blistered. It hurt even to look at himself.

He glared at Sister Rosemarie instead. "Bring me clothes. And notify the Prophet that I wish to speak to him on an urgent matter."

Sister Rosemarie moved briskly around the room. She opened a cupboard and brought him a folded stack of clothing, with socks and a pair of hiking boots. She hesitated, hovering beside the bed.

"What now?" he snapped.

"Did you find the girls?"

Maddox suppressed a wince as he tugged the IV out of his arm and let the tube-attached needle drop. Sister Rosemarie would take care of it. He carefully eased his arms into the crisp white shirt and buttoned it.

She had always favored Dakota over any of the other girls. Protected her, even. Lied for her once. Maddox had overlooked it out of compassion and nostalgia. Maybe he shouldn't have.

"That's none of your concern," he said. "Do as I ask of you, Sister. That's all you need to worry about. Find me the Prophet. Now."

36

EDEN

Eden woke up groggily. She'd been dreaming, though she didn't remember the specifics. Only that her foster parents had been with her, Gabriella sitting at her side, holding her hand; Jorge pacing in front of her bed, telling lame jokes until she finally laughed.

But when she opened her bleary, unfocused eyes, they weren't there. And she didn't feel like laughing. Her head and stomach hurt. Her arms and legs were weak and so, so tired.

She blinked up at the ceiling. The ceiling wasn't a ceiling—it was a white tent. She turned her head and looked to either side. She was lying in a hospital bed. A long row of identical hospital beds stretched out on either side of her. There was a narrow aisle at the foot of the row of hospital beds, then another row on the opposite side of the tent.

Each bed contained a person. Men, women, and children. Some were unconscious or sleeping. Others moaned in agony. IVs hung from hooks and dripped into tubes attached to their arms.

A man was missing both his legs. Ulcers marred his lips. A

woman's skin was seared a deep red, her eyes a filmy white—she'd been blinded by the light blast from the bomb. Her skull was knotted and bony, completely devoid of hair.

In the hospital bed to Eden's right, a five-year-old boy's arms, neck, and face were pocked with a spray of shrapnel wounds. Another girl cried as two doctors worked over her burned body. The raw, red flesh of her left leg looked boiled.

Eden looked away. Tears stung her eyes.

The bomb did this. A bomb that someone built and detonated on purpose. How could there be so much hate in the world? How could anyone do such a thing?

She glanced down at herself. An IV was inserted in her arm, too, attached to a bag of clear liquid. Her heart thumped against her ribs. How did she get here? Where was Dakota? And why was she alone? What happened?

Faint images swirled just below the surface of her memory. She reached up and touched her neck. The ugly, ribbed scar was there, and just above it, a slim butterfly bandage to cover the cut from her brother's knife.

She remembered the gangsters with guns, the car accident, remembered crawling beneath the truck and freezing, unable to move. The terror lodged in her throat. The blinding panic.

Doctors and nurses in white lab coats scurried back and forth between the aisles, carrying tablets, tending to the patients, and pushing strange-looking medical equipment around.

A nurse paused at the foot of her hospital bed. "Hey, you're awake. How are you feeling, honey?"

Eden signed, *Where am I? What happened?*

The nurse pursed her lips. "Oh, I'm sorry, dear. I don't know sign language. But I believe someone you know is waiting outside for you. Let me go get them."

Dakota. Eden's heart surged with happiness and relief, then

plummeted as more memories flooded in, everything Maddox had claimed she'd done. Dakota's betrayal.

"Hey," said a voice. But it wasn't Dakota.

Eden stiffened as Logan Garcia strode in and sank into a blue plastic chair next to the bed. He held a notepad and pencil awkwardly in his lap. In his big, scarred hands, it looked like a toddler's toy.

She couldn't stop staring at the tattoos snaking up his muscled arms. His bronze skin was damp with sweat, his jaw scruffy, his eyes dark and intent.

There was something intimidating and even frightening about him. He'd killed all those people in the ambush. They were bad people, but still...he was formidable. He looked like he knew ten ways to strangle someone in their sleep.

"You want Dakota. She's finishing up some oxygen treatment for her smoke inhalation. She sent me instead." He shrugged as if embarrassed. "Actually, she sent Julio. He's got a better bedside manner for kids, I guess. But Julio is sitting with Park in one of the other patient wards, so you're stuck with me."

She gave a small nod.

"Oh." He thrust out the notepad. "I guess you'll want this, right?"

She took it gingerly, careful not to graze his large, calloused hands. His knuckles were all scarred. His hands, arms, and face were covered in small cuts, scrapes, and bruises.

He saw her looking and drew his hands back into his lap, curling them into fists. His knee juddered. He was tense, his face taut, his body rigid. He looked as immensely uncomfortable as she felt.

She didn't want him here. She'd rather be alone staring at the ceiling.

That was a lie. She hated being alone. She'd hated every second she'd been trapped in that horrible bathroom. If she ever saw that bathroom again, it would be too soon.

Then she remembered that it had burned to the ground, along with the house she'd lived in for two years with Gabriella and Jorge.

They were probably dead now. Along with a hundred thousand other people in downtown Miami.

She looked down at her notepad. It wasn't hers. There was no rainbow or unicorn on the cover, none of the pages were filled with sketches. It wasn't bent and worn from hours and hours of use.

"Ah, they took your notebook thing during decontamination," Logan said. "Julio found you another one in a kiosk at the airport."

On top of everything else, she'd lost the last thing connecting her to her old life. All her drawings, the ASL hand signs she'd so meticulously crafted for Dakota—gone in an instant...

Tears pricked the backs of her eyelids. She blinked them away, opened the new pad to the fresh, crisp first page, and scribbled furiously. *Where am I?*

"We're at Miami International Airport," Logan said. "They've set up a bunch of field hospital tents both inside the airport itself and on the tarmac. There are decontamination, intake, and triage sections we all went through when we got here. We're in Ward F right now, on one of the concourses in the domestic arrivals area. I think. I'm not actually sure. This place is huge."

How long has it been?

Logan cleared his throat. "Three days."

Her eyes widened in shock. It felt like three hours. *Where is D?*

"D for Dakota? She's fine. Everyone's fine, I guess. Park's recovering from surgery on his arm. Shay had a few bone shards floating around in her scalp and some bleeding issues, but they gave her a blood transfusion and fixed her up." He tapped the IV bag. "We all got this concoction, too, but your case was more serious because you didn't have as much protection in that house."

Eden looked down at herself, expecting one of those thin, papery hospital gowns, but she wasn't wearing one. She wore an oversized pale pink T-shirt she didn't recognize. She pointed at her chest and raised her eyebrows.

Logan let out a nervous chuckle. "They ran out of hospital gowns, can you believe it? Or maybe they're saving them for the patients who really need them. Who knows? The Red Cross hooked up with a bunch of Goodwill and Salvation Army stores outside the hot zone. A butt-ton of church volunteers sorted through all the clothes and handed everybody those tiny shampoos and soaps and some plastic toothbrushes and toothpaste."

I don't remember anything.

"You blacked out in the army transport on the way here." He spoke rapidly, almost stumbling over his words. He kept raking his hands through his hair, his knee shaking, antsy and restless. "When you went in the decontamination tent, they took your old clothes and gave you these. Same with all of us. These jeans are a size too big, and this shirt is scratchy. The shoes fit like crap. But they're not contaminated, so that's a win." He hesitated for a moment. "How about you?"

She shifted, careful to keep her arm still, and lifted the hospital sheet. She didn't have a blanket, but she didn't need one. It felt like it was over eighty degrees inside the hospital tent.

The T-shirt was adult-sized and too big, but the soft pine-green jersey shorts fit okay, though the elastic band dug into the baby fat around her middle. She tugged on the shirt collar and checked beneath the shirt. Her cheeks went hot. She was wearing a bra and underwear she didn't recognize.

He cleared his throat uneasily. "Your—ah, Dakota—she helped with the girl stuff."

She wrote on her notepad. *The clothes r fine.*

"Uh, great," he said, clearly relieved.

"Can I have a moment?" A nurse stopped at the foot of Eden's bed. She was in her late forties, short and chubby with a kind smile. Her blonde, highlighted hair was angled in a crisp bob at her chin.

Eden nodded.

The nurse glanced at Logan and frowned. "Sir, are you family?"

Logan stood up hastily. The nurse's eyes widened as she took in the full view of him. He looked like he belonged on the streets or in an MMA cage, not a clean, sterile hospital.

"Uh..." he stammered. "I'll just take a leak and...I'll be back."

He lowered his head, brushed past the nurse, and hurried out.

37

EDEN

The nurse stared after Logan, then looked back at Eden. Her puffy, bloodshot eyes narrowed. She looked like she'd been crying. "You okay, honey? You sure you know him?"

Eden bit her bottom lip. Yeah, he looked a little terrifying, all burly and glowering and dangerous, but she remembered how he'd shot those bad guys. He'd stayed back and kept fighting right alongside Dakota so Julio could rescue her and carry her to safety.

Didn't that make him a hero, no matter what he looked like?

Once upon a time, her brothers or her father told her who was good and who was evil, who to trust and who to fear. They seemed to know without a shadow of a doubt, like God Himself had told them. Maybe He had. But he wasn't telling her, and none of them were here.

Indecision and anxiety swirled inside her. She hated making decisions. She wasn't any good at them, even now, three years after the compound.

Jorge and Gabriella had worked with her on that. Standing up for herself, making her own choices, finding her voice. That's what Gabriella always said—*find your voice*—without even a hint of irony.

Chiquita, she'd said once, *It's still there. You just have to work a little harder than everyone else to make it heard.*

"Honey?" the nurse prodded.

Eden forced a smile. *Yep,* she wrote. *He's good.*

"Okay, well, you can never be too careful. Especially at a time like this..." Her voice trailed off. For several long seconds, she simply stared down at her table, a vacant expression in her eyes.

"Sorry about that." She cleared her throat and wiped brusquely at her eyes. When she looked up, she was all business again. "Let me give you an update, honey. We've taken several blood tests over the last several days to help us look for drops in your disease-fighting white blood cells. We also looked for abnormal changes in the DNA of your blood cells to determine the degree of bone marrow damage. Luckily, you're a healthy young girl. The permanent damage should be mild."

That sounded good. Or at least, not bad.

"In addition to a cocktail of fluids and electrolytes, we gave you a protein called granulocyte colony-stimulating factor to promote the growth of white blood cells to help counter the effect of radiation poisoning on your bone marrow..."

The nurse kept speaking, but Eden couldn't follow. It was too overwhelming.

Everything was still slow and fuzzy. The woman's words all jumbled together in her foggy brain. *Radiation. Abnormal DNA. Bone marrow damage.* She could barely make out the words, let alone understand their meaning.

Back in the compound, she never saw a real doctor. The Prophet said hospitals usurped the will of the Lord, that only God could decide who lived or died. Dakota said he was full of hogwash, only she used a different word.

Eden didn't know who was right. Her social workers and foster parents had taken her in for exams and check-ups, and no bolts of lightning had struck her down in punishment. Not yet, anyway.

The nurse glanced down at her tablet and swiped a few times. "While I would love to keep you for a few more days to monitor your progress, we have thousands of people waiting to be treated. You'll be discharged in the morning. We'll send you with instructions for medical care when the onset of the overt illness stage begins, okay?"

Eden gave her a blank look.

"You'll feel better for a few weeks, but then the symptoms will return even worse, I'm afraid. Acute radiation syndrome can last for months. You have a good chance of recovery, but you may experience lifelong complications and an increased cancer risk."

Eden thought of Ezra and all his dire predictions. This was the kind of stuff he'd always warned them about. It'd seemed like the same doom and gloom that the Prophet and her father preached, just in a different way.

It had always scared her so much that she blocked it out and promptly forgot it, imagining the facts and statistics and probabilities draining out of her brain like a strainer.

Now it was real. The thousands of bodies burnt to ash. The radiated ruins of a dozen cities. The poison inside of her, eating away at her internal organs.

"I'm sorry," the nurse said in a strangled voice. She looked so, so tired. Dark shadows rimmed her haunted eyes. "We just don't have the resources to treat everyone who needs it."

Eden nodded again. She didn't know what else to do.

"You're lucky, honey," the nurse said finally. "The things I've seen in the last few days...just...awful, awful things. The suffering... you're sick, but you're going to live. Life is a gift. A precious gift."

She stepped to the side of the bed and squeezed Eden's hand.

Eden forced a smile she didn't feel.

"Are you hungry? I'll have someone bring you dinner."

Eden realized she *was* hungry. Her empty stomach rumbled painfully. The sour, wrenching nausea seemed to be gone. For now.

The nurse squeezed her hand again and left to tend to the next patient, faltering a bit as she walked. She was probably exhausted from multiple shifts tending to the sick and dying, on her feet for hours and hours.

A few minutes later, Logan returned. He sat stiffly in the plastic chair, as tense and uneasy as before, a pained expression on his face.

A different nurse brought her a plastic tray with a Styrofoam plate. There was a lump that looked a little like meatloaf, some cold, clotted gravy, a pile of shriveled peas, and a dollop of crusty mashed potatoes.

Eden prodded the mashed potatoes with her fork. They didn't move.

Logan let out a snort.

Eden looked at him in surprise. A couple of nurses glared his way.

He shrugged his broad shoulders sheepishly and leaned in closer to Eden's bed. "They say hospital food is always gross, no matter where you live or what hospital you're at. Guess the apocalypse doesn't change everything, huh?"

The smallest grin tugged at the corners of her mouth.

"Maybe it should give us comfort that some things never change." Logan pulled something out of his jeans' pocket and surreptitiously slipped her a king-sized Snickers candy bar. "It's half-melted, but it beats this slop."

Her smile widened. She took the candy bar and wrote on her notepad. *Thank you.*

He gave her a tight smile in return. It looked strange on his face —but it wasn't bad. He should smile more. Then maybe people wouldn't be scared of him.

What's the worst food you've ever had? she wrote.

He sat back and raked his hand through his unruly hair. "Hmm. A lima bean sandwich covered in tomato sauce. How about you?"

She wrinkled her nose. *Alligator-meat sandwich.*

"Nah. Gator's good. Tastes like chicken."

Pickles dipped in ketchup.

His stiff shoulders eased a little bit. The hint of a wry smile tugged at his lips. "You clearly haven't lived, kid."

BBQ sauce dripped over oatmeal.

"Now you're getting a little more creative. How about strawberries dipped in mayonnaise? Or chicken on waffles sprinkled with hot peppers? Or ice cream and French fries?"

Yum.

"Okay, that one's not bad."

Cheetos mixed with broccoli and covered in soy sauce.

He made a face. "Gross. You win."

She took a bite of the candy bar. The chocolate, nuts, and caramel melted on her tongue and stuck in her teeth. She wrote, *Dakota puts ketchup on rice.*

He smiled. "That should be a crime against humanity."

She tried to smile back, but it slipped off her face.

She wasn't brave or strong like Dakota. She couldn't kill bad guys with guns. She'd just hidden when all the shooting started, like a coward. Someone else had needed to save her. Again.

She felt useless, a burden, Dakota risking everything again and again to save her.

The truth was, she'd forgive Dakota anything, no matter what she'd done. She already had. Just like she'd already forgiven Maddox in her heart. She loved her brother. She loved Dakota.

She couldn't allow herself to be angry or bitter toward either of them. She didn't want to feel all those horrid things or think terrible thoughts about the people she was supposed to love, who were supposed to love her.

That dark thought was there in her head again, niggling in her brain. She couldn't ignore it this time. Confusion, dread, and guilt twisted her insides in a tangle of knots she couldn't unwind.

If it was true that Maddox had done bad things, if he'd really tried to hurt Dakota...then Eden had made a mistake. She'd messed up.

If Dakota knew the truth, it was Dakota who'd hate Eden, not the other way around.

And she couldn't handle that. Not after losing everything and everyone else. Even the thought made her sick with apprehension.

She was terrified of being alone.

Tears stung her eyes. She started to cry.

"What's wrong?" Logan asked hastily. He looked mortified. "What'd I do?"

She shook her head. It wasn't him. It was her. It was Dakota. It was everything.

"Do you want me to get the nurse?"

She shook her head again, sniffled, and wiped her nose with the back of her arm. She picked up her notepad.

I'm afraid.

He hesitated for a moment, his jaw working, like he was unsure what to say. "We're all afraid, kid."

Of everything.

Logan gave a heavy sigh. He sat there, big hands bunched uselessly in his lap, his shoulders hunched like he alone bore the weight of the whole broken world. "That, too."

3 8

DAKOTA

"They're late," Dakota muttered.

"Relax," Logan said. "They'll be here."

Hawthorne had asked them all to meet him after lunch without providing a reason.

Logan sat at the table next to her, finishing a cheeseburger. They were in Terminal D in the American Airlines Admirals Club lounge. They both sat stiffly in black cushioned chairs angled against the wall, facing the room and the airy terminal beyond them.

Neither of them liked open air at their backs. They were both alert and watchful, constantly scanning their surroundings.

Logan took a huge bite of his cheeseburger and washed it down with a Coke. Dakota had already finished her sandwich and fries. When you were a foster kid, you learned to eat fast or not at all.

The food was from Shula's Bar and Grill. Several of the restaurants in the airport had remained open to serve the hundreds of staff that made up the Emergency Operations Center, free of charge. At least to the people. She was sure the restaurants were keeping a tally for the government. The hotels, too.

Hawthorne had set them up in a couple of the rooms in the

Sheraton next to the airport alongside hundreds of government workers and officials. Hawthorne told them the Hilton, the Marriott, the Hyatt, and nearly every other hotel surrounding the airport were already over capacity.

Including the support staff, there were almost two thousand officials not including medical and military personnel. Additionally, she'd seen hundreds of agents with badges designating DHS, FEMA, ATF, Army Corps, EPA, and the Department of Defense.

Apparently, Hawthorne had some clout or serious connections, because the visitor's pass security badges he'd obtained enabled them to move freely around certain sections of the airport where most regular civilians weren't allowed. Hence, the government-funded hot meal in the Admirals Club lounge.

Dakota shifted restlessly in the leather chair. All this waiting around for days was driving her nuts. She was eager to get back on the road, to finally reach Ezra and his safehouse, to go home.

Here, she felt inert and unproductive. Like everyone had a purpose but them.

Well, everyone but the Wilburns. Carson and Vanessa had spent the majority of their time lazing around in their hotel room, apparently "recovering." Every time Dakota saw them, Vanessa was crying or curled in the fetal position, Carson bent over her, murmuring sympathetic encouragement.

They were both utterly useless.

Dakota barely even registered their presence. Maybe it was cold, but it was the truth.

Shay was somewhere in one of the hospital wards doing something helpful, but she'd promised to make it for Hawthorne's meeting. Julio was with Eden in Ward F. He'd insisted Dakota take a break from her vigil and shooed her out. The nurse had said Eden would be discharged in the morning.

Park hadn't been discharged yet, either. He was still recovering from his surgery to repair the shattered bones in his right forearm.

The doctor had explained that they didn't have the capabilities to perform microsurgery to repair the severed tendons.

Since almost every trauma center in the country was already overwhelmed with patients, they'd triaged him. Park's injury wasn't life-threatening. They'd chosen not to expend the resources to airlift him to an actual hospital. Permanent nerve damage and limited mobility was the most likely outcome.

It all sucked. But at least he was alive.

Dakota swirled a fry around the ketchup on her plate and sighed. "I should go check on Eden—"

"Did you not hear the part about relaxing?" Logan asked wryly.

"Yeah, yeah." She scowled at him. "Talk about the pot calling the kettle black."

He shrugged and gave her a lazy grin. It was the only lazy part about him. His body was tense, his shoulders stiff, his relentless gaze roaming the lounge and the concourse beyond. He hadn't let down his guard, not even here.

Her hand drifted to the empty spots on her belt. She missed her tactical knife and her pistol. She felt almost naked without them. Judging by the disgruntled expression on Logan's face, he felt the same way.

Her knife was back in the hotel room—security had let her keep it, but she couldn't bring it onto EOC grounds. She'd scrubbed the knife thoroughly in the decontamination tent upon arrival. The map, too, which had miraculously survived.

Before they'd arrived, Hawthorne had taken their firearms, including the two AR-15s, so they wouldn't be confiscated by security. He and Captain Kinsey had taken the F-150 somewhere as well.

He'd promised to keep everything safe.

They'd been forced to trust him. What choice did they have? But no one could make them like it. Dakota hated every second.

She'd rather be out on her own, controlling her own fate.

She glanced at Logan. He'd half-twisted to eye the bottle of Bacardi white rum sitting on the counter of the drinks bar behind them. There was a look on his face she recognized—craving and regret, mingled with a sour desperation.

The look of an addict jonesing for a fix.

But he didn't rise to the bait. He didn't make a move to get out of his chair.

She respected that. She'd known more than one drunken foster parent who never refused their baser instincts. Once sloshed, the slurred curses and sloppy punches started up, faithful as clockwork. She rubbed her jaw, recalling a long-healed bruise.

She should try to help him. Logan needed a distraction, but she had no idea what to say or do other than insult him, or maybe kick him in the shin.

A better diversion arrived in the form of Shay, who sauntered into the Admirals Club lounge wearing a white lab coat over her clothes, her grin tired but exuberant, as usual.

Hawthorne trailed closely behind her. He'd spent every spare minute he wasn't out in the field with Shay since she'd been discharged. As for Shay, she'd spent nearly every waking moment volunteering as a nursing assistant.

The hospital was already desperately shorthanded; they were accepting anyone with medical experience. Shay being Shay, she'd jumped at the chance to help.

Logan turned quickly, his face shuttered, his eyes flat. Whatever he'd been thinking or feeling, he'd locked it down hard.

"Nice glasses," Dakota said to take any attention off him.

Shay touched the square purple frames sheepishly. "One of the nurses found them for me. I'm just glad I could finally get rid of those awful contacts. After four days of stinging eyes, I could barely see. But I'm good now." She struck a silly pose, one hand on her jutting hip. "Is it my style?"

She looked adorable. Shay could make anything look adorable.

"You're rocking it," Hawthorne said.

Shay ducked her chin and gave him a wide, shy smile. She might have been blushing. "Thank you."

"How's your head?" Dakota asked.

Shadows still ringed Shay's eyes, but her gaze was bright and alert, her skin back to its rich, vibrant brown. Her familiar perky grin played across her face. The large bandage they'd wrapped around her head was gone, replaced by a small square of gauze. She'd parted her wild, wiry curls so they mostly covered the gauze—and the bald spot.

Shay grabbed Dakota's hand and squeezed it. "Much better, thanks to you."

She smacked her gum cheerfully. She was definitely back to her old enthusiastic self.

An unmarked door behind them opened, and a man dressed in a military officer's uniform decorated with awards and ribbons strode out. Hawthorne waved and the man walked toward them.

"There's someone I'd like you to meet," Hawthorne said with a grin. "This is my uncle, General Randall Pierce, State Coordinating Officer for the Joint Field Office and Emergency Operations Center. Basically, he's the guy in charge of everything."

In his mid-fifties, General Pierce was a formidable black man with short, wiry gray hair and a hint of gray beard stubbling his square jaw. He was as tall as his nephew but at least a hundred pounds heavier, large but not fat, and solid as a slab of concrete.

Logan shoved back his chair and stood hastily.

Dakota followed suit. "A pleasure to meet you, sir."

"You must be the folks that saved my nephew's life," General Pierce said in a deep baritone. "I asked Hawthorne to introduce us."

"It was Logan and Dakota, sir," Shay said, beaming at them. "They've saved my life several times now."

General Pierce shook their hands with a firm grip. "I can't thank you enough. Anything that's in my power to do for you, just let me know."

"Hawthorne has already helped us with anything we've needed," Shay said.

Hawthorne had gone above and beyond for them, but even though they'd saved his ass, Dakota figured it was as much for Shay's sake as hers and Logan's. The ATF agent could barely take his eyes off Shay. He had an obvious crush.

"I know you had questions about the state of things," Hawthorne said. "This is the man to ask."

"Who did this to us?" Logan said. "That's what I'd like to know."

General Pierce scratched at his stubble. "A basketful of loonies have crawled out of the woodwork to take credit. But most aren't what we'd consider credible intelligence. Still, Homeland is sifting through every single one of the three hundred thousand reports of suspicious activity we've received from the alphabet-soup agencies.

"Seems some of the chatter points toward radicalized Muslim extremists in Iraq and Syria. Other experts suggest there may be a domestic tie-in—deep cells hidden among us for years, maybe decades. Russia and China are suspects, too, of course. Or maybe some tiny rogue nation we haven't considered. North Korea did plenty of saber-rattling, but in the end backed down."

"So, we still don't have a clue," Logan said.

"It's a touchy situation. Plenty of generals want to bomb the hell out of the Middle East, evidence be damned. But the new president is cautious. Some despise her prudence as weakness; others applaud it as a strength. We don't want another Afghanistan and WMD fiasco on our hands, but the people are desperate for blood. Frankly, so am I."

"What about evidence?" Shay asked. "How would we even know who did it?"

"Ground zero is buried beneath millions of tons of rubble. Even if we could excavate, anything connected to the IND—the improvised nuclear device—would already be incinerated. But we have some leads. We're incredibly lucky that the fourteenth target—the IND in Chicago—didn't detonate. The CIA and Homeland are chasing leads with the bomb casing, the van's VIN registration, and the source of the highly enriched uranium. The rest is classified, I'm afraid."

"Understood," Dakota said.

The faint wrinkles lining the general's forehead deepened into crevices as he frowned. "Make no mistake, we'll get the bastards who did this."

"We have no doubt, sir," Shay said. "What about the recovery efforts?"

"To be blunt with you, we have a difficult slog ahead of us. We don't have the resources or the manpower to get this vibrant city back on her feet."

"What about the National Guard?" Shay asked.

"The president has federalized the National Guard across the nation. Florida has over nine thousand guardsmen and around two thousand airmen. Governor Blake begged the president to allow us ours to restore Miami, but New York, California, and D.C. are higher on the priority list. She deployed eight thousand for federal use and left us less than a thousand troops. That's not nearly enough," General Pierce said gravely.

"The governor reinstated the Florida State Guard as a state defense force, the state's own version of the National Guard, which doesn't answer to the feds. The SDF will be trained, organized, and deployed under the direction of the Adjutant General of Florida and the state military officers within the Florida Department of Military Affairs.

"They're accepting recruits into an expedited training program at Camp Blanding. This is the worst crisis our nation has ever faced.

We need good soldiers." The general stared at Dakota and Logan with a level, appraising gaze. "You two fit the bill."

"I appreciate the offer," Dakota said quickly, "but I'm headed to a friend of mine in the Glades. We'll be safe there."

General Pierce nodded and turned to Logan. "And what about you, Mr. Garcia? I heard you have skills to spare. You'd be a solid asset to the recovery efforts."

Logan's eyes went wide, like a deer trapped in headlights.

Dakota's gut tightened against her will. Was he going to say yes? For days, she'd been planning to ditch this guy. But now the thought of Logan abandoning her filled her with dread.

Somewhere along the way, she'd started to depend on him. Trust him, even.

He was a different person after he'd stopped drinking. Steady, strong, reliable—and a hell of a warrior. The way he'd cut down those Blood Outlaws at the checkpoint with relentless precision, no hesitation, no mercy.

Maybe he was someone she even *wanted* to stick around. Who was she kidding? She did want him around.

But whether he wanted to stay was another matter entirely.

39

DAKOTA

Dakota felt Logan's gaze on her. His eyes were dark and unreadable.

He raked a hand through his unruly black hair and shook his head. "Thanks, but I made a promise. I said I'd get this girl and her sister to their safehouse. And I intend to do that."

She couldn't help it—relief flooded through her veins.

Shay caught her eye and gave her a knowing grin. Dakota turned her face away to hide the warmth heating her cheeks. Stupid body— betraying her with feelings she wasn't even sure she wanted.

But she knew for certain that she didn't want him coming with her out of some misplaced sense of duty or because he owed her a favor. She didn't need any favors. Or pity.

She cleared her throat. "Don't feel like you have to," she said. "You don't."

He just shrugged. "I know."

General Pierce nodded, clearly disappointed. "The offer is a standing one. We have hot food, hot showers, and quality accommodations. Those amenities are in short supply right now and will be for quite some time."

"We'll keep it in mind, General," Logan said.

"What's happening outside Florida?" Dakota asked. "Can you tell us anything?"

"Of course," the general said. "In short, millions of refugees have fled the attacked cities, even those not affected by the radiation. Nearby cities that initially accepted refugees with open arms are now threatening to close their borders."

"Why?" Shay asked, appalled.

"For every hundred terrified families seeking shelter, there is one or two of the criminal persuasion, those without conscience or empathy, those who resent that they've lost everything and so take from others ruthlessly, without remorse, hesitation, or compassion. And I fear there are more of them in our society than we'd like to admit.

"Every city that has offered sanctuary has experienced an immediate and catastrophic rise in crime against their own citizens. Not to mention the dwindling food supplies in those cities as well. Everyone is only looking out for their own."

"What's going to happen with all the refugees?" Shay asked.

The general sighed heavily. "FEMA is researching potential areas in the Midwest to relocate the refugees in massive tent cities. We have five million displaced persons across the country and nowhere to put them. For context, that's like creating a city the size of Las Vegas overnight—times five."

"That's insane," Shay said.

"Yes," the general said. "Yes, it is. And that is only a portion of the problems facing us. With the rolling power outages and intermittent cell coverage, even citizens in unharmed states are panicking. The grocery store shelves in over sixty percent of cities nationwide are already bare. Our country's supply chain system has been crippled."

"It was intentional, then," Dakota said. "The terrorists hit port cities."

General Pierce nodded. "It appears that way. The loss of millions of lives to the blasts and radiating poisoning is devastating. But that was just the first round. What will truly devastate us is the long-term, critical disruption to the nation's supply chain.

"The Port of Los Angeles and the Port of Long Beach together bring in over a third of the entire country's imports. These two ports alone handle seventy percent of the container traffic for the West Coast. Both ports are shut down due to damage and heavy radiation. Cargo can't be relocated to Seattle; they were hit, too. Oakland doesn't have the capacity to take the increased load.

"And here in Florida, Miami and the Port of the Everglades bring in a third of the Southwest's oil. Both ports were heavily radiated. They're now too dangerous for human workers to occupy for months—possibly years."

"That's why gas is thirty dollars a gallon," Dakota said.

"And the price will only go up, I'm afraid," the general said. "The president enacted emergency measures requiring every single cargo container be inspected before leaving port, including every aid package delivered by foreign countries. I can't blame her for her caution, but it's causing even more of a slowdown in getting much-needed supplies to the people.

"Half the port workers across the country stopped coming to work. Who could blame them? They're terrified of another attack. There aren't enough people to offload or inspect the cargo deliveries we do have. The movement of food, gas, and other essentials has gone from a well-oiled machine to a sluggish crawl."

Everyone simply stared at the general, gaping.

For Dakota, it was a terrible confirmation. Ezra had been right. He was right about everything.

"We're receiving offers of significant aid from Canada, Australia, and the UK," General Pierce said. "Even Russia, surprisingly enough. Humanitarian aid, food, hygiene, medical supplies. Canada has offered to serve as an intermediary, setting a percentage of their port availability aside for U.S. aid. We're also diverting West Coast cargo ships to Anchorage to transport cargo by road down through Canada.

"But with millions of displaced people, hundreds of impassable roads, and more than a dozen cities either hot zones or burning with rioting and looting, the reality of getting that aid to the people who need it is...daunting."

"It's been a week," Dakota said. "Most people don't keep more than a week's worth of food in their pantries. Most, even less."

"You're right." The general wiped sweat from his shiny brow. "Stores used to stock three days' worth of goods for 'just in time' delivery. Now it's even less. Which means the rioting and looting will only get worse, not better."

"How can that be right?" Shay asked. "We have so many farms here in the States. Indiana's just one big cornfield."

"Not nearly big enough. Ninety percent of Walmart's shelves are stocked with consumables made in other countries, from China and Mexico and Brazil. What happens when our imports grind to a halt? It creates a domino effect, a systemic collapse where each falling domino affects all the others—food, transportation, energy, banking.

"Consider this single example out of hundreds of possible ramifications: shipments of industrial materials have been delayed, causing serious problems for critical facilities, such as water treatment plants. In a short period, city water may become unsafe for citizens to drink. Our entire country will turn into Flint, Michigan."

"That's America's weakness," Hawthorne said soberly. "Its Achilles' heel. If one domino falls, it topples all the rest with it."

For a long moment, no one spoke. There were no words that could encompass the enormity of the disaster looming over the United States and its people.

"While I don't wish to cause a panic," General Pierce said slowly, "I do believe the truth is the best resource with which to arm our citizens. And the truth is that this crisis is only beginning. It's going to get much, much worse."

Dakota, Logan, and Shay looked at each other, the same fear reflected in their eyes. Dakota shivered. Her whole body went cold. It was one thing to think about a national disaster and societal collapse in the abstract.

It was quite another to live it.

"We can't let this destroy us," Shay whispered. Her dark eyes gleamed wetly. "Then they win. Whoever did this, all those people who feed on hatred and suffering."

"It's fear." The general shook his head wearily. "Fear will be what destroys us, in the end. Terrorists can't destroy America and what it stands for. The only ones truly capable of destroying America are ourselves."

40

DAKOTA

"We can't lose hope," Shay insisted. "No matter how bleak things look."

"Don't mistake me," General Pierce said. "I will never give up. Neither will the fine soldiers who defend this country with their lives. There are good people still fighting the good fight. America is too strong to be defeated by this."

A woman in a rumpled, sweat-dampened pantsuit hurried up to General Pierce, a tablet clutched in her hands. "Sir, another checkpoint has been attacked. And the Recovery Logistics Officer and Public Assistance Branch Director are waiting for that meeting."

Behind the woman, Dakota glimpsed several men in the room General Pierce had exited a few minutes before—all in expensive, tailored suits, their heads bent in grave discussion.

Two men stood a little apart from the rest of the group. One was a short, burly white man with piggish eyes, his sharp, suspicious gaze darting around the room. The guy next to him wore a military dress uniform. He was broad and blonde, his leathery face pockmarked with acne scars. He was scowling as he gestured aggressively at a sheaf of papers scattered across the long mahogany table.

The woman saw Dakota watching and hurriedly shut the door.

General Pierce shook their hands again. "It was a sincere pleasure to meet all of you," he said in his booming baritone. He turned and gazed at Shay intently, then each of them in turn. "Whatever you do, don't give up."

Shay raised her chin. "No sir. We won't."

After the general strode away, Hawthorne glanced around warily and lowered his voice. "There's another reason I wanted to meet. I needed to warn you. The president's surviving cabinet members are urging her to declare martial law. So is Governor Blake. Some of the Joint Task Force bigwigs are pushing for all refugees to be placed in FEMA camps where they can be tracked and corralled."

Shay nibbled anxiously on her thumbnail. "What does that mean?"

"I mean it may not be a choice for much longer. State and local governments are so worried about crime and rioting, they're threatening to ban the camps within their borders unless FEMA promises to keep the refugees under control. The only way to do that is to place them inside the camps forcibly if they won't go willingly. And then keep them there under guard."

Dakota's chest tightened. "How much longer do we have?"

"I'm not sure. From the rumors I've heard, that's the meeting my uncle is headed to right now."

Logan stiffened. "Hell, no. I'm not getting stuck in some FEMA camp."

"Agreed." Dakota knew exactly what government-sponsored care looked like. She'd experienced the brokenness of the system firsthand. Gotten slapped around by it a few times, too.

She'd chew her own foot off before she went back to it.

"FEMA is helping," Shay said, wrinkling her nose. "Without them, all these families wouldn't have anywhere to go."

"I've read about the chaotic mess after Hurricane Katrina,"

Dakota said. "Thousands of scared, panicky, stressed people shoved together in close quarters for days, weeks, or longer is a special kind of torture."

"For some people, it's their only choice," Hawthorne said. "But if you have a better option—friends or family with a stocked home outside the city, for example—you should take it while you can."

"We do," Dakota said.

"I'll get our stuff from the hotel room," Logan said. "I'll meet you back here."

"I'll get Eden," Dakota said. "Julio is with her."

"Okay," Shay said. "Okay. I see what you mean. What about Carson and Vanessa?"

Dakota made a face. "What about them? As far as I'm concerned, we saved them from the Blood Outlaws, no thanks to their own stupidity. We don't owe them anything else."

"And Park?" Shay asked. "What about him? The doctors couldn't repair the damaged tendons without access to the instruments they needed for microsurgery. He may have permanently lost the use of his right hand. He hasn't been discharged yet."

Dakota actually liked Park. He was funny and resilient, and not nearly as annoying as most people. Plus, she felt guilty as hell over Harlow's death. She didn't want to leave him alone and helpless. "Damn it."

"We have to go," Logan said, already moving toward the lounge entrance, restless and antsy.

Shay bit her lower lip. "What if we pull him out early? If he wants to come, that is. Or at least give him a chance to decide. Otherwise, as soon as they discharge him, they'll ship him off to the nearest camp. I know we don't know him well, but that doesn't seem like his style."

"I'll help you," Hawthorne said quickly. "I can use my uncle's clout to get him discharged if I have to. But with the overwhelming demand for beds, I don't see that becoming an issue."

Shay touched Hawthorne's arm and gave him a grateful smile. "Thank you."

"It's...ah, nothing," Hawthorne stammered, shuffling his feet and glancing down at the floor like an awkward teenager.

Shay's smile widened.

Dakota cleared her throat. "You think we could get our guns back? And our truck?"

"Right," Hawthorne said, abruptly all business again. "Get your people and meet me outside at the domestic arrivals entrance D at sixteen hundred hours. That's three hours from now. Let's do this."

41

MADDOX

"**M**addox Cage! My man!"

Maddox jerked his head up as a large man jogged toward him across the clearing. "Reuben."

His cousin was a thick, burly guy in his mid-twenties. His face was square and wide as his neck, his mouth and nose flat. He wore lightweight camouflage pants, hiking boots, and a gray T-shirt already stained with sweat from the sweltering heat.

"We've been waiting for you to wake up for days!"

"Who's we?"

"Everyone who matters, of course." With a jovial grin, Reuben slapped his shoulder. "The Shepherds."

A burst of pain radiated all the way down his arm. Maddox couldn't help it—he flinched.

"You look like hell, man."

He forced a smile. "Feel like it, too."

Reuben stepped close to Maddox and scraped a hand through his dirty blond buzzcut hair. All the Cage boys were blond. "Hey, man. About that. No hard feelings, okay? I tried to warn you, soon as I found out it was happening early. Something went wrong in

189

Chicago. They delivered the van early and someone found it, reported it to the feds. It was out of our hands. We had to move everything up before the entire country went on high alert, you know?"

Maddox stared at him, his muddled mind still working to take in everything Reuben just said. What he'd suspected was the truth.

The Prophet—and the Shepherds—were behind the attacks. They'd done this. All of it. The bombs. The fallout. The destruction and death.

"I knew you'd be cool," Reuben said with another wide grin, even though Maddox hadn't said a thing. He was like Jacob that way —always bending others to his will, either through charm and cajoling, peer pressure, or sheer force.

"You made it back," Reuben said. "The Lord has blessed you. I'll put in a good word for you with my father. We need you with us."

Maddox peered over Reuben's shoulder. Several of the guys he'd grown up with were sitting at one of the yellow-painted picnic tables in the center of the compound. A dour-faced woman, Sister Ada, served them fresh sandwiches and lemonade from a large platter balanced on one hand.

They were all Shepherds, the chosen ones, the Prophet's inner circle of warriors. These young men had trained together since they were ten. Almost every boy in the compound was selected.

Except for Maddox. The black sheep. The disappointment. The doubting Thomas.

He turned away. "Where's Franklin?"

"He and Gerber are both in Montana finishing some stuff up."

Maddox knew there were other Shepherds, at least one other outpost, though that one was more paramilitary rather than a commune. The Prophet traveled between them, coming and going as he pleased.

On return, he was always greeted with the adoration and

worship of his flock. When he was away on other holy business, Maddox's father, Solomon Cage, remained in charge.

"What stuff?" Maddox asked.

"Covering our digital tracks or something. They're the internet experts." He shrugged like they were discussing fishing or golf—simply a hobby he enjoyed, not the destruction of entire cities.

But he hadn't seen the devastation firsthand. He hadn't lived it.

Reuben saw something in Maddox's expression he didn't like. The corners of his flat mouth twitched downward. He was a jocular guy—until he wasn't. "You know I'm not supposed to be telling you this stuff. You're not a Shepherd."

"Not yet," Maddox said.

The suspicion faded from his gaze. "That's the attitude the Prophet wants to see. Come on, man! Wake up! The judgment is finally here. The one we've been hearing about all our lives. And we get to be a part of it. We get to be the ones to build the new America. It's wild, man. Beyond imagining."

He couldn't tell Reuben how sick he still felt. How every inch of his skin was raw like it was being scorched by a merciless sun. The last thing he wanted was to be cast aside now, after he'd suffered so much.

"Where's the Prophet?" he said. "I need to speak to him."

"In the big house. I'll take you."

Maddox turned and scanned the property, taking in the familiar fishing and airboat docks on the western border of the swamp beside the boathouse. In the compound's center stretched the big grassy area rimmed by picnic tables painted in bright colors. Adirondack chairs encircled a giant fire pit.

Across from him stood the family cabins and the barracks that housed the single men. The big house where the Prophet stayed was set back a little way. Behind the family cabins were the kitchen and cafeteria, one-room schoolhouse, greenhouses, and laundry area where the women worked.

Clotheslines were strung between the stubby pines as several women washed and hung the linens. A couple of children too young to be taught in the schoolhouse played around their legs, their high, bright laughter echoing in the still air.

There were solar panels on the roofs, generators, and several tanks of propane behind the storage sheds—the compound had power, but the Prophet frowned on modern amenities. Laundry was handwashed. Food was grown, prepared, and cooked from scratch—by the women, of course. The men had more important things to do.

To the east, on a raised bump of land, sat the church: a simple, unadorned building with hard wooden pews, cement block walls, and a plain wooden cross hanging behind the hand-carved pulpit.

The other buildings were hidden from view behind a forest of cypress and live oak trees, located far back from the rest of the compound. There the men trained in weapons, combat, and tactical exercises—militia operations, patrolling, ambushes, raids, conceal-ment, and guerrilla warfare.

And where they learned the specifics of the Prophet's plans and carried out his instructions—instructions hand-delivered by God, of course.

There were men who traveled with the Prophet, men Maddox didn't recognize. They were all heavily armed, didn't talk much, and spent most of their time in the off-limits buildings.

Three of the Prophet's seven sons were trained soldiers in the United States Army. There were other soldiers who came and went. Former Navy Seals and Special Forces—all muscular, whip-smart killers who'd served in Iraq and Afghanistan.

They'd become disillusioned by the American military-indus-trial complex, good American boys dying in a desert so defense contractors and rich, fat-cat politicians could become even richer and even fatter.

The soldiers fought to defend America; the defense companies manufactured wars to turn billions in profits. The Prophet promised these weary, disenchanted warriors that they could save America—the real America, the one built on the backbone of good, hardworking, God-fearing people.

Maddox had seen the armory. Thousands of rounds of ammo of all different calibers. Dozens of semi-automatic and automatic weapons. Even a few RPGs.

They were prepared. They'd been preparing for almost twenty years.

And the Prophet was smart about it. They bought their weapons at gun shows. It was easy enough to purchase "collector's items," including a .50 caliber Browning machine gun able to shoot 500 rounds a minute with a muzzle velocity of 2900 feet per second at a range of two thousand yards. Each round was over five inches long.

Maddox stared hard through the trees. Had the bombs themselves been built back there? Or had they been hidden elsewhere? And where the hell had they gotten ahold of the radioactive materials?

"Maddox!" Reuben called. "You fall asleep back there? Come on!"

Maddox shook his head to clear his thoughts. He hurried across the property, wincing at his clothes scraping his tender skin and the sickening lurch in his belly—the nausea still hadn't completely subsided.

He opened the screen door to the big house and entered the darkened room. The living area was modest—wooden plank floor and walls painted white, lace curtains hanging over the windows, a beige sofa with a coffee table in one corner, a piano in the other.

On the far wall beneath a large metal cross perched a small desk. The Prophet sat at the desk, pouring over a pile of papers written by hand. A heavy leather Bible sat next to his left elbow next to a satellite phone and a battery-operated radio.

He looked up as Maddox came in. "Blessings be upon you, Maddox Cage."

42

DAKOTA

Heat and humidity blasted Dakota as soon as she stepped outside. At least it would rain soon. Dark storm clouds billowed on the horizon. The wind had picked up, whipping the palm tree fronds and blowing stray strands of her hair into her face.

She glanced at her watch. 2:45 p.m. The typical Florida summer rainstorm was right on time. It'd be over and sunny again in an hour or two.

Dakota hastened through the airport parking areas, passing soldiers, police officers, government officials, and security guards hurrying in all directions. Buses, shuttles, and army Humvees were everywhere.

A red-and-white medical helicopter descended to the east, its rotors thumping. On the other side of the airport, a military cargo plane swooped toward a nearby runway.

She passed tent after tent, all with different designations: radiology, ICU, emergency, triage, exam and decontamination tents, surgical, and at least three dozen large white mobile buildings in a row, all labeled "morgue."

Out by the tent hospital's entrance, a long line of people

stretched out as far as she could see. Hundreds were sitting or lying down in the road, too sick or injured to stand. Volunteers in Red Cross T-shirts were walking up and down the line with carts, offering food and water.

Several dozen Guardsmen armed with rifles stood outside the hospital tent's main entrance, keeping the peace. Dozens more guarded the entrances to the airport along with several military vehicles and a couple of tanks. They ensured no one who didn't belong— and who hadn't gone through the decontamination procedures—got inside.

By the time she reached patient ward F, she was panting, almost wheezing. At discharge, the nurse had warned her of long-term smoke inhalation effects like hoarseness, prolonged coughing, and shortness of breath. He'd recommended a few weeks of rest. Screw that.

The wind picked up as the storm clouds headed closer. She redid her ponytail to keep her hair out of her eyes as the first fat drops of rain splatted against her cheeks.

She flashed her visitor's badge to the soldiers guarding the entrance, slipped inside the tent, and made her way past a cluster of nurses and a long row of hospital beds filled with wounded and sick patients to Eden's bedside.

Groans and whimpers echoed throughout the tent. Someone was crying. A middle-aged woman with raw and blistered skin tugged thick strands of her own hair from her scalp and laid them in neat rows across her bedsheet. Three doctors bent over a writhing, moaning teenage boy clutching a gushing wound in his shoulder.

Dakota shut out the horrific sights and sounds of suffering and focused on Eden. The girl was sitting up, a new notepad on her lap opened to a page with several sketches of the ASL alphabet. The first six hand signs were shaded in near-perfect dimensions.

Eden was signing something, and Julio, who was sitting in the chair next to the bed, was trying to mimic it. He looked up with a smile at Dakota's approach. "Your sister's teaching me how to say 'I love you' in American Sign Language."

"Great."

"And 'I really have to pee!'"

Eden gave a hoarse, whispery laugh. She looked better—happier.

"Sounds fun," Dakota said. She stopped a nurse hurrying past. "Excuse me. Can my sister be discharged early? We have a friend who'll take us in."

"Eden Sloane, right?" She rattled off a date of birth. Eden nodded. The nurse frowned down at her tablet before turning to Eden. "It says discharge tomorrow morning, but your vitals are good. You're feeling better?"

Eden nodded again.

"We could sure use the extra bed." The nurse pulled out a folded piece of paper typed with instructions from a side pouch on her medical cart. She took a step closer to Dakota and lowered her voice. "This is only the first stage of radiation sickness. We estimate her body has absorbed between two and two and a half gray.

"She'll seem better for eighteen to twenty-eight days after prodrome, or the first symptoms. Then she'll likely experience anorexia, fever, weakness, increased bleeding and infections, and partial hair loss. It will last for several weeks, possibly longer."

Dakota's stomach tightened. She'd received the same warnings when she was discharged, but her symptoms—and exposure—were far less than Eden's. "I understand. Thank you."

Within minutes, the nurse had unhooked Eden's IV and released her. Dakota signed a discharge form on the tablet, and they were free to leave.

Julio helped Eden out of the hospital bed. "Careful now. There you go."

Dakota bent down until she was even with the girl's face. She placed her hands on her shoulders. "I know you're scared, but you have to be strong now."

Eden's eyes welled with tears. Her chin trembled. The girl looked terrified. Was she going to freeze up every time something bad happened? She was going to put them all in danger.

Dakota bit back her frustration. They didn't have time for this. They couldn't afford it.

"Don't be so hard on her," Julio said gently. "She's just a scared kid."

"She can't afford to be a scared kid anymore," Dakota said. Her mind flashed back to that moment during the shootout when she'd realized Eden hadn't run for cover behind the dump truck. "She almost got you killed, Julio."

Eden flinched like she'd slapped her.

Guilt pricked her, but she brushed it away. "It's true. You can't freeze like that again, Eden. Do you understand?"

Tremulously, Eden nodded.

Dakota straightened and turned away.

Eden tugged on her arm.

"What?"

Eden turned the page in her notepad and scribbled with her pencil. *Have to tell you something.*

Dakota forced down her impatience. "Later. We have to go."

Eden shook her head. *You don't understand.*

Dakota sighed. "Okay, fine. What?"

I'm sorry.

"For what?"

Eden bent her head as she wrote, her blonde hair falling like a curtain across her small, intent face. When she looked up again, her eyes were filled with sadness—and guilt.

Maddox asked me where we were hiding before, she wrote. *I told him. I told him about Ezra.*

For a second, Dakota just stared at her in stunned silence. Then anger slashed through her, sharp and furious. What the hell? What was Eden thinking? How could she do something so ridiculously stupid—

Something far stronger and deeper took hold of her: an intense, debilitating fear.

Not fear for herself, but fear for Ezra.

He was ex-military, but the grizzled old bear was seventy years old. Even the mightiest warriors were slowed and weakened by age. Even the most cunning fighters could be defeated by the element of surprise, by an unsuspecting ambush.

Maddox Cage was going after Ezra. She was certain of it. He'd be filled with rage that the old fool he'd mocked so often had been the one to harbor Eden and Dakota right under his nose.

He would see it as an affront. An insult. And he would demand payback.

And Maddox wouldn't go alone, either. Not that close to his home base. His father had a small militia at his disposal. Neither of them would hesitate to use it.

Maddox didn't care about fairness or justice or honor—only winning. He would descend on Ezra's cabin with fire and fury.

She had to warn him.

But the old man didn't have a landline phone or a cell, only the P.O. Box in town he checked once a week. He had his ham radio, but she didn't know how to find one to contact him.

Trying to warn him was futile and a waste of time. She had to get there first—

Her mouth went dry. Eden had told Maddox about Ezra four days ago.

Four days.

They were already out of time.

"We have to go." Dakota seized Eden's hand. "Right now."

43

DAKOTA

Dakota, Eden, and Julio exited the tent hospital and turned east toward the Sheraton. The sky above them darkened to charcoal. A light rain spat into their faces.

Everywhere was crowded with civilians—the roads, the sidewalks, the parking garages, the loading and unloading areas. People milled about, their expressions anxious, bewildered, shell-shocked.

"What are we doing for transportation?" Julio asked.

"Maybe the car rentals are still in business," Dakota said doubtfully. "Or maybe Hawthorne can get us the truck. I don't even know what they did with it once we got here. We'll find something. Let's find our people and get out of this mess first."

She pushed through the growing crowd toward entrance D in domestic arrivals, keeping a tight grip on Eden's damp hand.

It was raining harder now. People were groaning and shouting, covering their heads with their arms, and surging toward the arrival's doors beneath the overhang.

"Whatever happens, I can't get stuck in a FEMA shelter," Julio said urgently. "I'd never get back to my wife."

"Are you still headed north to find her?" Dakota asked.

"I finally got through to Palm Beach last night when Hawthorne let me use his sat phone."

"Is she okay?"

Julio grunted as a heavy-set man in a Marlins cap shouldered past him. "My wife and sister-in-law and her girls are okay. They're safe, for now. The radiation didn't reach them. But they're having the same power outages and gas shortages as we are. The grocery stores are almost empty. Luckily, my sister-in-law likes to be prepared. She's stocked three months' worth of food in their garage."

"Good. She's smart, then."

"She is. But if things continue like this for much longer...I fear what will happen." He touched his gold cross and closed his eyes briefly, like he was saying a prayer for them. He opened his eyes. "Their house is too urban. It's not a long-term solution."

"Not many places are."

Someone shoved into Dakota's back and almost knocked her over. Julio offered a steadying hand. Less than a minute later, Eden tripped, too. People kept knocking into them. It was way too crowded; something was going on.

Dakota's pulse thudded against her throat. Her palms were damp—and not just from the rain. She hated all these clammy, sweaty bodies pressed against her, bumping and jostling and shoving.

It made her feel helpless and out of control—two emotions she despised.

"Where's Hawthorne?" she growled. "We need to get the hell out of here."

One, two, three. Breathe.

Stay calm. Stay focused.

She just had to get through this. Get through and make it to Ezra before Maddox did. Because if he got there first...

She pushed down the fear tangling in her belly. Right now, she had to focus on escape. Then she could worry about Ezra.

"I'd like to bring my family to this safehouse of yours, Dakota," Julio said.

"I can't promise you anything," Dakota said honestly. She was sick and tired of lying. "I don't know for sure if Ezra will accept new mouths to feed."

"They're both hard-workers. Yoselyn, my wife, she's a cook at an elementary school. She knows how to make anything from scratch. My sister-in-law is a pediatrician. They have money and skills. Even the kids would help. They'd be assets. They're good people."

Everything had changed. She couldn't lead anyone into a potentially dangerous situation without their knowledge and consent again. She couldn't do it. She wouldn't. "There's more. There's something else I need to tell you—"

Before she could finish her sentence, Shay appeared in the crowd. "Dakota! There you are!"

She struggled toward them, her arm slung around Park's waist. His right arm was bent at a ninety-degree angle, wrapped in a cast, and cradled against his chest in a sling. He wore too-large khaki shorts and a loose yellow Minions T-shirt. His pallor was still a sickly yellow, but he was on his feet.

"Well, this sucks hairy coconuts, doesn't it?" he grumbled as someone bumped into him. He winced but managed a feeble grin for Eden. "Heya, kid."

"How're you feeling?" Julio asked.

"Like I was hit by a Mack truck. But the morphine they gave me is realllllllyyyy good." He slapped his pocket with his good hand. "I've got a prescription of oxycodone to keep me nice and numb for a while."

"Are you coming with us?" Dakota asked.

"Hell yes," Park said. "I'm all about the adrenaline high of a good thrill. Getting stuck in a crowded, stinky FEMA camp indefinitely isn't my idea of fun."

"It's no one's idea of fun," Dakota said.

Shay touched Eden's shoulder. "How are you feeling? Better?" Eden nodded with a tentative smile.

Shay turned to Dakota with her own grin, but it slipped from her face when she saw Dakota's expression. "What's wrong?"

"She hates crowds," Julio said.

"I hate people," Dakota muttered. "We need to go. Now."

"Dakota!"

Dakota peered anxiously through the crowd. She raised her free hand and waved. "Over here!"

Fifteen feet away, Logan shoved through the jostling bodies. They parted easily for him, swallowing their curses and insults when they caught sight of the scowling, formidable warrior inked in dangerous tattoos. He moved like a panther among rabbits.

Dakota exhaled in relief. His presence alone brought a measure of calm.

Logan stalked to her side, his scowl deepening. His damp black hair was slicked to his forehead, his clothes splattered with rain. "What the hell is going on?"

Vanessa and Carson followed behind him, both pale and terrified. Vanessa's perfect hair was matted. Rain dripped down her temples. She looked haggard and at least a decade older, her face drawn and her eyes haunted.

"They announced everyone had to exit the hotels and make their way here," Carson said.

From somewhere behind them, a woman shouted into a bullhorn. "Please make your way into the airport and follow instructions to your concourse. Buses will be waiting to take you to shelter."

"Wait—we don't want to—" Dakota started.

But it was too late.

There were too many people. Hundreds. Thousands.

It was like a strong tide, too strong to resist without risking falling and getting trampled. She might risk it for herself, but not with Eden.

Dakota and the others found themselves swept along whether they wanted to be or not.

Dakota clutched Eden's hand. "Don't let go!"

Shay wrinkled her nose and twisted around to look behind her. A huge linebacker of a man elbowed her in the side as he brushed past and almost knocked her over. "But I'm supposed to—"

"Just go with it," Julio said. "Otherwise, we might get crushed trying to get out of here."

They were pushed along by the crowd into the airport. Colorful murals and artwork and advertising shared the wall space. The lights in the large, airy spaces were dimmed to conserve energy.

They followed the sea of people through the main concourse, passing restaurants, snack shacks, souvenir kiosks, and designer shops, most of them shuttered with rolling, barred gates.

"This is certifiably insane." Park looked around wide-eyed. "They'd have better luck herding goldfish with chopsticks."

"It feels like that's exactly what they're trying to do," Dakota said.

"What's going on?" Julio asked an airport security guard.

The woman ignored him, just kept gesturing for people to continue on. "Keep straight, keep straight!"

"We need to fight our way out!" Dakota hissed. "Right now, before it's too late."

"It'll be too hard to fight our way out of here," Logan said, his voice tense. "There's too many guards and soldiers everywhere. We'll just get ourselves arrested."

Dakota glared up at him. Since when had Logan become the voice of reason?

"He's right," Julio said. "Just be patient."

Patient was the last thing Dakota felt right now. Her insides were a snarl of tension, worry, and dread. She wanted to punch something as hard as she could. Preferably a person.

They were crowded onto the Skytrain and herded off a few

minutes later in terminal D. The tile floor was slick from hundreds of wet shoes. Dakota tightened her grip on Eden. She was tempted to grab the back of Logan's shirt to stay close to him but resisted.

"Please take a seat in D10," another soldier directed a group in front of them, gesturing at the rows of quickly filling seats.

By the time they reached him, he was pointing right and ushering everyone into the next section. "Please have a seat in D11. Sit in D11, please. Thank you. Ma'am, please have a seat."

"Ladies and gentlemen, please settle down and we will explain the details to you," said a soothing female voice over the speaker system. "Please be patient. More information is forthcoming."

Out the huge windows, Dakota watched dozens of buses pulling onto the tarmac and lining up in rows: school buses, Miami-Dade County metro buses, and even some from Broward County Transit. Airport workers were rolling mobile stairwells to each of the gates.

Ice water flushed through Dakota's veins. The government was shipping them off to the FEMA camps, whether they wanted to go or not.

There were hundreds of people here. Thousands.

This was going to turn into an epic disaster, guaranteed.

They had to get out of here.

44

DAKOTA

"There's another soldier over there." Julio pointed at the check-in counter for D11, where a female soldier holding a clipboard stood close to two airport security officers, their heads bent in serious discussion. "I'm going to see if we can get anywhere with her."

He moved through the crowd, apologizing repeatedly as he accidentally jostled and bumped into people. Logan caught Dakota's gaze and rolled his eyes. He hadn't apologized to anyone.

"Sit down, ma'am," the soldier repeated to Dakota.

"We need to leave," Dakota said.

"Ma'am," the soldier said with a hint of impatience. "You need to sit down and wait patiently. The buses are already here. Pretty soon you'll have hot food and hot showers. A safe place to stay."

"I don't want to go to the FEMA camps. We don't need to go. We have someone to stay with. Do you understand?"

The soldier shifted uneasily. He was a young Irish kid, maybe twenty, with buzzed red hair and a constellation of pimples sprinkling his oily forehead and soft, stubbled chin. "I'm sorry, ma'am, but the city is full of civil unrest right now."

"We know," Logan said. "We experienced it firsthand."

"Then you of all people should understand we're trying to keep everyone safe. The city no longer has the law enforcement personnel to protect its citizens. We don't have the manpower for an escort."

"We're not asking for an escort," Dakota said through gritted teeth. "We understand the risk and we're willing to take it."

"We can't have refugees getting hurt or killed. Or engaging in looting and destruction of property for food and shelter. The government is going to provide what you need. You don't need to worry about that. We'll take good care of you."

"That's exactly what I'm worried about," Dakota muttered.

Logan stepped up beside her. "You can't keep us here against our will."

The man's face reddened. "I'm sorry, but as of an hour ago, the president declared martial law. Civil rights and laws are suspended, as is *habeas corpus*. By order of Governor Blake, all displaced persons must be placed in FEMA-sponsored shelters for their own safety and protection."

The soldier turned away for a moment, directing a Haitian family with two crying babies toward a few empty seats in the back along the windows.

Julio pushed through the crowd and returned to the group. "They're not letting anyone leave," he said in frustration. "You have to get on the bus and go to whatever place they've set up—Watsco and FIU stadiums, local high schools, one's at a big Jewish community center—then FEMA will assign everybody a case number and work through the files to figure out who has somewhere to go and who needs to stay for who-knows-how-long. It's a nightmare."

"This is ridiculous," Dakota muttered.

"Beyond ridiculous," Park said. "This is turning into a dumpster fire."

"FEMA isn't evil," Vanessa murmured. "The government's trying to help us."

"No one said they're evil on purpose," Julio said. "But they're unprepared and overwhelmed. That's not a recipe for a positive outcome, unfortunately. I truly hope I'm wrong."

"It's the best option for people who don't have somewhere else to go," Shay said. "But I don't think they should force people."

"I don't care," Vanessa said, shaking her head sharply. "I would rather be safe than stuck out there in that madness."

Carson nodded. "Seems like it's the lesser of two evils."

Dakota was surprised at their willingness to head to a FEMA camp. Maybe they thought their elevated social status would ensure them a cushy suite at the Ritz. They would be sorely mistaken. A hard, plastic stadium seat and a lumpy pillow was more like it.

Uncle Sam didn't care any more about them than he did anything else.

Dakota wanted to give a sarcastic retort, but she glanced down at Eden, who was frowning up at her. Eden liked these people.

Dakota sighed and swallowed her irritation for Eden's sake. "Go with FEMA. I hope it works out for you."

Vanessa squeezed her husband's hand. "Thank you. We will."

Carson wrapped his arm around her shoulder. She sank into him gratefully. It was good they were together. If they were going to make it, they would need to be a team.

Carson glanced at Logan and Dakota, his expression apprehensive, like he knew getting on those FEMA buses wasn't the best idea, but he was resigned to their fate.

He opened his mouth like he was going to say something, then closed it. He frowned and tried again. "I—I was wrong, back there, with the truck. We should have listened to you. Our actions put all of you in danger, and you still saved our lives. Thank you."

Logan gave him a small nod.

"We understand," Julio said, benevolent and forgiving as always. "It was a stressful situation for all of us."

Vanessa leaned down, pulled something out of her pocket, and pressed it into Eden's hands. "Take this, honey," she said quietly, her voice trembling. "You might need it."

It was a wad of wrinkled tens—at least a hundred dollars' worth. She must have snuck it through the decontamination center, or maybe the cash survived just like Dakota's map.

Eden offered a tentative smile and waved goodbye.

Vanessa hugged her quickly, and she and Carson moved into D11, searching among the groups of sullen teenagers, crying toddlers, and anxious families for two available seats.

Dakota stared after them for a moment, startled. Never in a million years would she have guessed those two were capable of such selfless generosity and human decency.

"What do you know?" Julio said. "Miracles happen every day."

Dakota rolled her eyes. "If I knew miracles were on the agenda, I would've wished for a different one."

The red-headed soldier stepped in front of them, his jaw set, fresh out of patience. "Ma'am, I don't want to hurt you, but if you don't obey my orders right now, I will be forced to escalate this situation."

"You gonna kick us out?" Dakota snapped. "That would be highly ironic."

Julio put a restraining hand on Dakota's arm.

She waved him off. "We already told you, we don't want to go."

The soldier's face hardened. "If you don't obey, I will be forced to detain you."

Dakota raised her eyebrows, incredulous. "You're gonna lock us up? Because we don't want to be extra mouths the government has to feed?"

His expression wasn't cruel, but annoyed and more than a little nervous. He was a grunt, an order-follower. It wasn't his business whether the orders were wrong or not. "Let me assure you, the United States government will do what we need to do to restore order and ensure the safety of the populace."

He placed his hand on the grip of his pistol at his side. He kept it low key, but his actions spoke volumes. He was done playing nice. "I will not ask you again."

Julio gripped her arm more forcefully. "We understand, sir."

"D11 through D19 are full now. Move along to D20." He gestured with his free hand. "I will personally escort you."

"We're going now," Julio said. "All of us."

Dakota was so startled at Julio's unexpected forcefulness she allowed him to turn her down the terminal toward D20.

Logan muttered a soft curse but didn't argue.

"We'll figure something else out," Shay said under her breath. "Don't worry."

"Wait just a moment, please." Another officer bustled up to them, glaring down at the tablet in his hands. "Stop right there."

45

DAKOTA

The officer wore a flak jacket stenciled with the letters ATF on the back. He was also incredibly tall.

Dakota found herself smiling. *Hawthorne.*

"This isn't the correct bus," Trey Hawthorne said as he swiped at the tablet. "Let me check your paperwork."

"What paperwork?" The soldier frowned and tilted his head up to look at Hawthorne. "No one has paperwork."

"This group does." Hawthorne flashed his security badge. "Over your clearance level."

Captain Kinsey jogged up beside Hawthorne, elbowing her way through the crowd, a big grin on her face. She glanced at the soldier's name and rank. "Thanks for all your help, Private McDonald," she said with a dismissive authority the rank and file knew not to question.

"Of course, Captain," Private McDonald said quickly.

"Follow me, please." Before anyone else could say anything, Hawthorne took off with a confident stride, weaving between the clumps of civilians, Kinsey jogging in his wake.

Luckily, he was a head taller than everyone else in the crowd. He was an easy man to follow.

"What are we waiting for?" Shay whispered. "Let's go."

She was right. This was their chance. Whatever plan Hawthorne had cooked up, it had to be better than this.

Dakota pulled on Eden's hand and scrambled after him. Logan, Julio, Park, and Shay quickly followed, leaving the disgruntled soldier behind.

A few minutes later, Hawthorne pulled them out of the stream of people into an empty concession kiosk full of healthy snacks, keychains and mugs emblazoned with photos of South Beach and the Miami skyline, and paperback bestsellers stacked on a center table.

"Hawthorne," Shay said breathlessly. "That was fantastic."

He beamed at her.

"What's going on?" Dakota said a little too sharply. This wasn't the time or place for these two to exchange batty-eyed lovelorn gazes.

With apparent difficulty, Hawthorne pulled his eyes from Shay and turned to Logan and Dakota. His expression grew serious. "I'm a patriot. I love my country. I've dedicated my life to serving America. To me, that includes its people. All of them."

He cleared his throat uneasily. "All this—FEMA, the National Guard, ATF, FBI, local law enforcement, emergency services—we're here to help. Seems like there's something wrong about forcing help on people via gunpoint."

"No kidding," Dakota muttered.

Hawthorne folded his tablet beneath his arm. "This whole thing seems counter to everything this country's supposed to stand for."

Kinsey nodded enthusiastically.

"General Pierce doesn't agree either, but the orders are from the governor," Hawthorne said. "However, seeing as the orders were just relayed today, it seems reasonable that not everyone would receive them at the same time. In fact, I believe my radio has been on the fritz all afternoon."

"Mine, too," Kinsey chirped. "Damn government hardware."

"If the president just now declared martial law, why are the buses already geared up to go?" Shay asked.

"Great question, Shay," Hawthorne said, grinning.

Dakota rolled her eyes.

Kinsey nudged Dakota in her ribs. "In the field, this guy is an ace shot and consummate professional. Would you believe it?" She smirked. "But get him next to a pretty girl, and he transforms into a love-sick puppy."

Shay dropped her gaze to the floor and bit her lip, clearly flustered—and pleased.

"I think it's mutual," Julio said.

"I can hear you, you know." Hawthorne cleared his throat, attempting to look all business and only partially succeeding. "As I was saying, the president resisted enacting martial law, pointing out that the loss of American freedom should be a last recourse. The governor, though, has been pushing hard behind the scenes for martial law for days. Especially after the gang warfare and the attacks on our checkpoints.

"He wants the populace under control so he can expend more resources to crush the uprisings and retake the sections of the city already gang-controlled. I'm sure he's been in close communications with the FEMA Housing Officer, Disaster Housing Coordinator, and the Logistics Section Chief getting everything ready before the president's official announcement this afternoon."

Dakota didn't care about all the political nonsense. She just wanted to leave. "Just tell us how to get the hell out."

"We'll escort you," Hawthorne said. "No one will stop us. Not in all this chaos."

Kinsey gave an almost giddy grin. "I checked your weapons out of holding. They've all been decontaminated and are packed in the rear seat on the floor of your F-150—which we also had washed by hand to within an inch of its life. It's parked outside the fence along Miami Dairy Road."

"We'll give you an official military escort off base," Hawthorne said, "but then you're on your own. I'd avoid any FEMA bus convoys from now on if I were you."

"No worries there," Park said.

Kinsey held out the key fob. Logan and Dakota reached for it at the same time.

Julio snatched it first. "It's my turn to drive."

"Fine with me. Can't be worse than Carson." Dakota allowed herself a tight smile. Things were finally going their way for the first time. With a truck full of fuel, they could be at Ezra's by nightfall.

Her stomach tightened. She had to tell the others what might await them. She had to give them the choice to stay or go. "There's something I need to tell you guys, first—"

"Whatever it is can wait," Logan said. "Let's go."

"I'm not coming with you," Shay said suddenly.

Everyone turned to stare at her.

"What?" Julio said.

Shay lifted her chin. "Yesterday, one of the doctors asked me to stay on as a nursing assistant. I can help here. I want to help."

"You're staying here?" Dakota echoed as Shay's words sank in.

"Yes. I want to be useful and do some good. I want to make a difference. I can do that here." She started to nibble on her thumbnail, glanced surreptitiously at Hawthorne, and dropped her hands to her sides. "I just—I came to say goodbye. I'm staying."

"Excellent idea." Hawthorne couldn't keep the grin off his face. "I'll take special care of her, I promise."

Dakota groaned. "I'm sure you will." She turned to Shay, a sudden, unexpected tightness in her chest. "What'll we do if one of us gets shot in the head?"

Shay's dark eyes glistened. "I'll miss you, too."

"Here." Hawthorne thrust something into Dakota's hand. "I was planning to give it to Shay." He shot her a wide, goofy grin. "But since she's staying here, I'll give it to you instead. It's a sat phone, since regular cell phones are hit or miss right now. It's got my personal number programmed. If you need anything, anything at all, don't hesitate to call. Good people have to stick together. And you're good people."

Dakota stuffed the phone in her pocket. "Thank you."

"Don't ever repeat this, but Kinsey is right," Hawthorne said. "We'd both be dead if you hadn't stuck your neck out for two complete strangers. I won't forget that."

Kinsey punched him in the shoulder. She had to raise her arm over her head. "Hell, yes, I'm right."

"We've got to hurry," Logan said.

They hugged quickly. Shay squeezed Dakota so hard her ribs hurt. She hugged Julio, fist-bumped Logan and Park, and had to bend to wrap Eden in her arms.

"Take care of Dakota for me, okay?" Shay whispered in Eden's ear just loud enough for Dakota to overhear.

Eden nodded soberly, her notepad clutched to her chest.

Logan shook Hawthorne and Kinsey's hands. "Thank you. For everything."

"We'll see each other again." Shay wiped at her eyes as they turned to go. "I know we will."

46

MADDOX

The Prophet smiled at Maddox. "Handwritten letters are a lost art, don't you think?"

"No idea," Maddox said. He'd never written or sent a letter in his life.

The Prophet scooped up the pile, straightened the bent corners, and slipped them into a drawer. Before the drawer shut completely, Maddox glimpsed a few scrawled lines.

It wasn't English. He couldn't tell what language it was. The Prophet spoke to God. Maybe it was Greek or Hebrew, the original languages of the Bible.

Brother Richard had tried to teach him Hebrew once. He'd failed—mostly because Maddox refused to attend class. He'd visited the mercy room for that.

The Prophet rose to his feet and smoothed his crisp white button-down shirt. "No one sends letters anymore. It's truly a shame."

Reuben grabbed an orange from the wooden bowl on the coffee table. He tossed it in the air and caught it. "Here's our boy. In the flesh, just like I promised."

"I see that. He must be blessed." The Prophet closed his eyes, as if he were communing with God that very moment. He opened his eyes. "He is."

Despite himself, Maddox flushed.

Solomon Cage stalked out of the kitchen into the living room. "You returned emptyhanded," he said flatly.

Reuben froze halfway through peeling a strip of orange peel. The Prophet gave a barely perceptible shake of his head.

"Catch you later, man." Reuben threw Maddox a hurried wave. "See you at dinner."

After he had gone, Maddox's father whirled on him. "You failed. Again."

His eyes were a cold, cruel glacial blue. His sandy blond hair and beard were trimmed short and peppered with gray. He was a hard man, a man of rules and consequences—quick to anger, even quicker to punish. Maddox had never seen him shed a single tear, not even at Jacob's funeral. He ruled with an iron hand, bending only to the Prophet.

The Prophet, on the other hand, was handsome, charming, and charismatic. He was a slim, tall man with a long, narrow face and wavy yellow hair to his shoulders. In his mid-fifties, his tanned skin was creased with laugh lines. An easy smile was always on his lips. Much as Jacob used to be—a natural leader. People just wanted to follow him.

One felt enlarged in his presence, made *more* somehow, when his benevolent but penetrating gaze was pinned on you, searching your very soul. People hung on his eloquent words. They were willing to give up their lives and their savings, anything to do his bidding, to receive his blessing, to be touched by his holy hand and hear the word of God dispensed by his silver tongue.

"I know. I'm sorry—" Maddox began.

The scorn Solomon Cage felt for his son was evident in every line of his face. "The Prophet needs his bride, as Christ needs His church. Did you not understand how important your mission was?"

His stomach cramped. He felt sick. He told himself it was the remnants of the radiation poisoning. Eden was of age. What did he care who married her? There were far more important things at hand. "Yes, Father."

"Your sister is incredibly important to me," the Prophet said softly. "God has given her to me as a token, as a sign of his grace for all of us, for the new world that we will create. Even her name bespeaks of her critical role. It is a great evil that she is trapped out in the wilderness of wickedness and destruction. God gave you the task of correcting that evil."

"I did everything I could—"

"It wasn't enough." His father sneered. "It's never enough with you, is it?"

Maddox kept his head up, his eyes straight ahead. He wouldn't fall prey to that trap again. He wouldn't rage and curse and scream back like he once had.

He knew full well that his father was punishing him, humiliating him purposefully. For his failures, yes. But also because he wasn't Jacob, could never be Jacob.

And that was the ultimate failure, the one thing his father would never forgive him.

"I know where they are," he said, willing his voice not to tremble. "Or where they will soon be. And it's only an hour from here."

His father stepped back, stunned by his words. The Prophet said nothing, only watched him closely, a faint, bemused smile ghosting his face.

"After that whore killed my brother and stole my sister, she sought refuge at the homestead of Ezra Burrows, off Mangrove Road on US 41. She lived there for several months before escaping again and fleeing to Miami with Eden."

"Ezra Burrows, that old half-mad ex-Marine who used to sell

rabbits at the farmer's market in Little Cypress?" His father's lip curled in disgust. "I thought you checked his place."

"We did. He said they weren't there. We had no reason to doubt him."

His father scowled. "And you just believed him? You just stopped searching?"

"We couldn't search every square inch of the Glades!" Maddox burst out.

"How do you know the girls were staying with him?" the Prophet asked calmly.

"Eden told me when I found her in Miami." He considered telling them about her mutilated throat and mangled voice. That, too, would be his own failure.

Maybe they'd see her as defiled now, impure. Would they send her to the mercy room? Or worse, cast her out? Though Maddox cared for little except saving his own skin, he did have feelings for his little sister.

He wasn't a monster. He wanted her home and safe and taken care of, just like before.

His father was already furious enough. He decided to keep his mouth shut on that count.

"I attempted to rescue her," he explained, "but I was sickened by radiation poisoning and overcome by the group with her."

"You found her but didn't bring her home?" his father spat, his face turning purple with anger. A vein in his neck pulsed. He took a menacing step forward, his fists rising. "You worthless piece of—"

The Prophet laid a gentle hand on Solomon Cage's shoulder. The man bristled but didn't dare shake him off.

"The past is the past," the Prophet said. "The future is what concerns us now."

Maddox cleared his throat. "I know—knew—Dakota Sloane better than anyone. Downtown Miami is in ruins. The city is falling into chaos. She's going to go where she feels safe. She's coming to Ezra."

"Are you certain?"

"I would bet my life on it."

"I knew we had underestimated your son," the Prophet said. His eyes shone with approval. "We'll need every soul dedicated to the cause to complete our task and achieve victory."

His father said nothing, just scowled—incensed but unable to speak his mind in the Prophet's presence.

"What happens after this?" Maddox asked. "What's the next step?"

The Prophet placed his arm around Maddox's shoulder and steered him out the front door to the wooden porch. "Do you see these people, Maddox? My flock?"

Dozens of people strolled across the grass toward the chapel for evening worship. The men chatted with each other, smiling and laughing. The women walked together quietly, their long skirts swirling around their legs, Bibles in their hands. Children dashed back and forth, shouting gleefully.

"Yes," Maddox said, unsure where the Prophet was going.

"America left them behind. They lost their jobs, their marriages, their families, their pride, their livelihood. Out there in the fallen world, they ran out of options. Life disappointed them, left them bitter, angry, and hopeless.

"But God never gave up hope on them. And neither did I. They found a purpose, a mission here. I gave them back their hope. I promised to give them everything they felt they're owed, that they deserve.

"America has become a whore, suckling the greedy mega-corporations, corrupt Wall Street, and criminal politicians. They cut wages and benefits and lay off American workers to hire foreigners and illegals. They outsource cheap crap that's made to break—intended to break, even from its very inception. Much like America.

"The America of today destroys everything she touches. She orchestrates wars to make billionaires even richer. She manipulates revolutions, insurgencies, and violent coups, plotting the devastation of entire countries to line her blood-stained pockets. America is soulless. She doesn't care.

"But we have made them all care—the corrupt politicians, their barbaric, warmongering military industrial complex—we have opened their eyes. As Isaiah 13:22 says, 'Babylon's days are numbered; its time of destruction will soon arrive.' That is the next step, my son. That is what is coming, what has already arrived. I am God's right hand. I have done this."

Three members of the Prophet's flock hurried up to him, their heads bowed in deepest respect, their hands held out beseechingly. "Blessings, Prophet," a bearded man—Brother Samson—murmured.

"Blessings be upon you." The Prophet took each hand with a magnanimous flourish and kissed them. "I bless you, my soul."

They raised their heads and gazed at him in adoration, almost in worship.

His smile was gracious, but there was something unnerving in those curving lips, that white flash of teeth—a smile so blindingly benevolent that it was also somehow menacing.

The Prophet watched the three men stroll away, that strange, disconcerting smile still fixed on his lips. "Now, a new nation will rise up, led by God's chosen Prophet—a prosperous America who knows her place. Be patient, my son. We have our Shepherds ready to enact the next step when the time comes. The Lord will provide."

Maddox nodded dully. Once, he would have saved the Prophet's pompous, vainglorious words in his mind to repeat to Dakota later, the two of them rolling their eyes in mockery. Now, though, he simply listened, awed and humbled.

The Prophet stared into his eyes, his intent gaze penetrating his very soul. "Are you one of us, son?"

"Yes," Maddox said without hesitation. "I am."

47

DAKOTA

"I have to be honest with all of you," Dakota said. "There's something I have to say before we leave."

Their group seemed so much smaller—it was only Dakota, Logan, Eden, Park, and Julio. Park rested in the backseat. The others were standing along the shoulder of Miami Dairy Road at the rear of the F-150, pausing for a few minutes to catch their breath and reload their gear.

The truck looked like hell—dented, scraped, and pockmarked with bullet holes—but it worked. They'd just completed a weapons check. Everything was there, along with a few boxes of 9mm ammo for the pistols and 5.56 mm NATO ammo for the AR-15s, both of which were NATO chambers, so they could use both 5.56 and .223 ammunition.

Hawthorne and Kinsey had also left them with two backpacks full of bottled water and MREs—military "meals ready-to-eat"— three headlamps, two LED penlights, a first aid kit, and a can of DEET for the killer mosquitoes. They'd even shoved a rusty old toolbox in the truck bed.

While she and Logan had been working on their gear, Julio had managed to connect with his wife for a few minutes on Hawthorne's cell before service went out again. He looked happier just hearing her voice, his expression radiant.

He slipped the phone in his pocket and turned to her, a satisfied smile still on his face. "We're listening, Dakota."

Dakota sheathed her knife and slipped two loaded magazines into an ammo pouch on her belt. She rezipped the backpack and slung it over her shoulder.

Then she turned and faced the others. "I promised you a safehouse, but I don't know what we're going to find when we get there."

This was it. Time for candor. Time to try a little trust. It didn't matter that she sucked at both of those options.

She owed them the truth, no matter what.

One, two, three. Breathe. She took a breath, let it out. *Here goes nothing.*

"The truth is..." she began haltingly, "the guy who was after us before—Maddox Cage—he knows now that we were hiding out at Ezra's cabin after we ran away from him and his people. He knows that's where I'd head now. He hasn't bothered to track us because he knows exactly where we're going. He may have beat us there."

"What if we don't go to the cabin?" Julio said. "Will that keep your friend safe?"

"No." Dakota swallowed the sudden lump in her throat. "These people are vindictive. As soon as they find out Ezra kept Eden from them, they'll attack him whether we're there or not. Ezra is a former Marine. He's no joke. He's the bravest, crabbiest, most cunning bastard I've ever met. But he's getting old. He's not as quick as he used to be.

"Your typical trespasser or thief—Ezra can handle that, no problem. But a surprise multipronged assault from who-knows-how-many trained guys with semiautomatic rifles? I don't know."

"What do you think we're gonna see when we get there?" Logan asked soberly.

"If Maddox made it back or was able to contact his people...it might already be over. Ezra will be dead, and those guys will be waiting for us in an ambush."

"Maddox is half-dead himself," Logan said.

"He's not alone. There's at least thirty trained men at that compound. They all know how to shoot and fight, and they all do the bidding of the Prophet."

Julio raised his bushy eyebrows. "The Prophet?"

"You don't want to know."

"Holy hell," Park muttered. "He sounds like a madman."

"Something like that."

Logan folded his arms across his chest. "And if they're not there yet?"

"Then we arrive in time to warn Ezra. That cabin is a bunker. If we're prepared, we can defend it. I know we can. It's still the best option out there."

Eden wrapped her arms around her ribs and stared down at the ground, her blonde hair falling over her face. She sniffled quietly.

"I'm sorry." Dakota turned to Julio and Logan. "To both of you. You never asked for any of this. I promised you safety, Julio. And all the booze you can drink, Logan. I lied on both counts. Ezra is a teetotaler. He doesn't even drink."

Logan sputtered out an incredulous laugh. "That figures."

"I knew I was in danger, but I thought I could keep my past hidden. I was wrong, and Harlow got killed. I don't want any more death on my conscience. I don't have any expectations that either of you should come with me. You don't owe me anything."

"And if we don't go?" Logan asked. "If we part ways right now?"

"I can drop you off at any point between here and the Glades. I'll give you the rest of my cash and you can check into a hotel, rent a car, go find your family, do whatever you need to do. You can even go back to the airport and throw your lot in with FEMA. I'm—I'm sorry it got this far."

"And what about you?" Logan asked.

Dakota slipped the last magazine into her belt pouch. "I'll go by myself. Ezra Burrows saved me once. I'm not turning my back on him now."

Logan gave a rueful shake of his head. "Why am I not surprised?"

She couldn't look at the others, couldn't bear to see the judgment in their gazes.

She glanced up at the cloudy sky. The afternoon thunderstorm had already passed. Beads of water clung to the blades of grass and dripped from the palm fronds. The pavement was still wet, but it wouldn't be for long. The sun peeked through the clouds, already beginning its descent toward the western horizon.

Julio leaned against the truck and sighed. "This is an awful lot to take in."

Dakota had already apologized more times in the last five minutes than in the last five years. She couldn't bring herself to do it again. She simply waited for their decision—calm on the outside, a sea of nerves on the inside.

"If we defeat these guys, what happens then?" Julio asked.

"Ezra owns over fifty acres. He has years' worth of stored food, plus he has a well, a greenhouse, chickens and rabbits, and the man can hunt anything that moves in the swamp. Ducks, wild hogs, racoons, gators.

"If we help him defend his place, he'll have to let us in," she said, more in desperate hope than certainty. "There's room for all of us—and your family, Julio." She hesitated. "Whatever's happening in the cities, we can outlast it."

Julio tossed the key fob into the air and caught it. "I was really looking forward to driving this beast."

"You still can," she said. "Come with me to Ezra's. After the dust settles, we'll figure out how to bring your wife there, too."

Her heart pounded in her ears. She didn't dare look at Logan or try to guess what he was thinking. He would walk away. She knew he would.

He and Julio both would, and Park with them.

What she was asking of them was crazy, especially after she'd lied and deceived them. It was too much.

The thought left her feeling hollowed out and empty. Bereft. No matter how terrifying it felt to trust these guys, being without them was worse.

Logan stomped around the side of the truck. He opened the door, climbed inside, and slammed it shut.

She looked up, startled. What was he doing? He wouldn't try to steal the truck, would he?

Of course, he would.

She'd overestimated him, erroneously believed he'd discovered some shred of honor deep inside his twisted ex-convict heart.

Stupid, stupid, stupid.

Anger flared through her veins. She should've known better. She should've known never to trust—

The rear window on the driver's side buzzed down. Logan stuck his head out and stared at her. A slow, lazy smile spread across his face. "Thought you'd want shotgun."

She glanced at Julio, too surprised to speak.

Julio grinned, shrugged, and jogged over to the driver's side. "What's one more dance with death?"

Park opened the rear passenger door. "I used to gamble for a living, you know. I've ridden every rollercoaster on the east coast. I've jumped out of airplanes. You give me long odds, I'll take the risky bet every time. Big risk, big reward. But the house always wins in the end.

"Still, if you're wise, if you know when to go all in and when to fold, and if you're smart enough to take your chips and go home—in the short term, you can win."

Dakota stared at him. "What the hell are you saying?"

Park rolled his eyes. "I love to beat the odds. I'm saying I'm in."

"What's taking so long?" Logan grumbled. "Are you coming or what?"

48

DAKOTA

"It's getting dark," Julio said.

"We're not stopping," Dakota said.

Julio kept both hands on the wheel, his gaze straight ahead. "Agreed."

They'd been driving for two hours. Julio had the wheel; Dakota took shotgun while Logan watched their left flank and rear from behind the driver's seat.

Park slumped in the middle seat, his head flung back against the headrest, his cast cradled to his chest. He was doped up on plenty of painkillers, but he still looked like he was hurting.

On the other side, behind Dakota's seat, Eden leaned against the window. She should be sleeping, but instead, she was drawing. Dakota could hear her pencil scratching. She didn't have the heart to tell her to stop.

They had taken Miami Dairy Road beneath the Dolphin Expressway and gradually made their way past the Mall of the Americas and turned west along Tamiami Trail, aka SW 8th Street, aka Calle Ocho as the Cubans famously dubbed it.

Dozens of vehicles still littered the shoulder and occasionally blocked one of the westbound lanes, but a week after the terrorist attacks, the traffic jams from those fleeing the fallout had mostly cleared.

Julio was right. He was a much better driver than Carson. The ride was a smooth one, even though they were forced to swerve and weave to evade all the stalled and abandoned vehicles.

"Do you remember where to go?" Julio asked.

"Pretty much." She still had the paper map, but she didn't need it if they stayed straight west. "There aren't many roads crisscrossing the Everglades. Only two main ones go east and west—Tamiami Trail and Alligator Alley.

"Tamiami Trail is a two-lane, eighty-mile strip of road connecting Miami with Naples. In between is nothing but swamp and snakes, gators and mosquitoes. There are a few rural settlements, old-timer gladesmen and Indian land, but they're remote and difficult to reach."

"Let me guess, that's where we're headed."

"When SHTF, you want to be hard to reach."

"Can't argue with that."

Only a few moving cars were visible at any given time on either side of the highway. Trash and debris littered the asphalt—a black garbage bag full of clothes; a stroller tipped on its side; large suitcase unzipped—shirts, shorts, and underwear scattered along the road for a couple hundred feet.

It was like people had simply shed their belongings as they fled.

"Well, that's creepy," Park said.

It *was* eerie. Unnatural, almost sinister in its silence, the enormous emptiness of a city devoid of the rush and crush of humanity.

Very few people had returned to work or felt safe enough to leave their homes or neighborhoods. It was like life itself was on pause, everyone holding their breaths, waiting for the other shoe to drop.

Their world was broken. It had always been broken. People like her and Logan knew that already. The rest of them were just figuring it out while the comfort and security they'd always trusted in shattered all around them.

Park began to hum the R.E.M. song, "It's the End of the World as We Know It."

"You seem in good spirits, considering," Dakota said.

"Why shouldn't I be?" Park said, his voice dripping with sarcasm. "My arm's gone to the crapper. Probably won't be able to pick up a spoon with that hand ever again. But at least I'm a lefty. What I should be doing is counting my lucky stars, I guess."

"Hey, man—" Julio started, already trying to soothe frayed nerves.

"I got ahold of my parents in New York and my aunt in Houston last night." Park took a breath. When he spoke, his voice was flat, emotionless. "My brother is dead. So are my uncle and two of my cousins. Well, presumed dead. They were all in the middle of ground zero when it happened. My parents won't even have a body to bury at the funeral. Well, neither will a million other families, so it's like I don't even have a right to grieve, you know?"

"I'm sorry about your brother." Julio touched his cross with one hand. "And your cousins. Every life is precious. Every life is a tragedy. That others are suffering doesn't negate your own pain."

"The whole country's gone to hell in a handbasket," Park continued, as if he hadn't heard Julio. "What's left if we can't find a way to laugh in the face of hell itself? Humor's a coping mechanism. It's gotta be. Otherwise, you'd best send me to a padded room, because none of us are ever gettin' out."

Dakota didn't say anything. She agreed with him, though she'd rather spit in the face of hell than laugh at it.

But everybody had to figure out their own way to survive. Not just physically, but psychologically, too. Otherwise, it'd crush you.

The movies and books always overlooked the psychological toll of extreme disasters. For once, Dakota was thankful she didn't have a network of friends and family who were dead or missing. She had no one to grieve.

Hundreds of thousands of families would never know for sure how their loved ones had died. They wouldn't have a body to bury, would never have the comfort of absolute proof.

The loss of family, friends, co-workers, and neighbors combined with the destruction of thousands of homes and businesses and communities...and not by accident, not an act of God or nature—but the cruelty of human beings committed unconscionable acts against one another.

The entire country was floundering, tormented by grief and despair. How long until the reports of skyrocketing suicides started coming in?

Maybe it wasn't the ones with the most skills and resources or the strongest physically who survived in the end—it was the resilient ones. The ones who got knocked down just like everyone else, but they always got back up.

49
DAKOTA

"Can we turn on the radio?" Park asked, clearly done with discussing his own misery. "See if there's anything not about the demise of civilization as we know it?"

Dakota leaned forward and switched it on. "...Chase banks in Houston closed their doors after opening for a little over three hours Friday morning when angry customers exploded into rioting. Two tellers were injured...Fears continue to rise over rumors of a snowballing financial crisis...NASDAQ is scheduled to open Monday, but forecasters are predicting another rapid shutdown if gun-shy investors cause another freefall..."

Dakota flicked to another station. "...MS-13 gang members attacked a Red Cross convoy delivering humanitarian aid from Russia, the U.K., and Canada yesterday in Richmond, Virginia... The National Guard in Washington D.C., New York City, and L.A. worked throughout the night to disburse supplies as thousands of hungry citizens waited in lines as long as twenty-four hours..."

She turned the dial again. The news was all the same, just spouting different facets of a country balancing on the knife's edge of chaos.

"...The National Weather Service reports Tropical Storm Helen is strengthening off the coast of Puerto Rico with sustained winds reaching sixty-five miles an hour. It is predicted to become a Category One hurricane sometime tonight. If it remains on its current path, it could strike Florida's east coast as early as Sunday."

Dakota stopped channel surfing and listened.

"Meteorologists with the National Oceanic and Atmospheric Administration predict a possible trajectory from the Keys up through Daytona Beach. However, if Helen were to hit Miami as a Category Two or Three hurricane, the impact on an already devasted city could be catastrophic—"

"Mother Mary and Joseph," Julio murmured.

"Hot damn," Logan said.

"We're still reeling from the nuclear attack, and now this?" Park asked, incredulous. "It's almost...apocalyptic."

"Armageddon" was the word that slithered into Dakota's mind. Plagues and destruction of Biblical proportions. Doomsday.

She pushed those traitorous thoughts deep down. Those were the words of a charlatan. A liar. A madman dealing in beautiful falsehoods and lethal deception.

"It won't hit us." Julio took one hand off the wheel and crossed himself. "I have faith that it won't."

"Keep praying, then," Park said. "And maybe send up a prayer for us while you're at it. I'm an atheist, but in times like these...It can't hurt, right?"

"I already have, and no, a few prayers definitely can't hurt," Julio said.

"...In international news, the conflict in Syria escalated overnight," the radio announcer continued. "Russia continues to claim U.S. interference in the attempted coup of Syrian President Bashar al-Assad. Five American soldiers were attacked and killed by insurgents on Monday, inciting intense criticism that U.S. soldiers belong in the U.S., addressing their own humanitarian crisis that has now claimed over a million lives—"

Dakota switched the radio off. She felt sick. Numbed. The enormity of it was overwhelming. Paralyzing. It made her want to curl into a ball and block out everything—the fear, the chaos, the suffering and loss.

"We can't get distracted," Logan said. "We have to focus on what's right in front of us. That's how we keep from becoming another statistic. That's how we stay alive."

They drove past housing developments and low-rise condominiums painted in tropical yellows, oranges, and blues. Most of the streetlights weren't working. On Dakota's side, a canal of dark water about fifteen feet across paralleled the road. The large palms growing from the center islands dividing the east and westbound lanes rustled gently in the early evening breeze.

"There's a red Porsche that's been behind us for the last several minutes," Logan said from the back seat. "And I think I've seen that same orange sportscar, too. Can't make out what it is from this distance."

Julio whistled. "A Porsche 911 Carrera?"

"Can't tell," Logan said. "Maybe."

"That's a sweet ride. Up to 690 horsepower. Top speed over one-ninety an hour. Not a lot of trunk space, though."

Dakota twisted around. "How far back?"

"A hundred yards, maybe," Logan said. "They haven't gotten any closer. And they're both too far away for me to make out identifying characteristics of the drivers."

"We're on a main highway," Julio said mildly. "There's no other roads to turn off. Everyone is headed to the same place."

He pointed out his window as they passed a black Dodge Grand Caravan loaded to the tops of the windows with suitcases, bags, and whatever else the family could squeeze inside. A toddler in a rear-facing car seat peered out the window at them with big brown eyes.

"Maybe," Logan said darkly. "I still don't like it."

50

DAKOTA

R ed and gold streaks ribboned the sky as the sun began to set. Very few lights appeared in the shopping plazas or big box stores. They passed a Jiffy Lube, a Goodwill, a gas station that read "No Gas. No Cash. Closed." All dark.

"How are you doing?" Julio asked Dakota, so quietly Logan and Park couldn't hear them in the back over the low rumble of the diesel engine. "For real?"

"Fine," she said automatically. She glanced across the road and watched the squat buildings of Florida International University slide past them on the left. On the right, neighborhoods crowded behind the canal.

"I miss Shay," Julio said with a sigh. "She was more talkative."

Dakota snorted. "And way too chipper."

"Admit it, you liked her."

"She might have grown on me a bit," Dakota said with a tight smile.

"Me, too. I understand why she stayed, but I still wish she was here with us. At least we can check in with her on Hawthorne's phone."

To the right, the housing developments finally gave way to scrubby pineland, though the opposite side of the road still bristled with restaurants, grocery stores, autobody shops, and sad little houses crowded together.

They were close to the end of civilization.

"I hope you don't take offense at this," Julio said hesitantly, "but I want you to know that I wasn't being facetious before. I do pray for you. For you and Eden. For all of us, but especially for you."

She rolled her eyes. "You pray to Jude, the patron saint of lost causes?"

"Very funny. And impressive. You know your saints."

"Only that one." It was what Sister Rosemarie, a former nun, used to say to her back at the compound. She always had a wry smile on her wizened old face when she said it, though. *I'm sending up a prayer to Jude for you, girl. You're the queen of lost causes.* And Dakota, with her smart mouth, would always retort, *If you think there's any hope for me, doesn't that make you the lost cause?*

It was always whispered, never spoken aloud, for praying to anyone other than the Lord was an abhorrent sin, punishable via the mercy room. It remained a small secret between them, a bit of pleasant commiserating in a harsh life filled mostly with draconian rules and restrictions, hard labor, and shame—always the shame.

Dakota ran her hand along the stock of the AR-15. That was a long time ago. A lifetime ago. And yet, it wasn't lost on her that every mile they drew closer to Ezra, they also drew closer to the compound.

"You still a praying man?" Dakota asked Julio. "Even after all this?"

"I am now," he said grimly.

"I don't do religion. It just causes more harm."

"Maybe," he allowed. "Maybe that's why I strayed for so long. Religion isn't the same as God. Religion isn't faith. It took me a long time to understand that. Religion can be a lot of rules and traditions to follow. It's not always bad, but it's not always good, either."

"You got that right."

"When God spared me in the blast—I knew I was here for a purpose, you know? There has to be a reason."

Dakota stiffened. That sounded all too familiar. "You think God caused this?"

"No," Julio said swiftly. "Absolutely not. God doesn't cause evil. But God can work through something terrible to make something good come out of it. That's what I believe. That we were put here to ease each other's burdens, to help each other."

Dakota stared out the window. "I hope you're right."

"Throughout time, there have been religions who've claimed to speak for God who instead heaped great harm and suffering upon others. But God isn't in those people, whether they call him God or Allah or Jehovah. God is a God of love."

"The only God I ever heard of was a god of wrath and judgment, fire and brimstone. A god just waiting for you to mess up so He could punish you with torture and misery."

"That's tragic," Julio said softly. "And wrong. God *is* love. A man or woman who doesn't show love in everything they do doesn't know God."

"Maybe," she allowed, noncommittal.

Julio's god seemed antithetical to the one they'd crammed down her throat at the compound. Which one was the right one? Maybe they were both wrong.

Maybe God didn't give a single crap about all the little humans scurrying around on planet Earth, destroying the world and each other. It sure as hell seemed that way.

"Look at everything you've survived," Julio said. "I'm smart enough to know that I don't know the half of it. Someone up there is watching out for you, even if you don't see it."

They drove quietly for a while.

Julio removed his hand from the wheel and touched Dakota's arm. This time, she didn't flinch.

"I'm asking your forgiveness in advance for butting into your business," he said. "I'd like to say something to you, something you may not like."

"Spill it," she said tightly, glancing at him. "We both know you're going to do it, anyway."

A smile flickered across his face before his expression grew serious. "I sense some animosity between you and Eden. Anger and hurt feelings. Maybe some things you didn't tell each other that you should've. Am I barking up the right tree?"

She hesitated, again fighting her instinct to close up and shut everyone else out. The classic M.O. of the abandoned, defensive, bitter foster kid. Jeez. She wasn't even original.

It hadn't worked so great for her so far, either.

She sighed. "Pretty much."

"I don't know what happened to you. But after our run-in with Eden's brother, I imagine it wasn't pleasant, whatever the details."

The scars crisscrossing Dakota's back tingled and itched. She could feel every single one. Her throat tightened.

"Seems to me, the very fact that you managed to find each other in the midst of utter chaos and destruction is a miracle in itself. You two have been through hell and back. Whatever hurts you've both suffered, the only thing that's gonna heal you is love. God's love, and love from others. That's all that matters."

"I think you missed your calling, bartender. You should've been a preacher."

Julio chuckled softly. "I should've been a mechanic, with my own shop. But that's a sob story for another day. My point is, you've got to get over whatever's between you. Forgive your sister."

"You called her my sister."

"How many people live their entire sad, lonely lives and never know the loyalty and love you two have for each other? I don't care whether the same blood runs through your veins. What does that matter? When I look at both of you, all I see is family."

She blinked at the sudden stinging in her eyes. Julio was right. Eden was her sister, no matter what anyone else said.

Other people only held power over your own mind when you gave it to them. They might be able to beat and brand and destroy your body, but they couldn't steal your thoughts, your beliefs, your truths.

Not without your consent.

Eden was her sister. And she was Eden's.

They were family. And family—the family you chose—never gave up on each other.

Dakota couldn't remain angry at Eden for telling Maddox about Ezra. It wasn't fair or right. She was the one who'd withheld the truth from Eden in the first place. The only one she could blame was herself.

All she could do now was vow to be better. For Eden. But also, for herself.

"Thank you." She swallowed the lump rising in her throat. "I mean it."

They drove on.

Shortly after they passed the Seminoles' Big Cypress bingo hall, the road narrowed to only two lanes: one westbound, one eastbound, metal guard rails bordering both sides. More abandoned cars cluttered the road, making less room to navigate. Julio slowed to fifteen miles an hour, easing carefully between the vehicles like some twisted obstacle course.

As the sky faded to indigo, stars appeared. The lights in the review mirror seemed even brighter. Almost like pairs of eyes—harsh, searching, predatory.

"Those same cars are still behind us." Logan's voice was tense. "They've closed the gap, maybe fifty yards now. Those two cars have stayed close together this whole time. And now there's a third one right behind them. Looks like a blue sportscar...a Maserati. Not sure of the model."

Julio flicked his gaze to the review mirror. "That orange one's a Jaguar F-TYPE SVR for sure. The red one is a Porsche 911. And a Maserati GranTurismo. Each of those retails over a hundred and fifty grand."

"Three expensive sportscars driving together," Dakota said uneasily. "What are the odds?"

The hairs on the back of her neck prickled, and she tightened her grip on the AR-15.

Logan had good instincts. If he was worried, so was she.

"You think we're being followed?" Julio asked.

"I think we're being hunted."

51

LOGAN

There was nothing ahead or around them but wilderness and darkness.

The vehicles pursuing them grew bolder. They drew closer, revving their engines, then fell back only to speed up again, tires squealing in protest as they swerved to miss random cars.

The Porsche switched on its brights. The two cars behind it followed suit.

"You think it's the Blood Outlaws?" Julio asked.

Harsh light blared into the cab. Logan squinted through the window, his adrenaline surging, his muscles tensing. "Yeah, I do."

"Mother Mary and Joseph," Julio said. "Why do the bad guys get all the best cars?"

"Take that one up with the man upstairs," Park said. "We've got bigger concerns."

"They were searching for us," Dakota said. "For the truck. It's hard to miss with the front fender dented and all the bullet holes. They could've been lying in wait for us. Or had patrols out scouting, circling the EOC, hoping to get lucky."

"We obliterated twenty of their guys," Logan said. "They want revenge. They want to make a statement. Gangbangers like these, they can't let nothing slide. Otherwise, they look weak just when they need to solidify their domination over competing gangs. If they look like they can't handle their business, someone else'll take their place."

"It's like King of the Mountain," Park said, "but with machine guns."

"It's exactly like that," Logan said.

They passed a rickety billboard advertising alligator wrestling, airboat tours, and rare snake exhibits along with a roadside food shack and concessions. Fields of stubby pine forests rose up on both sides of the road. On the right, the canal had stretched to thirty or more feet across.

"This is just a straight road for eighty miles," Park said. "Nothing but swamp on either side. How are we going to lose them?"

"We stop and fight," Dakota said.

"Three cars packed full of crazy psychos against the two of us?" Logan said. "You *are* nuts, girl."

"We can end this thing right now," Dakota said fiercely. "I know we can."

"Settle down, Rambo," Park said.

"I can shoot if I have to," Julio said. "I'm not very good, but I know the basics."

"We need you to drive," Logan said.

"Okay, fine," Park said, his voice squeaking a little. "If we're doing this thing, let's do it. Give me a pistol. I've still got one good hand."

"Have you ever fired a gun before?" Logan asked.

"I have incredibly steady hands—hand, I mean. Sleight of hand is a requirement in my job. I'm good under pressure and learn fast. I know what to do: keep my finger off the trigger and don't aim at anything I'm not prepared to kill, then point and shoot."

"Only if we're desperate," Logan said. "And we're not there yet."

Dakota twisted around in her seat. He could barely make out the wide whites of her eyes in the dark. "What's the plan?"

She wasn't automatically taking charge. She'd asked his opinion —like she'd actually wanted it.

"We don't stop," Logan said. "Not unless we have to."

"We can outrun them," Julio said.

"Those are fast sportscars," Dakota said, dubious. "We've got a beat-up truck we're lucky even runs."

"We can still do it," Julio said confidently.

Logan raised his eyebrows. "In the dark? With all these stalled cars everywhere?"

"It's like the obstacle course of doom," Park muttered.

"Exactly," Julio said. "Last car standing wins."

The realization struck him. "You want to use the cars. Get the gangbangers to crash into them."

Julio nodded tersely. "We don't have to outrace these guys, just outlast them. If they're no longer mobile, they can't chase us anymore. We leave them in the dust."

Julio drove fast and steady, with precision and skill. The Ford responded like a well-trained horse under his control. Unlike Carson, whose barely contained panic had made the drive jerky and precarious, like a rickety ride at the fair.

A car horn blasted. Twenty yards behind them, the Porsche unrolled its windows. The barrel of an assault rifle poked out.

"Trust me," Julio said. "I can do this."

Dakota and Logan exchanged another tense glance. They could crash just as easily as the gangbangers. If they were injured, they'd be unable to defend themselves. It was a risk.

It was also the best option. Maybe the only one that gave them a legitimate chance.

The Porsche blasted its horn again. It swerved around an SUV parked along the narrow shoulder and sped up, pulling to within thirty feet of the truck.

The Jaguar and the Maserati roared into the oncoming lane. The Jaguar came up alongside the Porsche, honking angrily.

Every time the truck tried to pull ahead, they ate up the distance like it was a Sunday drive in the park. Damn, they were fast. Incredibly fast with their jacked engines and sleek, aerodynamic forms. The Ford was a clunky junker in comparison.

Park twisted around in his seat, gritting his teeth as the top lip of his cast caught on his seatbelt. "One of those turd-blossoms is hanging out the window. He's aiming a gun right at us."

"We're doing this," Logan said. "You drive, we'll shoot."

"Aim for the tires," Dakota said.

The crack of a gunshot exploded behind them.

They were under attack.

M addox stopped outside the chapel. Muffled noises echoed through the wooden door, which was only partially closed. The hairs on his neck prickled.

Above him, the wide bowl of the sky was turning to indigo. Bats darted above the trees. Cicadas buzzed. The whole compound was quiet. It was dusk; everyone was inside the cafeteria for dinner. Everyone except for whoever was inside the chapel.

He silently opened the door and peered inside.

At the front of the chapel, a figure knelt before the first pew, his hands folded, his head bent. He recognized the broad, stiff back, the graying blond hair, the hard, stern profile. Solomon Cage.

His father.

A woman knelt next to him. Long, braided black hair and narrow, hunched shoulders. His stepmother, Solomon Cage's second wife, was a severe, humorless woman Maddox avoided as much as possible.

He called her Sister Hannah, not Mother. Never Mother.

Maddox's own mother had died here in the compound, during

childbirth with Eden. No one summoned a doctor. God's will, everyone said.

His father was mumbling something. His voice was strange— somber, apprehensive, almost... grieved.

Maddox strained to listen.

"Those people...all those lives...the whole country is burning to the ground," his father murmured. "What...What if..."

He left the words unspoken. *What if we were wrong?*

Sister Hannah leaned closer to her husband. She placed her small hand on his quaking shoulder. "It is not our place to question."

"I know—"

To doubt is to sin, Solomon."

"I know. It's just—"

"The Lord gives us difficult tasks to test us, just as he gave the Israelites. He ordered them to slay the wicked Canaanites, instructing them to kill men, women, and children. Even babies." Sister Hannah's pious voice grew louder, full of vicious zeal. "Why did the Lord do this? Because those people were idolatrous pagans, vile and grotesquely evil.

"They had to die before the Israelites could claim the promised land. It is the same now, Solomon," she said fervently. "The wicked in America must die so the Prophet may birth a new America, the one where *we* are the ones chosen to lead and rule in a land of prosperity, a land flowing with milk and honey."

"You've been blessed with holy insight, woman," his father said gruffly, appropriately chastened.

Maddox moved closer to hear better. His foot struck the bottom of a pew with a thud.

His father rose swiftly and spun around. Tears trembled in the man's eyes.

Maddox stared at him, gaping, too stunned to be embarrassed for eavesdropping. He'd never seen his father stricken with grief, regret, or uncertainty. Had never seen him doubt himself, their faith, or the Prophet. Not once.

His father wiped furiously at his eyes until they were dry and there was no sign he'd ever felt anything but zealous devotion. His expression darkened. "What're you doing here?"

"He should be whipped for his disobedience," Sister Hannah said, her voice dripping with disgust. She was an attractive woman but dour, always frowning, like her incessant misery was a public declaration of her piety.

She had never loved Maddox, had only seen him as a burden—had detested him as furiously and passionately as he detested her.

Sister Hannah pointed a bony finger at Maddox. "Send him to the mercy room—"

"Silence!" his father boomed.

She pressed her lips together and obediently dropped her gaze to the floor.

"We will speak alone," his father ordered. "Now."

Sister Hannah scurried down the narrow aisle, passed Maddox without a word or glance, and slipped out the door, her long skirt swishing behind her.

Maddox took a step toward his father, his mind reeling. He was still muddled and thickheaded from the radiation poisoning, but one thought pierced through the fog: if his father harbored doubts over what the Shepherds had done, maybe he also doubted Eden's calling.

Maybe they could stop this. Maybe she could come back and just be a kid, not some wrinkled old patriarch's seventh wife. "Eden—"

"Has been set aside for...for a holy purpose."

"Do you really believe that?" Maddox whispered. "What if he's wrong?"

His father took two long, swift strides to reach him. He slapped Maddox hard in the face.

5 3

MADDOX

M addox staggered back against the pew, his hand flying to his face. His cheek stung. One of his blisters burst. Pus leaked down his neck.

"The Prophet may be my brother, but he is no mere mortal!" His father glowered at him. "He is the voice of God. Do you understand that? We must obey. There is no choice in the matter. None."

But of course. The Prophet had already announced that it was God who commanded Eden be set aside for him. If the Prophet allowed Eden to slip through his grasp, then God was wrong—or else the Prophet was.

And maybe that was all it would take to cause his devout followers to doubt him. Maybe it would plant a seed of uncertainty, a question of the most dangerous kind, one neither Solomon Cage nor the Prophet could abide.

Absolute faith—and absolute obedience—were required above all else. Even if his father was allowed a moment of weakness, of unbelief, certainly no one else was.

His father glared at him in disgust. Like he was repugnant,

rotten to the core. Beneath the man's disdainful gaze, Maddox felt something inside himself shrivel.

He bowed his head, the dutiful, compliant son once again. Jacob's replacement. "Yes, Father."

For a long moment, there was silence. Maddox did not look up. He was still dizzy and lightheaded, but he dared not show it.

Would his father continue to berate him? Or would he order him to the mercy room for his insolence? The lash wounds striping his back were mostly healed into ridged, wormy scars.

But Maddox did not fear pain. He never had. He simply waited.

Finally, his father spoke. His voice was gruff, but no longer laced with revulsion for his remaining son. "I have ordered Reuben to send a contingent to the Burrows' homestead. They'll take care of things and bring Eden back to us."

"Reuben?" Maddox sputtered, looking up. "But it's my job—"

"You're barely on your feet. Your presence would compromise the mission, if not outright ruin it." He placed a heavy hand on Maddox's shoulder. His stern expression softened. "You must recuperate. I have need of you. This holy war is just beginning.

"As soon as we close this loose end and return the Prophet's bride to her rightful home, we can focus on the glorious future at hand. We will rule this country. We will build it anew, but better this time. Pure and holy, and above all, obedient."

Maddox heard his words but couldn't focus on them.

"We must remain faithful," his father said. "The most difficult task is already over."

"You could...spare the girl." He didn't know what he was going to say until the blasphemous words were already spilling out of his mouth.

He longed to strangle Dakota Sloane himself, with his own two hands. He'd dreamed it, again and again and again. She was his. After her betrayal, after all the pain and suffering she'd caused him, he deserved that.

And yet...

An image flashed into his mind—the two of them out in the airboat, drifting free in the river of grass, laughing about nothing. He saw the sunlight reflecting off the auburn strands of her hair, the way her tough features softened when she smiled at him.

Out there, together, they could just be. She was the only person in the world who'd never expected him to be anything but what he was.

"You could show her mercy," he whispered, hating the words even as he spoke them, despising himself for his weaknesses, his myriad impotent flaws. "One last time."

His father's eyes flashed with fury—and seething contempt. His fingers dug into Maddox's trapezius muscle until it hurt. He squeezed harder. "That little slut killed your brother. Have you forgotten?"

"No...no, of course not."

"And that paranoid old fool harbored her." Solomon Cage bared his teeth, his face a rictus of hatred. "I won't rest until I see them both dead."

"I know, but—"

"You're unwell," his father said sharply. "Your words are nonsense. You don't know the profanity of which you speak. I will ignore it due to your illness, nor will I mention it to the Prophet. This time."

"Thank you," Maddox said, but he felt anything but grateful. He forced himself to accept his father's will—God's will. "When will it happen?"

"Tonight." His father released his grip on his shoulder and moved past him. "They've already left."

"What are Reuben's orders?"

Solomon turned and stared at him. There was no trace of doubt in his eyes now. No sorrow, regret, or guilt. There was nothing but hard, steely purpose. "Attack the Burrows' homestead. Get Eden. Kill everyone else."

Maddox said nothing.

His father's expression changed again, this time shifting to paternal affection and concern. He reached out and touched Maddox's still-stinging cheek, his fingers gentle. "Whose side are you on, boy?"

An ache started somewhere beneath Maddox's ribs, a throbbing pain, a desperate longing for something he'd never had. "Yours."

"Do not disappoint me, son," Solomon Cage said, "and you will take your dead brother's place and serve at my right side, as you deserve."

An overwhelming shame filled him. Shame and bitter self-loathing. She had done this to him. It was her fault. It had always been her fault.

No longer.

Maddox lifted his chin, strangling the wriggling shame, shoving it deep down, allowing a cold, cleansing resolve to fill him instead. "I won't."

54

LOGAN

Julio jerked the wheel, pulling a right turn so hard the truck went up on two tires as he slid into the oncoming lane. Someone was screaming.

Everyone was thrown against each other, against their seatbelts, against the door. Park's elbow jammed into Logan's tender ribs. He barely registered the jolt of pain.

He tugged his loaded Glock 43 out of its holster and thrust it at Park. "Use it only if you have to."

Park nodded tightly. "Got it."

Julio grunted with exertion. He wrestled the wheel straight again. The tires touched down on the blacktop, and he stomped on the gas. They lurched forward.

The seatbelt seared Logan's neck, but he didn't care. That cold, detached calm washed over him. He thought only of what he needed to do next to keep everyone alive. He braced his left hand against the door frame, trying to keep the rifle steady against the window as he flicked off the safety.

The truck accelerated to twenty-five, thirty, then forty. Their headlights were twin beams piercing the thick blanket of darkness.

The shining hulks of cars appeared and disappeared as Julio veered out of harm's way.

Behind them, tires squealed as the gangbangers struggled to maintain control of their vehicles. The Porsche was still in the lead, with the Jaguar right on its tail.

The Maserati lagged a bit further behind. It kept fishtailing across both lanes, braking then accelerating like the driver was indecisive, or overly cautious.

The sportscars were sleek, well-oiled machines, designed for elegance and speed. If not for the obstacle course of doom, as Park had called it, they would've already been overrun.

Over the rumble of the engines came the distant *pop, pop, pop* of gunfire. All three vehicles had their windows down now; Logan caught the gleam of moonlight off the barrels of rifles and pistols waving in the air.

The occupants of the Porsche were close enough for Logan to make out the heavy ink swirling across their arms, chests, and faces. Definitely Blood Outlaws.

"You got your side?" Logan said.

Dakota lifted her AR-15 and flicked off her safety, too. "Got it."

Logan and Dakota buzzed their windows down simultaneously. The hot wind rushed in, buffeting him, whipping his hair, his shirt.

With the windows down, the sounds of gunfire grew louder. The fast, steady *pop, pop, pop* of a handgun. The *rat-a-tat* of semiautomatic gunfire. They were aiming for their back tires and simultaneously trying to blow out the rear window.

"Get down on the floor!" Dakota screamed at Eden.

There was a click and a dull thump as the girl unbuckled her seatbelt and threw herself against the floorboards. He glimpsed her out of the corner of his eye, cowering behind the seat, her hands wrapped over her head, letting out harsh little gasps.

Park scooted down to keep his head below the headrest. He clutched Logan's Glock to his chest with his good hand.

Most of the Outlaws' shots went wildly wide and high. It was extremely difficult to aim and shoot in a fast-moving vehicle. This wasn't the predatory drive-by shootout against competitors' unsuspecting family members they were used to.

This felt like balancing on an exploding rocket while trying to nail a three-inch target.

Eventually, though, a bullet would find its mark.

Logan released his seatbelt. He braced the rifle against the window frame, his spine wedged against the back of the driver's seat, his legs bent awkwardly and feet anchored against the lip of the rear seat so he could properly angle his shots and give himself some sort of leverage. If the truck crashed, the impact would severely injure him, if not kill him outright.

He punched off several shots. Missed them all.

The Porsche returned fire. Logan flinched but refused to duck.

He fired another volley. The stock kicked against his shoulder. Three shots missed. The fourth struck the windshield, punching a hole through the safety glass right above the driver's head.

The Porsche skewed left as the driver ducked instinctively. He righted himself, sneering and shouting words Logan couldn't make out. They sped up, lurching so close they nearly kissed the Ford's bumper.

In the passenger seat of the Porsche, a hulk of a man the size of a linebacker leaned out the window and aimed his semi-automatic with both hands. *Boom! Boom! Boom!*

The Ford's rear window exploded.

55

LOGAN

Gummy safety glass sprayed across the backseat, raining harmlessly over Logan, Park, and Eden. Logan squeezed his eyes shut. A few shards struck his face and neck and fell to the floor. He felt nothing more than a mild sting.

"Damn, damn, damn!" Dakota chanted, squeezing off a shot with every curse.

Julio veered the truck sharply to the right to avoid a stalled white Volvo in the dead center of the road. Logan's shoulder exploded in pain as he smacked against unforgiving metal.

"Damn it, Julio!" Dakota shouted.

"I'm doing the best I can!"

His best was good enough. Julio had waited until the last possible second to swerve, while the Porsche was so focused on ramming them that the driver didn't even see the stalled Volvo.

Its tires screaming in protest, the Porsche slammed its brakes and slewed sideways before smashing into the Volvo at fifty miles per hour. The front of the Porsche crumpled like a soda can. Metal ripped and tore. Glass shattered. Smoke poured into the night sky.

Logan whistled. "Hot damn."

"Yeehaw!" Park pumped the Glock above his head. "They're not walking away from that one."

"Yes!" Dakota shrieked, giddy as a little girl. "I take it all back, Julio. You're the man!" It was the happiest Logan had ever seen her.

"Where the heck did that come from?" Logan asked Julio.

A glimmer of a smile flickered across Julio's face. "I told you I could drive."

"No kidding!" Park shouted gleefully. "That was awesome!"

"One down, two to go," Dakota said, already back to business.

The Jaguar and Maserati didn't stop to help their wounded compatriots. They didn't even slow down. The Jaguar swung into the lead, roaring after the truck with a renewed fury.

The Jaguar driver wasn't as cautious as the Maserati or as skilled as the Porsche. He weaved crazily over the narrow road, barely maintaining control.

Julio kept his eyes straight ahead, his hands so tight on the wheel his knuckles were white as paper. The wind shrieked through the opened windows. The inside of the cab stank of gunpowder. Logan's ears rang from the percussive blasts in such close quarters.

He breathed in, breathed out, steadied his nerves.

His head was clear. He wasn't sick. He wasn't drunk. He could do this.

He was made for this.

It didn't matter that he was a terrible person, that he could barely maintain a normal conversation let alone a healthy relationship with another human being, worthless at anything but killing.

Violence was in him, dark and seething, infused in his pores, his very bones. There was no way to escape it. The only way was to embrace it—the cold, the dark, the monster.

In this world, killing was what was needed.

He didn't look down at the tattoo inked on his forearm, the Latin inscription warning him of an abyss he'd already leapt into, feet first. The words were just marks now. Meaningless.

Everything was meaningless but the task before him.

That cold, mechanical calm descended. His senses sharpened. Emotions, thoughts—everything faded away. Logan blocked out the wind, the darkness, the spearing blaze of the headlights—and focused on his target.

Inhaled, exhaled. Squeezed the trigger. Logan fired at the Jaguar's right front wheel. The bullet hit home, punching through its target and blowing out the tire. Black rubber exploded.

He unloaded five more shots into the front windshield.

The Jaguar slewed hard to the left, rising on two wheels and coming down hard on its ruined rim. The vehicle crashed through the guard railing, pitched off the road, and careened headfirst into a pine tree.

The deafening crash echoed in the night as metal caved and twisted. Steam boiled up from the bent, distorted hood, the sportscar shuddering in its death spasms.

Logan stuck his head out of the window, blinking against the stinging wind.

Behind them, the battered passenger door wrenched open. The big linebacker stumbled out. His rifle dangled at his side. He took a single faltering step before collapsing to the pavement.

The Maserati zigzagged furiously to miss the huge man lying in the middle of the road like a felled tree trunk. Logan couldn't tell from that distance, but it looked like the Maserati lurched over an arm or a leg as it sped past.

Either way, the linebacker didn't get up.

Logan shifted his attention from the dead guy to the final sportscar. The Maserati roared after them, throwing caution to the wind now. Logan and his group had taken their guys out multiple times. It was an insult to their very existence.

Hellbent on it, they'd do anything to get their revenge.

"Two cars ahead!" Park yelled in warning.

Julio hit the brakes. He had to slow to squeeze between a lemon-yellow Volkswagen Love Bug on the right and a burgundy hatchback—its hood propped open—on the left, giving the Maserati time to catch up.

The Maserati barely tapped its brakes. It burst through the two cars with a screech of metal, the fender and hood crumpling, and kept on coming.

The gangbangers squealed to the right and pulled up alongside them, nudging the Ford's rear fender and forcing them into the oncoming lane. The Maserati jerked hard to the left, jolting into the side of the truck. Metal scraped against metal.

Eden let out a frightened gasp.

"He's trying to shove us into the guard rail," Julio cried.

"Not if I can help it." Dakota dropped the AR-15 and reached for the Sig at her side.

Logan shifted, swung his rifle around, and re-aimed. The Maserati was on his opposite side now.

"Get down!" he shouted at Park. Park's eyes went round and he flattened himself against the seat cushions. Eden was already huddled on the floor.

Logan aimed into the Maserati's rear passenger window just as a thug leaned out, a pistol clutched in his hands. His pulse spiked as he recognized the inked face, the teardrops blackening the gang-banger's left cheek.

Teardrop sneered in triumph and pointed his pistol at Logan.

Logan was faster. He fired three quick shots.

Blood spurted from a hole in Teardrop's neck. He flew back-ward, the back of his head striking the metal frame above the Maserati's window. The pistol dropped from his hand and clattered away into the dark.

The Maserati lurched forward and slammed into them again. Julio swerved, fighting to maintain control, as the left side of the F-150 grated against the guardrail. The truck juddered and bounced.

"Car ahead!" Park shouted.

The Ford's headlights illuminated the back of a red Land Rover stalled in the oncoming lane not fifty yards ahead of them.

Julio grunted. But his hands remained steady, his knuckles white on the wheel, the rest of his body shaking like a leaf. He wrenched the truck to the right, smashing as hard as he could into the side of the Maserati.

The sportscar jolted sideways. It wasn't enough. They were still blocking the truck from the safety of the empty right lane. The Land Rover loomed like a crouching beast in the headlights as the truck raced toward it at over fifty miles an hour.

"Hold still!" Dakota pointed the Sig down at the Maserati flanking them and fired twice, then twice more.

Someone inside the Maserati shrieked in agony.

The sportscar skidded across the road, smashed into and then through the guardrail with a wrench of tearing metal, bounced through a few yards of thick underbrush, and plowed nose-first into the canal.

"Look out!" Park cried.

Julio slammed the brakes. He spun the wheel sharply to the right. The truck skidded and fishtailed. The vehicle slowed rapidly as it turned. But not rapidly enough.

The front fender struck the right corner of the Land Rover's bumper and jolted to a sudden, jarring stop.

Logan smacked into the rear of the driver's seat. The back of his skull bounced off the doorframe. Stars exploded behind his eyelids.

The engine ticked, stuttered, and went quiet.

For a long second, no one moved.

Julio winced and rubbed his chest. "Everyone alive? Airbags didn't go off. Kinda wished they had."

Park moaned. "I'm definitely alive. Hurts too much not to be."

"Sore, but I'll live." Dakota leaned over the back seat. "Eden?"

Eden sat up, brushed a tangle of blonde curls out of her face, and gave them a shaky thumbs up. She had a cut across her cheek but seemed okay.

Logan moved his arms and legs gingerly, grimacing at the flash of pain gouging into the back of his head and radiating down his neck. He'd have a nice case of whiplash, but nothing was broken.

"We've got to check the canal," Dakota said tersely. "They could still be alive."

Logan and Dakota wrenched open their doors and hopped out first. Julio and Park climbed out, stumbling dizzily, and followed behind them.

The truck's headlights were still blaring like searchlights in the night. The moon peeked out between a break in the cloud cover, bathing the road, trees, and the canal in a silvery glow.

"Stay in the truck until it's safe," Dakota said to Eden.

They sprinted back to the spot where the Maserati capsized into the canal, Dakota with her Sig out and ready, Logan with the AR-15. He ejected the half-used magazine, pulled a new one from the pouch at his waist, and slapped it in.

They approached the accident site slowly and cautiously in case one of the thugs was still alive. They moved side by side, Dakota tense and alert beside him.

His body humming with nerves, he scanned the road, the banks along both sides of the canal, the scrubby pine trees, and the underbrush. The guardrail was a wreck of twisted metal. The sportscar was nowhere in sight. It had already sunk below the surface of the canal.

No movement.

"What just happened?" Park asked from behind them, awe in his voice. "I thought for sure we were goners."

"I got the driver," Dakota said breathlessly. "Nailed him right in his hand."

"Nice one," Julio said.

"I was aiming for his head."

"We can't all be ace shots," Logan said.

She grunted. "Speak for yourself."

Cicadas buzzed in the night. A mosquito whined in his ear, but he didn't slap it away.

Dakota reached out and grazed his arm.

An electric charge surged through him at her touch. He felt it like a bone-deep pull inside him, that primal craving to be a part of something, to connect with another human being. To belong.

That same urgent need had lured him to the gang as a teenager. Before it all went sideways, they were the family he'd never had—brothers who cared for him, unlike his absent father he'd never even met, or his addict mother who'd barely bothered to feed him when she was high or gone on a bender in some crack house.

"*Ven aquí mi gordis,*" she would mumble, opening her arms for a goodbye hug before she went out for a night or two on the town, abandoning her eight-year-old son to an empty apartment bristling with real and imagined terrors.

Dakota squeezed his forearm, dragging him back to the present. Without speaking, she pointed at a moving shadow.

Two figures popped to the surface on the far side of the canal about twenty yards downwind. They clambered up the slick bank, coughing and spitting water, splashing wildly.

"Logan—" Dakota said.

"I know." Logan didn't hesitate. He nestled the stock against his shoulder. He could see clearly enough in the moonlight to get the job done. He pressed the trigger and unleashed a rain of bullets. Water sprayed as lead peppered the canal.

Both bodies slumped and collapsed backward. They sank beneath the black water. A few scattered bubbles drifted to the surface, then nothing.

Logan stared at the water for a long moment, breathing heavily, letting the adrenaline drain from his limbs. More dead bodies to add to the tally.

The violence was in him. There was no going back from it.

He could harness it to protect the people he was beginning to care about, but that didn't make him safe. He could only protect them from outside threats; he couldn't shield them from the darkness in his own heart, the savagery and death in his own two hands.

"It's done," Dakota said gently, bringing him back to the moment. She was looking at him, something like concern on her face. "It's over."

He nodded grimly.

"They're gator chow," Park said, sounding extremely satisfied.

DAKOTA

"So, this is the Everglades," Park said. "Confession: I grew up in south Florida, but I've never been out here."

All around them was endless vistas of flooded, boggy wetlands stippled with stubby slash pines and underbrush.

"This isn't the real Glades," Dakota said. "You've got to go further in."

She took a step down the embankment. Something large and heavy splashed in the middle of the canal. Moonlight glimmered off the ripples of black water.

Dakota flicked on the LED penlight and scanned the canal. A pair of glowing eyes shone back at her just above the surface of the water. Another smaller pair drifted along the far bank.

Her stomach tightened despite herself. Would the beasts eat the bodies? She imagined massive jaws tearing at flesh and bone and repressed a shudder. Good riddance. Besides, it was just nature, doing what nature did best. Still, the thought sent chills racing up her spine.

"Gators," Logan muttered. "Don't like 'em."

"I do," Park said. "They're fascinating creatures. Like primeval dragons living right alongside us. They only attack four or five people a year. In seventy-five years, there's only been a few dozen fatalities. They prefer to eat turtles, fish, and birds."

"Tell that to those few dozen 'fatalities.'"

"What about now, though?" Julio asked, gesturing at the ruined guardrail, meaning the corpses of the thugs floating somewhere beneath the dark water. "They've never had a human buffet like this."

"Fine point," Park said. He took a step back.

Dakota couldn't disagree. She climbed back over the guardrail, choosing the relative safety of the road.

"I'm incredibly grateful we're still here," Julio said quietly. He crossed himself. "We all could have died. Maybe we should have. I'll be sending up some grateful prayers tonight, that's for sure."

"We're alive, thanks to you," Dakota said.

Julio shook his head. "I told you, Dakota. God is watching out for you."

Dakota rolled her eyes.

"How about we just thank everyone?" Park swatted at his neck with his good hand. "Except these awful mosquitoes."

Logan turned to Julio. "You should've told us you could handle a car like that."

"I did."

"You should've told us again, apparently," Logan said wryly. "That was some damn fine driving."

"Thank you, Logan. That means a lot to me." Julio cleared his throat and glanced back at the Ford, its hood still steaming. "We ready to get this show on the road? We've still got somewhere to go."

"You think the truck's okay?" Park asked, his expression doubtful.

"Only one way to find out." Julio jogged the twenty yards back to the Ford. He slid into the driver's seat, leaving the front door open. The ignition wheezed like an asthmatic smoker, struggling to catch. He put the truck in reverse and pumped the gas. It made horrible grinding, scratching noises...and went nowhere.

Julio got out, moved to the crumpled front fender, and wrestled the dented hood open. "Give me a few minutes, and I think I can get this beast purring like a kitten again. Park, can you grab that rusty old toolbox out of the back? And Logan, can you bring me some more light?"

While Julio worked on the truck, Dakota stayed next to Eden.

She imagined the Everglades she couldn't see from the road but knew was there, just beyond the darkness—beautiful, haunting, ugly, dangerous. Water the color of tea flowed for hundreds of miles, south to the tip of the mainland all the way west to the Gulf of Mexico. Millions of watery acres covered in endless waves of sawgrass.

Here were gators and manatees, spoonbills and herons, mangrove swamps and cypress trees. And the mosquitoes—clouds and clouds of them, buzzing and biting with that horrid, high-pitched whine in her ears.

Outside of malaria and the host of other deadly diseases they spread, mosquitoes couldn't kill you outright, but sometimes it felt like they could. She swatted one on her neck and flicked another bloodsucker from her arm. She pulled the can of DEET out of the backpack Hawthorne and Kinsey had left for them, filled with gratitude at their thoughtfulness.

"Here." She sprayed herself and Eden before passing the can on to Park to give to Julio and Logan.

She glanced down at Eden. At her sister. The girl had climbed out of the truck and now sat cross-legged next to the wrecked guardrail, her notepad limp on her lap, staring blankly into the canal. She looked utterly terrified.

Dakota's heart twisted. Julio was right, as usual. Tomorrow wasn't promised to anyone. The next ten minutes weren't promised to anyone. Certainly not in this life.

Eden was her sister, and that was all that mattered.

She squatted down next to her. "Hey."

Eden looked up at her with wide, unblinking eyes. She formed a fist with her right hand, her thumb peeking out, and rubbed her chest in a circle.

Dakota swallowed. "What does that mean?"

Eden picked up the notepad and opened it to the half-finished drawing of a raccoon scurrying across a rotted log, a baby raccoon clinging to its furry back. She flipped to a new page and scribbled two words.

She held it up. *I'm sorry.*

"No," Dakota said. "You don't have to say that." She took a sharp, ragged breath. Her eyes were hot and stinging. "I'm the one who lied to you. I'm the one who didn't tell you the truth about… what happened, about your own life. That wasn't fair. It's not fair.

"You didn't know Maddox had turned against us because I didn't tell you. It's not your fault that Maddox knows about Ezra. Do you understand? It's not your fault."

Eden stared at her for a moment. Finally, she nodded, her eyes glassy with unshed tears.

Dakota had to look away. It hurt too much, like a hot poker skewering her insides, twisting slowly with agonizing precision. "I…I don't expect you to forgive me. I've messed up so much. I don't know if I can make it right—"

Eden pulled her into a giant hug. She buried her face in Dakota's chest and wrapped her chubby arms around her neck. Her tears dampened Dakota's shirt.

Instinctively, Dakota stiffened. This was okay; this was a good thing. She let herself relax into it, into the warmth, the comfort. She drew her sister close and held her tight. They sat there, together, rocking back and forth, Eden crying and Dakota holding back her own tears.

Dakota pulled away. She tightened her hand into a fist, her thumb poking out, and rubbed it in a circle over her own chest.

Through her tears, Eden's face lit up.

"I'm sorry," Dakota said. "I'm so, so sorry. I'll do better. I'll be better. And I want you to teach me this, okay? I want to learn sign language." She exhaled a breath, her chest expanding. "I was an idiot for refusing to learn. I—it made me feel like I was losing you."

Eden shook her head and frowned.

"I know, I know. It's stupid. More than that, it's selfish. You're my sister. You always will be. I shouldn't—I can't—" She swallowed hard. "I will never hurt you again. I promise. Never, ever."

Eden nodded eagerly and enveloped her in another crushing hug. She sat back, gestured something, and then wrote it down. *I forgive you.*

The hot poker in Dakota's gut twisted deeper. Despite the horrors they'd been through, her sister was still sweet, kind, and trusting, quick to forgive. Too quick.

There was something almost pathological in it—like Eden didn't believe she had the *right* to be angry. More of the Prophet's brainwashing. Sometimes it felt like they'd never be free of that place.

Dakota bit down hard on her own bitter rage. She couldn't allow herself to direct it at her sister. "Don't—you can't say that yet. Not until you know exactly what I did."

Eden widened her eyes, confused. She touched the ridged purple scar at her throat.

Dakota nodded miserably. "You have to know what I did to you. You have every right to be furious at me. To hate me, even. You need to—"

On the road, the Ford's engine coughed, sputtered, and finally roared to life.

"Well," Julio said with a tired sigh, "it's uglier than ever, but this American-made baby still runs."

Park cheered. "We're back in the game!"

"Come on, ladies," Logan called. "Last chance for a pit stop if you need it. Time to get the hell out of here!"

Dakota climbed to her feet. "As soon as we're safe," she promised. "I'll tell you everything."

She reached out her hand. Eden took it.

58

DAKOTA

Dakota glanced down at the map on her lap and traced her finger across the thin line bisecting the giant green blob that was the Everglades.

Due to urban development and the overeager destruction of Florida's natural habitats, the wetlands were half their original size now, but still stretched over two thousand square miles.

To the south of them was Homestead, Florida City, and Everglades National Park. To the northwest was Big Cypress National Preserve. They'd passed Shark Valley and Miccosukee Village several miles back. If they kept going, they'd hit Everglades City and then Marco Island and eventually, the west coast.

They were less than ten miles from Ezra's fifty acres.

Her gut tightened. What would they find there? *Please let us get there in time.* She didn't know if she was praying, and if she was, to who. To anyone who was listening. *Please let him be okay.*

The cab still smelled like gunpowder mingled with the sweeter odors of the MREs they'd just eaten—spaghetti and beef with sauce for Logan and Eden, chili with beans and cornbread for Julio, and mushroom fettuccini for Park and Dakota.

They needed the energy for what might lay ahead.

They'd already checked and rechecked their weapons, reloading the pistols and rifles and the four spare magazines. Logan and Dakota each took two of the magazines. They were as prepared as they were going to get.

She pointed ahead. "Right there, at that road. Turn right."

"What road?" Julio asked, peering through the spider-cracked windshield. "I don't see a road."

The headlights illuminated a narrow dirt track that looked more like a wagon trail, overgrown with weeds and wild tropical plants. They followed the path, the truck jostling and bouncing over ruts and roots, for what felt like twenty miles.

Park pointed at one of the giant cypress trees laden with moss that loomed on either side of the road. "What are those called?"

"That's a hammock of cypress trees."

"A hammock? Like for napping?" Park asked.

"It just means a forest of trees." Dakota rolled her eyes. "Don't you people know anything about the state you live in?"

"Not the wild parts," Park said. "Nowhere with mosquitoes."

"You're out of luck here, I'm afraid," Dakota said. "Turn left here, on Mangrove Road."

Julio squinted. "I don't see a road sign. This barely looks like it qualifies as a road."

"It does. It's an eight-mile dead-end drive. There are four homesteads on this road. Ezra's is the last. His property backs up to a huge area of wetlands. You can boat or kayak for miles and miles if you want."

"I love paddle boarding," Park chimed from the backseat. "Especially with gators."

"We should cut the lights," Dakota said.

The headlights switched off. Darkness pressed in on every side. Julio slowed the truck to a crawl as they waited for their eyes to adjust. Thick underbrush scraped the vehicle's undercarriage, leaves and branches slapping the doors and windows.

Dakota leaned forward and looked up through the cracked windshield. A sliver of moon peeked through the straggly clouds, bathing everything in a blur of faint, silvery light and black shadows.

"When we're a mile from his driveway, we'll park the truck off the road, out of sight, and hike in."

"You think that's a good idea?" Logan asked quietly. "What if this friend of yours sees shadowy figures lurking on his property and decides to take a shot at us?"

"We'll stay out of sight. And I know where the tripwires and boobytraps are."

"Tripwires?" Julio sputtered. "Boobytraps?"

"Cool," Park breathed.

"He's well prepared," Dakota said.

"You mean, you *knew* where the tripwires and boobytraps *were*," Logan said. "Hasn't it been two years?"

Anxiety pressed against her chest. "Yes. But it's the best information we have right now."

"It's the *only* information we have," Logan muttered. "I don't like this. Not at all."

Julio drummed his fingers against the steering wheel. "Why can't we go the normal way and just knock on the front door?"

"If Maddox and his people beat us there," Dakota said, "they'll greet us with a face full of lead."

"She's right," Logan said with an unhappy sigh. "We've got to scout the area first. If it's a trap, we need to know."

"Park here." Dakota pointed to an area thick with wild plants but free of trees. "Far enough in to hide the truck."

They climbed cautiously from the truck. Logan came around and helped Eden, holding her arm carefully so she didn't smack her head on the doorframe or lose her footing on the way down.

Dakota raised her brows in surprise.

He shrugged. "What? I'm not a complete animal. I've got manners."

"You should practice them sometime."

He snorted. "Now there's the pot-and-kettle thing again."

They were joking, using humor to diffuse the tension, but it didn't entirely work. They were all on edge, taut with nerves, their expressions strained.

They shut the doors quietly and gathered their gear in silence. Dakota checked her pistol, made sure a round was chambered, ensured she had her extra mags close at hand.

Logan came up beside her, silent and lithe as a panther. His body radiated heat. She felt his presence thrumming through her own cells.

In the dim moonlight, his eyes shone like black marbles. He was alert, ready. There was no anger or resentment in his face, only steely determination.

She'd thought he would hate her, but he didn't. She'd thought she didn't want him around, but she was wrong.

She felt herself drawn to him almost against her will. His presence calmed her, strengthened her. She wanted him here. With her. She wanted him by her side.

He stood only inches away, studying her face in the darkness. "I'll follow your lead."

She nodded.

He started to turn away, but he stopped himself. He licked his lips like he was suddenly nervous. "I've got your back, you know."

Her cheeks flushed, but she refused to look away. She'd been alone for so long that learning to depend on someone else—to trust them—felt foreign. And terrifying.

But she wouldn't be here without him. Neither would Eden. It wasn't just that she owed him--it was something else, something far deeper.

Something that scared her too much to look at straight on.

But Dakota had never allowed fear to rule her. She was too tough for that.

Trust was a risk, but maybe risking everything was the only way forward, the only way to discover the beginning of something else.

"I've got yours," she said. "No matter what."

The End

SNEAK PEEK OF INTO THE FIRE!

D akota Sloane was prepared for battle. She gripped her Sig in one hand, the AR-15 slung over her shoulder, the extra magazines tucked into a pouch at her belt.

"Let's go," Logan Garcia said gruffly. He carried his rifle, the Glock 43 tucked into its concealed holster at the small of his back, his combat knife strapped to his belt. "You ready?"

She nodded tightly. She was as ready as she'd ever be.

The group followed Dakota across the road. They hiked into the dense, dark forest with only the two small penlights to see by. Dakota had one; Julio de la Peña the other.

An owl hooted overhead. Unseen creatures scurried through the leaves.

Anxiety scrabbled up Dakota's spine. Doing this at night was a terrible idea.

But they had no choice. If Ezra was in trouble, he'd be dead by morning. If anything happened to him, she'd never forgive herself.

They couldn't wait. They had to reach the cabin tonight.

Ominous shadows crouched all around them. They kept tripping on roots and vines. Mosquitoes whined in their ears. The air smelled dank and damp, peat mixed with rotting vegetation.

Half-jungle, half-swamp, the Everglades was a land of haunting beauty. Wild and foreboding, primordial and ancient—here long before humans, and probably long afterward.

Ezra loved this place. Dakota loved it, too.

This mosquito-infested swamp was the only place in the world that had ever felt like home.

She and the others had escaped the radioactive ruins of Miami in search of the safety she knew she would find here. But now Maddox Cage and the Shepherds were threatening everything she held dear.

Her heartbeat quickened, thumping against her ribs.

Almost there.

She was trekking purely by memory, the cabin in the clearing fixed in her mind: the oak, pine, and cypress forests surrounding it. To the north, a wide expanse of sawgrass and brackish water that turned into a million miles of swampy marshlands.

"What are you looking for?" Logan whispered behind her.

She'd explored these woods dozens of times, but not for two years, and seldom at night. Everything looked different—strange and dangerous.

"Ezra has a buried cache near here. If I can find it, I can orient myself and know exactly where we are. Plus, the cache will have more nine mil ammo, and if we're lucky, another gun."

She was searching for a particular live oak tree with the branches locked in a weird, twisting shape that resembled a heart. There were two smaller scrubby pines on either side. The three rocks pushed up against the roots looked natural—unless you knew what to look for...

It was ridiculously hard to see in the dark. Shadows wavered just outside the penlight's halo. The moon still shone high in the night sky, but the trees blocked most of its light.

Twigs and thorns caught at her clothing. She nearly twisted her ankle on a tree root. The others stumbled behind her, Logan cursing softly.

She paused and glanced behind her, making sure Eden was keeping up.

Behind Logan, Julio trudged next to fifteen-year-old Eden, holding her hand to keep her from tripping. She looked so small and vulnerable. The girl had been through so much already. She needed Dakota by her side.

But Dakota had to lead them. She had to reach Ezra first and make sure he was safe. Then she could tend to Eden's needs. Until then, Julio was standing in the gap for her.

Her chest tightened. Julio was a good man. Steady and dependable—a loyal friend.

"I'm too out of shape for this," Julio huffed, but his tone was good-natured and self-deprecating. He rubbed his round, middle-aged belly with his free hand. "Too many *Cubanos*. What I wouldn't give for a delicious ham and cheese sandwich right now."

Eden looked up at him and signed something with one hand. It was hard to tell in the shadows, but it looked like she was smiling a little.

"Count me in." Yu-Jin Park took up the rear, but only slightly. Even with his broken arm, he managed to keep up. "I've never been hungrier in my life."

"We need to stay quiet," Logan reminded them.

Dakota returned to her task. Even at night, the heat was oppressive. She breathed in the dank, familiar scent of moss, peat, and wet leaves. Every passing minute felt like an hour.

Please, please find it...

Finally, her gaze snagged on something familiar.

She rushed forward, fell to her knees, and pushed the stack of three rocks aside. One of the rocks was long and flat, and had three short lines etched into it. It was perfect for digging, chosen by Ezra specifically for that purpose.

The others crowded behind her as she handed Eden the penlight. Eden kept the light trained on the ground where Dakota needed to work. She dug frantically for a few minutes until the rock scraped against something.

She brushed away the dirt, twigs, and leaves, and twisted the top off the five-gallon bucket—one of several Ezra had buried within a few miles of the cabin. This was the closest one on the southwest side of the property.

Ezra always said you couldn't keep your entire stash in one place. You might be returning home when you surprised an intruder. Maybe you'd be forced to flee without your weapons.

Ezra Burrows always had a backup plan.

Dakota reached in and pulled out a Springfield XD-S pistol wrapped in a Ziplock-type bag with anti-corrosion lining, made specifically for long-term firearm storage.

She could've wept with joy. It was close to the same model as her old gun, the one she'd lost with her bugout bag in the moments after the nuclear blast rained hell down upon Miami.

That was almost three weeks ago, but every day felt like a lifetime.

There were two spare magazines for the pistol—both preloaded and wrapped in the protective lining—and a box of 9mm ammo. She handed the box to Logan, who slipped it in his cargo pocket.

She moved aside some packaged protein bars, bottles of water, a small first aid kit, and a tin box she knew contained fire starter tools. She pulled out a folded tactical knife and held it out to Eden. "Take it, just in case. Keep it in your pocket."

Eden obeyed without protest.

Dakota handed a second, smaller pocketknife to Park. He stuffed it in his pocket with his good hand. The last item she took was a pair of binoculars.

She closed the lid, but didn't rebury the bucket. It would piss Ezra off—he was fastidious about stuff like that—but there wasn't time. She'd come back later and take care of it.

Suddenly, it was hard to breathe. It felt like some giant hand squeezed her heart. She hoped he'd be pissed at her. It meant the ornery old bear was still alive.

Dakota climbed to her feet, brushing the dirt off her knees, and slung the binoculars' strap around her neck. She handed Park the Sig, who returned the Glock to Logan. Dakota kept the XD-S.

"Point and shoot, remember?" she said to Park.

Park took it gingerly. "Okay, yeah. Got it."

"Now you've got a gun and a knife. Never bring a knife to a gun fight, they say, but when you need stealth and surprise in close quarters, it still works."

Park nodded soberly, his face round and pale in the shadows.

She held her finger to her lips. No more talking. They were close.

Within ten minutes, she'd led them safely through the woods and past a tripwire, the thin wire invisible in the darkness. But she knew it was there.

Ezra didn't use fishing line. Rather, it was a low-stretch, high-strength cord he'd previously sprayed with a flat, grayish green spray paint to dull the shine and blend in with the foliage.

She suppressed a tight smile. Everything was the same. Just as if she'd never left.

Her heart lifted with a hope she hardly dared believe. Maybe Ezra was safe. Maybe everything would be fine.

When she glimpsed the glint of the fence ahead, she scanned the area for a tree to climb. She gestured for Logan and the others to remain where they were, then swung herself up on the low branch of a live oak.

Swaths of Spanish moss tickled her skin. Tiny bugs crawled up her arm, but she couldn't brush them away. She grunted, muscles straining, bark scraping against her belly and arms as she clambered into a sitting position, then carefully stood, leaning against the trunk for balance.

Her pulse hammering in her ears, she peered through the binoculars. Ezra's cabin squatted in the middle of the wide clearing. There was the big shed, the chicken coop, the garden, the well, and the outhouse buildings, with the dock and the fishing boat in the distance.

Ten yards in front of the cabin, Ezra's familiar pristine 2004 Dodge Ram SRT-10 pickup sat in the dirt driveway. But two other trucks were parked in the drive. Strange trucks she didn't recognize.

The front gate was dented, hanging half-open.

Her heart stopped beating and her mouth went dry. Her hands were trembling, but she forced herself to keep looking. To see it all, no matter how terrible.

Three dead bodies littered the driveway. Dark, unmoving blobs in the moonlight. None of them were him—she was sure of it.

Two trucks meant more people. More enemies, more danger. They were inside. With Ezra.

Her worst fears had come true.

The Shepherds were already here.

To be continued...

ACKNOWLEDGMENTS

Thank you as always to my awesome beta readers. Your thoughtful critiques and enthusiasm are invaluable.

Thank you Becca and Brendan Cross, Mike Smalley, Lauren Nikkel, Michelle Browne, Jessica Burland, Sally Shupe, Jeremy Steinkraus, and Barry and Derise Marden.

To Michelle Browne for her skills as a great developmental and line editor. Thank you to Eliza Enriquez for her excellent proofreading skills. You both make my words shine.

And a special thank you to Jenny Avery for volunteering her time to give the manuscript that one last read-through and catch any stray errors. Any remaining errors are mine.

To my husband, who takes care of the house, the kids, and the cooking when I'm under the gun with a writing deadline.

And to my kids, who show me the true meaning of love every day and continually inspire me. I love you.

ABOUT THE AUTHOR

I spend my days writing apocalyptic and dystopian fiction novels.

I love writing stories exploring how ordinary people cope with extraordinary circumstances, especially situations where the normal comforts, conveniences, and rules are stripped away.

My favorite stories to read and write deal with characters struggling with inner demons who learn to face and overcome their fears, launching their transformation into the strong, brave warrior they were meant to become.

Some of my favorite books include *The Road, The Passage, Hunger Games,* and *Ready Player One.* My favorite movies are *The Lord of the Rings* and *Gladiator.*

Give me a good story in any form and I'm happy.

Oh, and add in a cool fall evening in front of a crackling fire, nestled on the couch with a fuzzy blanket, a book in one hand and a hot mocha latte in the other (or dark chocolate!): that's my heaven.

And I never say no to hiking to mountain waterfalls, traveling far-flung locations, kitting out my bugout bag and practicing at the range, or even jumping out of a plane (parachute included).

I love to hear from my readers! Find my books and chat with me via any of the channels below:

www.Facebook.com/KylaStoneAuthor

www.Amazon.com/author/KylaStone

Email me at KylaStone@yahoo.com

Or join Kyla Stone's Book Lovers Fan Group HERE!

SNEAK PEEK OF THE LAST SANCTUARY

Terror coiled in the pit of Amelia's stomach. The polished marble corridor stretched ahead of her, silent and empty but for the bodies.

The rat-a-tat of gunfire exploded from somewhere above her.

In just a matter of minutes, the whole world had fallen to pieces. Now there was nowhere to run. Nowhere to hide.

Amelia strained for any sound over the crashing thunder of the storm. She crouched behind the counter of a coffee bar along the corridor of Deck Ten of the *Grand Voyager* luxury cruise liner.

The voices came again. Two or three of them, from somewhere down the corridor. Terrorists. Ruthless killers.

They were hunting her.

Because of her father, the powerful leader of the Coalition. Because of what he'd done.

If they found her, they would use her as a bargaining chip, a pawn to get whatever they wanted from her father. They'd torture her. Then they'd kill her.

She sucked in her breath. She had to ignore the pain, the mind-numbing fear. She had to *think*.

The voices grew louder. They'd be on her in thirty seconds or less.

Her heart leapt into her throat. She was cornered. Trapped. Out of time.

Thunder crashed. Waves rocked the ship. Rain lashed the glass of the floor-to-ceiling windows on the far side of the corridor.

She had believed the terrorists were the deadliest threat on this ship.

She was wrong.

Grab the box set and binge read the entire series now. Get it HERE!